11/05

Crazy About Lili

BOOKS BY WILLIAM WEINTRAUB

Getting Started: A Memoir of the 1950s
City Unique: Montreal Days and Nights in the 1940s and '50s
The Underdogs
Why Rock the Boat?

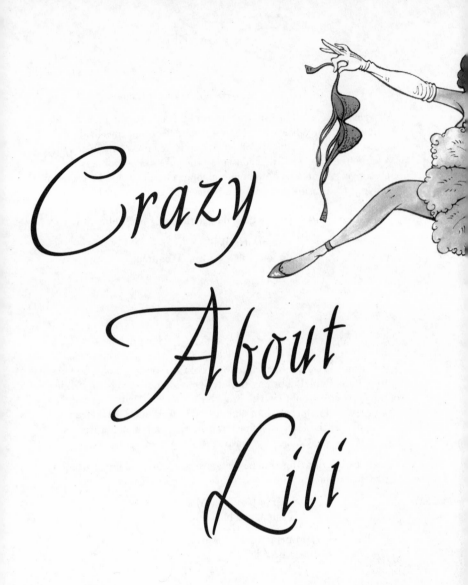

Crazy About Lili

WILLIAM WEINTRAUB

[A DOUGLAS GIBSON BOOK]

M&S

Library and Archives Canada Cataloguing in Publication

Weintraub, William, 1926-
Crazy about Lili / William Weintraub.

"Douglas Gibson Books."
ISBN 0-7710-8916-3

I. Title.

PS8545.E43C73 2005   C813'.54   C2005-900988-8

We acknowledge the financial support of the Government of Canada
through the Book Publishing Industry Development Program and that
of the Government of Ontario through the Ontario Media Development
Corporation's Ontario Book Initiative. We further acknowledge the
support of the Canada Council for the Arts and the Ontario Arts
Council for our publishing program.

This is a work of fiction. Names, characters, places, and incidents either
are the products of the author's imagination or are used fictitiously.

Typeset in Janson by M&S, Toronto
Printed and bound in Canada

This book is printed on acid-free paper that is 100% recycled,
ancient-forest friendly (100% post-consumer recycled).

A Douglas Gibson Book

McClelland & Stewart Ltd.
The Canadian Publishers
481 University Avenue
Toronto, Ontario
M5G 2E9
www.mcclelland.com

1 2 3 4 5   09 08 07 06 05

For Magda, as always

I

1948

It was a warm Friday night, late in August. The boys were sitting in their usual booth at Gagnon's, having ice-cream sundaes – the extravagant Pistachio Surprise, the reliable maple-walnut with hot fudge sauce, the understated but seductive Choco-Mint Parfait. These confections, in their fluted glasses, were exquisitely sweet, but the mood in the booth was heavy with the misery of being seventeen years old in 1948.

"So what we have here is yet another failure," said Stanley.

"That's right," said Martin.

"But it looked very promising, didn't it?" said Harold.

"It couldn't have started better," Martin said. "There I am at the party, dancing with her, very close. I feed her a couple of beers and I say, casual-like, 'Why don't we zoom up to Summit Circle and look down on the twinkling lights of the city?' And she says, 'Hey, that sounds romantic.'" Martin paused thoughtfully to take a spoonful of Pistachio Surprise.

"So you're parked up there in your daddy's Buick," Richard said, "and you're necking away vigorously."

"That's right," said Martin. "And after a few minutes I'm playing with her tits."

"Was it through the brassiere," Harold said, "or did you manage to get bare tit?"

"I got bare tit," said Martin. "She let me unhook."

"And what could be more promising than that?" Stanley said.

"Absolutely," said Martin. "So at this point I feel it's permissible to move on to the next stage. And so I go down, slowly and gently, with my sensitive fingers. With old Frankie Sinatra on the car radio." He paused again for more green ice cream. The others waited impatiently.

"Then up ye olde skirt?" Stanley asked.

"Well, gentlemen," said Martin, "I get three inches above the knee when she takes my hand away and puts it back on her tit, which by now is getting pretty boring."

"And that's it?" said Richard.

"That's it," said Martin. "The way she says, 'Please don't,' I know she means it."

"You must have been only eight inches away from the Garden of Eden," Harold said.

"I figure seven and three-quarters inches," Martin said angrily, slamming his fist down on the table and almost knocking over Richard's Choco-Mint Parfait.

"Were you talking to her at all, while you were doing all this?" asked Stanley.

"Of course not," said Martin. "I was too busy."

"You should have been whispering sweet nothings in her ear," said Richard. "Especially when you reached her knee."

"What the hell is a sweet nothing?" said Martin.

"That's something you're going to have to figure out, my boy, if you want to play in the big leagues," Stanley said.

"Thanks for your advice," said Martin.

"Let's face it, she's just another little cockteaser," said Harold.

"A miasma of virginity hangs heavy o'er the land," said Richard, who was a poet.

"Every night there's guys who drive away from Summit Circle with a severe case of blue balls," said Martin. "You've got to take yourself in hand as soon as possible, right after you drive her home."

"Our health is at serious risk, and I'm not kidding," said Stanley.

"Her flashing eyes, her shining hair," said Richard. "Beware, beware."

Later, walking home from Gagnon's, Richard started sketching some new lines in his head. *Behold, my laughter curls in agony*, he composed. *My laughter is sardonic*. Others would laugh too if they knew how pathetically little experience he'd had with girls, even less than overweight Harold. He winced as he recalled what had happened last Saturday night. Parked in his father's car, he and that hateful Amanda Cooper had been necking passionately – or he thought it was passionately. But everything had come to a screeching halt when she uttered those terrible words, "Watch your hands, Richard," when he attempted to fondle one of her breasts. It would have been a first for him. And that damn Martin had experienced not only tit, but bare tit, and had even come close to the gates of the Garden of Eden.

The ache of Richard's chastity would become even more acute after lunch on Sunday, thanks to his encounter with his Uncle Morty. Richard's mother seldom invited Morty to her elegant Sunday luncheon parties, but he was, after all, her brother, and she felt compelled to have him over at least twice a year. But she could never stop worrying that he might suddenly utter one of his vulgarisms at the table. Would he tell one of his horrid jokes about the travelling salesman and the farmer's daughter? And would he pat the maid on the behind, as he had once done, almost causing a serious soup-tureen accident?

Mrs. Lippman shuddered at the thought of this kind of behaviour in the presence of guests whom she described as "refined."

Richard's father's family was highly assimilated, having been in Montreal since 1804, when there had been only a handful of Jews in all of Canada. But his mother was a child of the shabby St. Dominique Street ghetto, the daughter of immigrants who came from Romania in 1906. As a girl, Shaindel Mintz had been phenomenally beautiful, and when Gerald Lippman of Westmount discovered her and asked her to marry him, Shaindel immediately became Sheila and hired an elocution teacher to iron out her accent, to rid her English of every vestige of Yiddish singsong.

By contrast, her brother Morty was an unreconstructed son of St. Dominique Street, with no cultural affectations of any kind. Now, at lunch in the dark mahogany dining room, as Sheila Lippman looked across the table at her brother's crude manipulation of his knife and fork, she worried what her other guests might be thinking of him, guests that included prominent lawyers and their soignée wives. But actually, these guests were thrilled to be in the same room as the legendary Morty Mintz, boss of Montreal's biggest illegal gambling operation, a man who had the police and the city council in his pocket.

Uncle Morty seldom got up before noon, and now, at that Sunday lunch, he dozed off over the dessert, slumping forward with his eyes closed and his mouth open. But he awoke with a start when the maid asked him if he wanted cream and sugar with his coffee. It took him only a moment to get his bearings and to rise abruptly from the table.

"It was sure nice meeting you folks," he said, disengaging his napkin from his fleshy neck. "I sure enjoyed our conversation."

But the conversation, Richard reflected, had been utterly boring. If only they could have asked Morty about the goings-on in his lavish casino, up on Côte St. Luke Road, it could have been a fabulous lunch, but it was an unwritten rule that one must never allude to Morty's colourful occupation. Officially he was "in the clothing business."

"And now Richard and I will bid you a fond farewell," Morty told the luncheon guests.

"Where are you taking him, Morton?" Mrs. Lippman asked suspiciously. She always called Morty Morton.

"We're going for a walk, in Murray Park," Morty said. "To aid the digestion." He hadn't asked Richard if he wanted exercise, but Richard was delighted with the prospect of some talk with this fabled uncle he so seldom saw, the only interesting member of the family.

When they got out onto the street, they went not to Murray Park but to Morty's car, parked at the curb. It was a glistening two-tone brown-and-beige Packard Phaeton. During the war, Packard had been building tanks, but as soon as they started turning out cars again, Morty had managed to get one of the first ones out of the factory. It was a marvel of luxury, with automatic transmission, hydraulic brakes, and sealed-beam headlights. It cost five thousand dollars and was, Morty was fond of saying, the Rolls-Royce of automobiles.

"Where are we going?" asked Richard, as he settled into the glove-leather bucket seat.

"We're going to get something to eat," said Morty.

"But we just had lunch."

"Lunch?" said Morty. "Christ, I'm starved. Your mother has become so fancy that she doesn't serve real food any more. Most of it, I couldn't get down. What the hell was that green stuff at the beginning?"

"That was avocado vinaigrette."

"And the main course, the white stuff?"

"That was *blanquette de veau*."

"Christ, this is no way for Jews to live," said Morty. "Just because your father has a lot of money, and you live in a big house in Westmount, your mother wants to look like a goy, sound like a goy, eat like a goy. Even if you could digest that fancy-schmancy junk she puts on the table, her portions are so tiny you could starve to death. And there's no seconds. Did you ever notice that gentiles basically don't eat?"

They were driving along Sherbrooke Street when Morty pointed to two tall, lean, middle-aged men on the sidewalk. They were striding along briskly, apparently out for their Sunday afternoon constitutionals. "Look at those two gentiles," Morty said. "Mr. McNish and Mr. McPish. Take the Harris tweed off their shoulders and they're thin like skeletons. They basically don't eat. A cup of tea and a cucumber sandwich. Then they ask the butler to bring in the Scotch." As a fat man, Morty was always contemptuous of people who were slim. Now, gunning the Packard's motor, he gave Mr. McNish and Mr. McPish a toot on the car's musical horn, causing them to jump, then look at him resentfully.

"Didn't you even like Ma's dessert?" Richard asked. "The profiteroles?"

"For dessert please give me a piece of honey cake, a strudel, something that will stick to the ribs, not that tra-la-la Frenchy stuff," said Morty. "No, the only thing I liked about that lunch, to be quite frank, was the little maid that was serving. I would have liked to have given her a quick feel, but your mother was watching me. I trust your brother Arthur is getting into that little maid now and then, Ricky-boy. It's his prerogative, you know, as the eldest son."

"Arthur?" said Richard. "Don't make me laugh."

Continuing along Sherbrooke Street, they sped eastward, past the museum, the Ritz, McGill. At St. Lawrence they headed north and pulled up at Freda's Restaurant, where Freda herself came out to greet Morty as though he were royalty.

"We have cholent today," said Freda.

"Excellent," said Morty. "We want cholent, we want *kishke*, we want *varenikes*. You know what we want, Freda."

"I know, I know," said Freda, and she rushed off to the kitchen.

"Notice this tablecloth," said Morty, as a waiter put a large bottle of seltzer in front of them. "Notice this yellow stain, probably from chicken soup. This, I like. This is human. Your mother's tablecloth is so white it blinds you. You can't relax. Her napkins are so starched it's like wiping your mouth with cardboard. But Freda's is human."

And dingy, thought Richard. The wallpaper was starting to peel in several places and the door leading to the kitchen squeaked loudly when it swung open. The heavy aroma from the kitchen was complex, challenging the nostrils to analyze how much of it was onion, how much cabbage, how much cauliflower.

"So tell me," Morty said, "what sports are you doing these days? Some baseball? Basketball? I guess you didn't make the football team, did you?"

"No," said Richard. "I don't do much sports."

"I didn't think so," said Morty. "Your mother tells me you've always got your nose in a book. Is that good for your health?"

"No, I guess it isn't," said Richard.

The waiter now brought the half-sour pickles and Morty started slicing them deftly. "So how's your love life, Richard?" he said. "Do you manage on occasion to dip the old wick?"

"Yeah, I'm doing okay," said Richard casually, thinking that here was a moment when a novelist would have his hero laughing inwardly, bitterly, perhaps sardonically. Didn't Morty realize that Richard was more virginal than his mother's starchiest dinner napkin?

"I bet you go down to De Bullion Street with the boys on Thursday night, eh?" Morty was saying. "In my day we went on Thursdays, never on Friday. Friday is payday and it's crowded as hell. You have to wait and wait, and once you're finally upstairs the girls are in such a bloody hurry it makes you nervous. No, Thursday is the night, a quiet night. But they tell me it's five dollars now. It was a standard two bucks in my day, but this is inflation, eh? That war didn't do anybody any good, did it?"

"Uh, Uncle Morty, we don't go to De Bullion Street," said Richard, suddenly alarmed that some of this might somehow get back to his father, thanks to Morty's propensity for blabbing.

"You don't patronize the cat-houses?" said Morty. "You mean you're not getting serviced professionally? Next you'll be telling me you're getting it amateur, from the girls in the private schools, when they're not eating their goddam cucumber sandwiches."

"That's it, Uncle Morty," said Richard. "It's those cucumber girls." Damn it, what would this man-of-the-world uncle of his think if he knew how meagre Richard's experience actually was? What would he think if he could see Richard, squirming in bed at night, visualizing the breasts of the hateful Amanda Cooper and able to find relief only by using his God-given right hand, moistened with a bit of spittle? And now he was telling Morty that he was in the habit of seducing girls from the private schools.

"I look into your eyes and I can see you're lying," said Morty. "Those girls keep it locked up tight, saving it for the honeymoon. If you're getting it at all in the leafy streets of Westmount, it's from the young housewife whose milkman is too busy to look after her."

The food was arriving at the table now and Morty sprang into action. He dribbled olive oil onto the chopped liver and called loudly for more fried onions. He ladled Romanian eggplant onto Richard's plate and onto his own. He sent the coleslaw back to the kitchen, asking for the spicy and not the creamy. He held glasses under the spigot of the seltzer bottle and hit the lever too violently, sending the bubbly water foaming over the glasses and onto the tablecloth. He handed Richard one of the glasses, which had a faint smudge of lipstick on it.

"So you're growing up hoity-toity, up on Murray Avenue," said Morty, reaching for the *kimmel* bread. "But do you ever get downtown, where life is real? I don't mean the whorehouses, I mean Montreal in general. You know, the bright lights, the big city. I'm worried you're too sheltered. You've got to prepare for the great battle that is life, Richard."

"Well, I admit that my gang doesn't get downtown much," Richard started to say, but Morty was ploughing on.

"For instance, do you boys ever go to the Gayety?" he said.

"No, I hear it's pretty sleazy."

"Sleazy?" said Morty indignantly. "Where the hell did you hear that? The Gayety is one of our great institutions. All over North America they say, 'When you're in Montreal, make sure you catch the show at the Gayety.' The Gayety is more than a theatre, it's a shrine, it's a temple for the worship of the female body, it's striptease like nowhere else."

"Sounds interesting," said Richard.

"It's more than interesting," said Morty, jabbing his fork into a plump little knish. "You ever heard of Lili L'Amour?"

"Vaguely," said Richard.

"There's nothing vague about Lili," said Morty. "Believe me, she is the greatest. As you will see for yourself at the Gayety, when she takes it off. You'll come, eh, tomorrow night?

We'll be in row three, centre. I have tickets. You'll be looking at a pair like you never saw in your life, Ricky-boy." Still chewing his knish, Morty cupped his hands and held them out in front of his chest, to show Richard the magnitude of what he could anticipate.

"After the show," said Morty, "we'll go backstage and you can meet her."

2

Over the years all the great ones came to Montreal, to take their clothes off on the stage of the Gayety Theatre. Each had her own reputation, her own sobriquet. Jennie Lee was the Bazoom Girl, Evelyn West was the Treasure Chest, Ann Corio was the Epic Epidermis, Peaches Strange was the Queen of Quiver. There were comic strippers too, like Peppy Cola and Apple Pie, the All-American Dish. Each had her own style, her own dance. Some were fast strippers, some were slow teasers. Each had her own variation of the classic bump and grind, but it was always punctuated by the same crash of drums from the orchestra.

After the show, aficionados would gather in the Taverne des Sports to discuss the performance. "What about that Ann Corio?" one fellow might say. "Did you ever see a swivel like that? It's a work of art."

"Swivel?" another might say. "Don't give me that artsy-fartsy swivel. What I want is a real grind. I want my coffee beans in there getting ground real fine – and real fast. Like Tempest Storm does, God bless her."

There might be some debate whether Tempest Storm was indeed the greatest of the grinders, but there was unanimous agreement that when it came to the bump – the pelvic thrust – nobody could compare with the frenetic Georgia Sothern. As one student of the art put it, "When Georgia throws it, you can catch it in the second balcony." So remarkable was this thrust that a certain McGill physiology professor would send his students down to the Gayety to see if they could discern which muscles Georgia invoked to achieve it. Was it the *rectus abdominis*? The *lineae transversae*? The *quadratus lumborum*?

While future physicians studied Georgia Sothern, McGill's engineering students came to observe Ginger Snapp, the Texas Tornado, who was renowned for her mastery of the tassel. Other strippers could attach tassels to their breasts and make them twirl clockwise or counter-clockwise, but only Ginger could get one of them going clockwise and the other one counter-clockwise – and keep them both going that way at the same time. For young engineers who were studying aerodynamics, it was a revelation.

"I've seen them all," Morty Mintz said to his nephew as they settled into their seats, third row centre. "They've each got their little specialty, Richard, but none of them can touch Lili L'Amour. You wait and see."

But they would have to wait for a while before Lili would appear. First, of course, as in any theatre, the orchestra would strike up "God Save the King" and the audience would have to rise and sing. Then the show would start, with a number of variety acts to be endured before the featured disrobing began. In the best tradition of burlesque, a comic called Bozo Snyder opened the show by bursting onto the stage, wearing baggy pants that kept falling down. He bellowed jokes about the female anatomy and brandished a large rubber bladder at shrieking chorus girls. But most of the other acts were more refined. There was a ventriloquist, a juggler, Mephisto the Magician, a trio of tap dancers, a singer called Maggie Mayne, and finally, Antonio and Suzanne. Antonio was the knife-thrower and Suzanne was the target he had to miss as he threw his twenty knives. There was a murmur of relief from the audience when his last knife whizzed into the cork board behind Suzanne, missing her by inches. She and her tormentor took their bows to hearty applause.

There was now an important drum roll from the orchestra as the master of ceremonies strode onto the stage. "Ladies and gentlemen," he said, "the Gayety Theatre now has the honour to present, direct from New York, Chicago, and Los Angeles, the remarkable, the unequalled, the unsurpassed interpreter of the terpsichorean art, Montreal's sweetheart – we can't see enough of her, can we? – ha, ha – the one and only Miss Lili L'Amour."

Again there was applause as the audience waited to see what surprise Lili had in store for them this time. It was four months since she had last played Montreal and this was her first night back in town. She always came with a new act. What would it be this time? Aficionados knew that her dances always told a little story, of her own concoction. Montreal had adored routines like Slave Girl in the Harem, the Jilted Bride, and Locked into a Chastity Belt. Her stories often dealt with a woman in peril, a woman with a terrible problem that could only be solved by getting slowly undressed. Tonight would be no exception.

"I wish she'd do Jungle Goddess again," Morty whispered to Richard. "The way she fights off the animals is something to see."

As they waited for Lili's entrance, the music from Len Howard's orchestra was slow and sensual. When she finally appeared, she was enveloped in more clothes than her admirers had ever seen. She glided to the centre of the stage in a huge hoop skirt of rose-coloured silk, a long-waisted bodice, a flowing scarf to conceal her bosom, and an enormous hat decorated with birds and butterflies. Aha! She was Marie Antoinette, dressed with the extravagance that had infuriated the starving peasants and hastened the French Revolution.

Oblivious of her political effrontery, the French queen was dancing a stately minuet, her feet invisible under the floor-length hoop skirt. But the minuet seemed to go on a bit too long, and Richard detected some restlessness, as well as a few coughs, from the audience. "Take it off!" some lout shouted, and his neighbours looked at him resentfully. You might shout that at Bombshell Betty, if she kept you waiting too long, but you just didn't do it with the great Lili L'Amour.

But now things were going to happen. From the orchestra came spooky violin scrapings, like movie music heralding the imminence of catastrophe. Then he arrived, the Executioner, wheeling in his portable guillotine. He was a huge, muscular, bare-chested brute wearing a black mask. With a flourish, he ran his finger along the guillotine's blade, to assure himself of its sharpness. As a further test, he produced a large cabbage, placed it on the block, and sent the blade crashing down on it. The cabbage was neatly sliced in two, one half falling into the head basket. Marie Antoinette's remaining moments on this earth would be few.

Seeing the guillotine, Lili recoiled in horror. She retreated to a corner of the stage and stood there, trembling, as the music became quiveringly plaintive. But then a smile came to her lips. She had a plan. As the music quickened, she glided to the centre of the stage, took off her huge hat, and hurled it into the wings. The audience immediately understood her strategy. She would reveal her naked body to the Executioner, who would be so overwhelmed by her beauty that he would have to pardon her. And beautiful she certainly was, more beautiful than any woman, or any photo of a woman, that Richard had ever seen. He drank in her glowing skin, her wildly high cheekbones, her extravagantly arched eyebrows. Visualizing what he suspected was about to happen, he felt the familiar tingle in his trousers.

Now Lili was dancing close to the Executioner and flaunting the hoop skirt in his face. Unimpressed, the masked monster brought his blade down on another cabbage. Lili now drifted to centre stage and, with the help of a clever spring-loaded mechanism, sent the voluminous skirt flying away from her body. With a quick motion, she tore the long gauzy scarf away from her neck, revealing that under her bodice she was encased in high-waisted stays, which, in the appropriate eighteenth-century mode, thrust her bosom as high as it could go, revealing most of it. Applause from the audience.

The Executioner was taking notice now. Distracted, he fumbled with his next cabbage and almost cut his finger in the slicing. The audience laughed appreciatively. As she danced, sometimes slowly and sometimes fast, Lili gradually escaped from the constriction of the bodice and the whalebone stays, revealing her breasts. In deference to the police, Marie Antoinette's nipples were concealed by small circular pasties. These were the first naked breasts Richard had ever seen, and they were beyond his most fevered imaginings.

"Notice she doesn't do the old bump and grind," Morty whispered hoarsely. "She doesn't have to. But you don't miss it, do you?" But Richard was too entranced to reply, or to ask what bump and grind was.

From the waist down, Lili was now clad in long, beribboned eighteenth-century pantaloons, and, as connoisseurs of the art knew, slipping pants off gracefully was always a challenge. But Lili, whirling like a dervish, divested herself of the pantaloons without anyone knowing how it was done. She was a magician, and the hips were quicker than the eye.

Marie Antoinette was now wearing only frilly black lace panties, secure in the knowledge that her audience would not be troubled by this historical inaccuracy. She was circling the Executioner now, with slow, writhing motions. Flustered and irresolute, he mopped his sweaty brow and fumbled his next cabbage, which rolled across the stage unchopped.

The guillotine blade now came crashing down on the empty block, and as it did so, its thud mingled with a crash of drums from the orchestra. That was the signal for Lili to whip off her black panties and stand there wearing nothing but the minimal G-string demanded by the law. For the Executioner, it was too much. With a sudden violent push he sent his wheeled guillotine careering off stage. His sweaty torso was now glistening in the spotlight as he approached Lili with arms outstretched, in the grip of lust. But Marie Antoinette was still a queen, even without crinoline and bodice, and with an imperious gesture she ordered him away. The orchestra obliged with a *nyah-nyah-nyah* sound as the wretched brute, defeated by beauty, shuffled off the stage.

The audience was on their feet now, applauding long and loud, as their beloved Lili L'Amour, pristine and glowing in G-string and pasties, took four curtain calls before the final blackout. Unhappily, Richard was unable to applaud as his right hand was in his pocket trying to control the erection that had sprouted in his pants.

"Let's go backstage, say hello to Lili," said Morty as the audience started filing out.

"Gee, can we really do that?" asked Richard nervously.

"Sure," said Morty. "We're old friends."

Moments later they were walking down a dingy backstage corridor. When they came to a door with a star on it, Morty knocked.

"Who's there?" came Lili's voice from inside.

"It's Morty. You were terrific, sweetheart. Can we come in?"

"Go away," said Lili. "Get lost."

"Hey, what's the matter?" said Morty.

"You know damn well what the matter is," said Lili. "So just disappear, will you?"

"I don't know what you're talking about," said Morty. "But look, I've got my nephew with me. He's come all the way from Winnipeg to see the show. Two thousand miles. He's dying to meet you."

There was silence from inside and then Lili, wearing a dressing gown, opened the door. "Come on in," she said, pointing to Richard. "You," she said, pointing to Morty, "you stay outside." And she closed the door in his face.

"Look, Lili," Morty shouted through the door, "it had to be done, believe me."

"Tell him I do not wish to speak to him," Lili said to Richard.

"Uh, Uncle Morty," Richard said, addressing the door, "Miss L'Amour says she does not wish to speak to you." Lili was obviously very angry, and Richard, caught in the middle of something, felt himself starting to tremble. Despite being so close to this sex goddess, his erection was now gone. There is nothing like terror to bring on a shrivelling.

"So how did you like the show?" Lili asked, sitting down in front of a mirror to take off her makeup.

"Oh, it was just wonderful," said Richard. "Fantastic."

"A little more interesting than that Ann Corio who was here last week, don't you think?" said Lili.

"Oh, definitely," said Richard. "There's no comparison." Ann Corio must be another stripper, Richard decided. Lili must have assumed that Richard was a regular patron of the Gayety.

"Where were you sitting?" Lili asked. "Was it close to the stage?"

"We were third row centre," said Richard.

"Did you hear anything the Executioner said, the son of a bitch?" she asked unexpectedly.

"No," said Richard, "I didn't hear anything. Was there supposed to be dialogue?"

"I never do dialogue," said Lili. "But that son of a bitch, every time I dance close to him he says something, something disgusting. He thinks I'm just another little stripper that wants to be screwed by a man with muscles. But I'm not a stripper, I'm an artist, and I don't want anybody to forget that." As she said it, she threw Marie Antoinette's wig down on the floor. She was furious again and, unreasonably, seemed to be directing some of her anger at Richard.

"You should get the bastard fired," came Morty's voice. He obviously had his ear to the door.

"Tell your uncle to shut up," said Lili.

Richard went over to the door and addressed it in a loud voice. "Morty, once and for all, will you please be quiet?" he said. He hoped his formidable uncle wouldn't take offence. He would explain later that he had to be sure Lili understood that he was on her side and wasn't one of the nasty adversaries who were arrayed against her.

"Now I guess you want a photo, and an autograph," Lili said.

"Oh, yes, I'd love that."

She opened a drawer in her dressing table and rummaged in it. "Damn it," she said. "I don't have any more. And they were supposed to send me some."

"Just my luck," said Richard.

"And you came all the way from Winnipeg," she said.

"Yeah, it's a long way away," he said. If he revealed that Winnipeg was a lie, albeit a lie of Morty's, she would surely fly into another fury.

She pondered for a moment and then said, "Well, you're a nice boy, so you deserve a souvenir." She turned her back to him, but in the big mirror he could see her opening her dressing gown, revealing that she was naked underneath. With a slight wince of discomfort, she peeled the pasty off her left breast. She closed the dressing gown, turned, and handed him the little blue pasty, sparkling with sequins. "This will help you remember Lili L'Amour," she said.

"Gee, thank you," Richard mumbled, visibly trembling now.

"I'm sorry you saw me being so mad," she said, opening the door for him. "I'm really a very nice person."

"She's a lovely person," said Morty, who had been waiting outside. "But could we talk for a minute, Lili baby?"

"No, we can't," she said, and with a smile for Richard as he left, she closed the door.

As he walked down the backstage corridor with Morty, Richard examined the pasty she had given him. This keepsake was going to be as sacred to him as the bones of Saint Anthony of Padua would be to a devout Roman Catholic.

"She gave you that?" asked Morty, noticing the pasty.

"Yes," said Richard.

"You must have made a good impression," said Morty. "Usually she just gives a picture."

"What did you do, Uncle Morty, to make her so mad?"

"I had her barred. But it was for her own good."

Richard's questions revealed that it had happened four months ago, during Lili's last gig in Montreal. She had arrived one night, after her show, at Morty's lavish illegal casino, to gamble at the barbotte table. But the doorman had turned her away, on Morty's orders.

"Every night for a week she was losing heavily," Morty said. "I can tell a customer's losing streak when I see it, and usually it makes me very happy, because it means money into my pocket. But this was different. Call me sentimental, but I don't want to see a girl wiped out on my premises, especially if she's got tits like that. So I say to her, 'Lili, baby, don't play barbotte, play roulette, play blackjack, play something I can control and I'll see to it that you don't lose, and maybe you'll even win a bit. But barbotte is beyond my control. It's the players that throw the dice, not my own boys.'

"But no, Lili wants to play barbotte. When she's in Montreal she only wants to play this crazy game, which is played nowhere else in the world. She doesn't like roulette. She doesn't like *chemin de fer*. She loves barbotte, even if it's cleaning her out. She does not want anybody telling her what to do, not even Morty Mintz."

"She was very mad," said Richard, as they got into Morty's Packard Phaeton to drive back uptown.

"She can be a wildcat," said Morty. "I once saw her hit a guy in the bar at the El Morocco. Knocked him right off his stool. But Lili is not like the other strippers. She's not chewing gum all the time and she talks fancy."

"She says she's not a stripper," Richard said. "She's an artist."

"That's what I mean," said Morty. "She talks fancy."

That night, sleep was impossible for Richard. The few words Lili had addressed to him in the dressing room kept echoing through his mind. She had treated him like an adult, confiding in him her contempt for the son-of-a-bitch Executioner. She had used the word *screw*, which he had never heard before from a girl or woman. As Richard turned her words over in his mind, the fragrance of the dressing room came back to him, the flowers of her perfume mingling with the exciting scent of her perspiration, from her exertions on the stage. But above all, it was the memory of the green eyes, the fabulous eyebrows, the gorgeous lips.

He was, without doubt, deeply in love. He had been in love before, with girls at school like Gloria, Sybil, and Edith, but those loves – never declared and thus always unrequited – now seemed shabby and infantile by comparison. He turned on the light beside his bed and took the pasty out from under the pillow, to examine it for the twenty-sixth time. And suddenly he knew what he had to do. He had to write a poem about Lili, a poem that he would send to her.

Leaping out of bed, he went to his desk and turned on the lamp. He took his yellow legal pad from the drawer, carefully filled his fountain pen with Parker Quink, and started to write: "Whenas in silks my Lili goes, / Then, then, methinks, how sweetly flows / The liquefaction of her clothes!" But what if she recognized it, as something Robert Herrick wrote – to his Julia, of course, not his Lili – three hundred years ago? No, it would be too dangerous to work that into the poem. Still, by old Herrick's next few lines you'd think he'd been right there in the Gayety, watching Lili: "Next, when I cast mine eyes and see / That brave vibration each way free . . ." When it came to brave vibration, who could match Lili?

But no, he had to be original. After a moment, the beginnings of an idea came to him, and he wrote: "Curvilinear, passion-tipped, your smiling breasts . . ." No, "smiling" was corny. Besides, the last time he had seen them, in the dressing-room mirror, they looked angry, not smiling. "Your angry breasts . . ." No, that wouldn't lead to anything lyrical. "Your even-tempered breasts . . ." No, no, no. And then he realized that he ought to forget about breasts, and any stuff like that, which could easily lead him into the poetry of horniness. He had written too much of that in the past. No, for Lili it would have to be pure, lofty. He would write about respectable body parts like her brow, eyes, lips. He would use good poetry words like alabaster, carmine, azure.

But beyond that, no pure ideas were coming. So, to recharge his creative batteries, he went downstairs to the kitchen to brew himself a cup of Ovaltine. And as the water started boiling, it came to him. He would bring back the beautiful women of history, who would take one look at Lili and realize that they were nothing in comparison. Lili would upstage Helen of Troy, Anne Boleyn, and many another. Some of these classical beauties would weep, some would rage. Grabbing the pad where his mother made her grocery lists, he quickly wrote: "Venus de Milo, in deep despair, her robe would rend / If only she had arms to do the rending."

Back upstairs, at his desk, ideas started coming thick and fast: "Even the Moon weeps, her beauty eclipsed / Her tears do fall on the parchèd earth . . ." Yes, Lili would have them all weeping. Quickly he made a list of historic lookers that he could use: Aphrodite, Persephone, Ariadne, Leda. No, maybe not Leda. She'd been involved with a swan, which always struck Richard as being a bit too odd. And everything with Lili had to be pure. But Dante's Beatrice, yes. "When Dante did sweet Lili espy / He said to Beatrice, 'Goodbye, goodbye.'"

Richard added Anna Karenina and Margaret of Navarre to his list, and then, to bring it up to date, threw in Greta Garbo, Marlene Dietrich, and Carole Lombard. Then he went to work, methodically forging lines to show how Lili's splendour put them all in the shade. By five in the morning his hand-written ode was finished. He fed a sheet of his best bond paper into his Smith-Corona portable and started typing.

"What are you typing?" his mother called from the hall. "You're waking us up."

"It's for school," Richard said.

When he finished, he folded the poem, put it into an envelope, and addressed it to Miss Lili L'Amour, Gayety Theatre, 94 St. Catherine Street West, Montreal. On his way to school he dropped it into a mailbox – and then immediately wished he hadn't. Surely she would think he was some kind of idiot.

Three days later his mother called him to the phone. "There's a female wants to speak to you," she said.

It was Lili. "Your poem is wonderful," she said. "You have a great talent."

"Thanks," said Richard. "I hoped you'd like it."

"Will you have lunch with me on Saturday?" she asked. "At the Ritz?"

"That would be great," said Richard, his heart thumping.

"Who was that?" Mrs. Lippman asked from the doorway, after he hung up. "And what was it you hoped she'd like?"

"A girl from school," Richard said. "We're working on a class project."

3

"*Mais c'est quoi, exactement, la striptease?*" Father Prud'Homme asked.

"*C'est une danse, mon père,*" said Trépanier, "*dans laquelle la danseuse se déshabille.*"

"What is her name, this woman?" asked the priest.

"She calls herself Lili L'Amour, *mon père,*" said Trépanier.

"Does she take everything off, this Lili L'Amour?" asked the priest. "Her underclothes as well?"

"So I am told, *mon père.*"

Father Prud'Homme inhaled the aroma of his cognac. He was always happy to be invited to dinner at the Lafontaine Club, and he only wished it happened more often. The setting here was elegant, the food was excellent, and, he noted, when the waiter came round with the cognac decanter he poured considerably more of it into Father Prud'Homme's snifter than into the snifters of the other men at the table. Was this deference to the Church? the priest wondered, with a little inward smile. Raising the snifter to his lips, he tasted this very old Courvoisier. This would be a moment of golden serenity, if only he didn't have to listen to the irritating voice of Maurice Trépanier.

"*Il y a toujours des jeunes dans l'auditoire,*" Trépanier was saying. "*C'est effrayant!*"

"But you have not seen this Lili L'Amour yourself," the priest said.

"Certainly not, *mon père,*" said Trépanier, who was chairman of the new Public Morality Committee. "I could never permit myself to enter into a place like that." Here again, Father Prud'Homme reflected, was Trépanier's holier-than-thou tone of voice, something that could be immensely annoying to a clergyman.

Adelard Robitaille, at the head of the table, had not seen the show either. He was president of the League of the Sacred Heart and host of this dinner meeting, which had been called to plan a massive crusade against vice in Montreal. The committee was proposing an all-out attack on the city's hundreds of brothels, gambling dens, after-hours drinking establishments, stores purveying pornographic literature, and immoral theatres, like the Gayety. The support of the Church was essential and that was why Father Prud'Homme had been invited, along with dignitaries from organizations like the Catholic School Board and the Knights of Columbus. But none of those present had actually seen the degrading spectacle being put on by this Lili L'Amour. Except, of course, Galipeau, the private detective who had been hired to do research for the committee.

"Monsieur Galipeau can answer your questions, *mon père,*" said Adelard Robitaille.

"How much of her clothing does she take off?" asked Father Prud'Homme.

"I would say 95 per cent of it, *mon père,*" said the detective.

"What remains, the 5 per cent?"

"I would say 1½ per cent of it is affixed to each breast, a small circle of cloth to conceal the nipple, pasted on. These are called pasties and they sparkle when they catch the light."

Trépanier and Robitaille exchanged a nervous glance. They had instructed Galipeau to withhold nothing, but was he going too far? But then again, priests were used to hearing worse than this in the confessional, were they not?

"And the remaining 3½ per cent of the clothing," said Father Prud'Homme. "I presume that is down below?"

"Yes, *mon père*. It is called the G-string. It is a narrow band of cloth, barely enough to conceal the pudendum." The detective hesitated, with a small cough. But he was a professional, and he plunged on. "Of course the hair down below," he said, "has been shaved."

"Montreal has become a cesspool," said Trépanier, thumping his fist on the table.

"So it would appear," said Father Prud'Homme, sipping his cognac and reaching for a cigar. The waiter who was bringing round the cigar box, he noted appreciatively, was wearing white gloves – another nice little touch in the Lafontaine Club. The service here, and the decor, was just as luxurious as in the exclusive men's clubs downtown, the Mount Royal Club, the Saint James, the Mount Stephen. Those places, the refuge of Scottish railway barons and English insurance tycoons, did not welcome French Canadians into their deep leather chairs. It was in response to this prejudice that a group of resentful French businessmen and lawyers had founded the Lafontaine. And a good thing it was, too, thought Father Prud'Homme, as he watched his cigar smoke curl up toward the glittering chandelier.

"Let us come to the point, *mon père*," Trépanier was saying. "We know you have the ear of the archbishop. So would you be kind enough to put this into his hands?" He handed the priest a thick document, the blueprint for a blitzkrieg against vice.

"Thank you," said Father Prud'Homme, wondering whether on his way home he could contrive to forget this document in the taxi. A crusade against vice was, of course, out of the question. The priest's task now was to show these naive zealots that they must face the facts of life.

"Of course the Church will join you in your noble work," said Father Prud'Homme, contemplating the glowing tip of his cigar. "But there are a few things about the problem of vice that you may not know. For instance, Monsieur Trépanier is not accurate in saying that Montreal has become a cesspool of vice. Montreal has not *become* a cesspool. Montreal has *always been* a cesspool, back since the days of New France. Our countryside has always been pure, with its simple habitant farmers, but in the metropolis the putrefaction of drinking and dancing and whoring has been with us since the earliest days. The reports in the archives are so lurid that even historians are not allowed to see them."

The committeemen nodded sagely as they sipped their *pousse-cafés*.

"For three centuries the Church has been unceasing in its efforts to drain this cesspool that is called Montreal, to dig it up, or to pave it over. But we are struggling with the devil, gentlemen, who often comes in the guise of a naked woman, and that is never an easy contest. While I am very appreciative of your desire to pick up the challenge, I must say that you are new to the game and have much to learn. For instance you say that the doors must be nailed shut on every brothel in town. But is that really a good idea, gentlemen?"

The committeemen looked at each other, puzzled.

"Montreal is a seaport," the priest continued. "There are foreign sailors pouring off ships every day, sailors who have been at sea for a long time. I need not tell you what they are looking for. But if they cannot find an outlet for their bestial urges on De Bullion Street, or Charlotte Street, will honest women, walking on honest streets, be safe from the attacks of sexually crazed brutes from Marseilles or Mozambique? Would your wives be safe? Would your daughters be safe?"

"Are you suggesting that the bawdy houses be allowed to remain open?" Jean-Pierre Pomerleau asked nervously. He was the representative of the Order of Jacques Cartier.

"No," said the priest, "I am suggesting that a few be allowed to function, as a safety valve. But how few? It would not be easy to arrive at a number. There should be a survey – number of ships arriving, number of sailors, average time taken by each sailor to satisfy his lust, all this divided by number of staff in the average brothel, etcetera, etcetera. I bring up this matter, gentlemen, simply to show you that the struggle against vice is a subject more complex than you might think."

Father Prud'Homme beckoned to the waiter for another cognac, noting with satisfaction that his remarks seemed to have surprised the committeemen, who were now busy whispering to each other. Galipeau, the detective, had taken out his notebook and was entering some figures in it, perhaps starting to calculate how many whorehouses should be left open.

Leafing through the document that Trépanier had given to him, the priest noted that the committee wanted the archbishop to launch a noisy citywide campaign, with blistering homilies from every pulpit every Sunday, with leaflets distributed at the church door, with petitions, with picketing of the Gayety Theatre. But above all, they wanted the archbishop to sit down with J. Alcide Tourangeau, chairman of the executive committee of the city council, and demand action – or else. The police must be sent out to raid, to arrest, to padlock.

"We must have protest marches," the Knights of Columbus

delegate was saying. "I shall personally lead my Boy Scouts through the red-light district, with placards."

It was time now, Father Prud'Homme decided, to bring these enthusiasts down to earth. He would do it suddenly, boldly. He brandished the blitzkrieg document. "Do you realize, gentlemen, that this campaign, at this moment, could gravely injure the Church?"

The committeemen looked at him blankly.

"As you must know," he said, "the corruption engendered by the brothels and the gambling dens extends very high into the police force and the city council. Our highest officials turn a blind eye on this stinking cesspool, and in return they become rich enough to build for themselves handsome residences in Ahuntsic, to buy large boats and cruise Lake St. Louis, to escape winter on the sands of Florida. There is much, much money involved."

"That is exactly what the archbishop must denounce!" Trépanier exclaimed.

"Let us change the subject slightly, but only slightly," said the priest. "I need not tell you that now that the war is over, building materials are again becoming available. I happen to know that the archbishop wishes to build, to build massively. He wants to see, in various parts of the Island of Montreal, at least two new seminaries, as well as two nunneries, eight new churches, and an orphanage. For this he will need land, city-owned land. He can only afford this land – hundreds of acres – if the city will sell it to him at a nominal price, say one dollar per acre. Now I ask you, gentlemen, if the archbishop were to sit down with J. Alcide Tourangeau and the executive committee of the city council and say, 'Messieurs, I am about to launch a campaign that will eventually close the brothels and sink your cabin cruisers on Lake St. Louis. Your wives will no longer be able to go to Florida in winter. Now in return, would you please give us several hundred acres of free land?' If the archbishop were to say this to Monsieur Tourangeau, what do you think the response would be?"

Father Prud'Homme lit another cigar as he watched the committeemen whispering to each other uneasily. What he didn't tell them was that he suspected that the archbishop very much wanted to be made a cardinal, and knew that if he achieved a reputation as a massive builder of churches, this would probably come to the attention of the pope. Great builders could become cardinals, but you could hardly imagine His Holiness putting the red hat on the head of a cleric whose main claim to fame was to have closed down a few whorehouses, or even, in the case of Montreal, a few dozen whorehouses.

"So despite all our planning we cannot launch our campaign," Adelard Robitaille was saying.

"Not for the moment," said Father Prud'Homme. "But we can do it later." He did not add that it might be much, much later. But now, he noted, the committeemen looked crestfallen. It meant so much to them to become cleansers of the city. Taking pity on them, he decided to throw them a bone, something that would make their pain easier to bear.

"There is something we *can* do, gentlemen," he said. "We can at least strike one blow for decency. We can have this Lili L'Amour thrown out of Montreal, once and for all. This would be symbolic and would get us excellent publicity."

"How could we have her thrown out, *mon père?*" Robitaille asked.

"Well, gentlemen, as you may know, I sometimes write articles in the newspapers on religious matters," said the priest. "*Le Devoir* is always glad to hear from me, and I shall offer them a blistering denunciation of the depravity that permeates this Gayety Theatre. I shall demand that the police arrest this

Lili L'Amour on grounds of obscenity, indecent exposure, and the corruption of youth. The police will have to act."

This small move against one stripteaser would in no way disturb the real powers that be, the bosses of the brothels and the gambling dens. But the committeemen were fascinated by the idea.

"On behalf of the committee," said Trépanier, "may I congratulate you, *mon père*, on this very imaginative initiative."

"Thank you, thank you," said the priest. "But first I must have more information about this lady." He took out his notebook and turned to Galipeau, the detective. "Is she perhaps from the L'Amour family of Berthierville, which has given us so many criminals over the years?"

"No, *mon père*," said Galipeau. "She is from the United States. She is not even French. Her real name is Anna Holmquist."

"Then she is not a disgrace specifically to Quebec womanhood, she is a disgrace to all womanhood, everywhere. Or perhaps girlhood. How old is she?"

"Twenty-seven," the detective said. He produced a photograph from his briefcase and handed it to the priest. It was a publicity shot by Bruno of Hollywood and it showed Lili standing tall and completely nude, except for a small triangle of cloth, studded with sequins, which hung from a thin belt around her waist.

Father Prud'Homme studied the photo carefully. "Is this the G-string device that you described to us?" he finally asked.

"No, *mon père*, she calls this her chastity belt. In her dance she implores the gods to unlock it for her so she can commit adultery."

"I have seen chastity belts in the museums of Europe," said Father Prud'Homme, whose passion was medieval history, "and this device in no way resembles them. For one thing, they were designed to go underneath as well as in front. And they were made of iron."

"Iron?" asked Robitaille, shuddering.

"Yes," said Father Prud'Homme. "They were made by the same armourer who would construct the nobleman's suit of armour – his helmet, his visor, his breastplate, his greaves, his vambrace, and so on." The priest was on his feet now, quite excited as he demonstrated how the parts of a suit of armour fitted together. "If the nobleman was going off on a crusade," he continued, "which might keep him away for several years, he would ask his armourer to fabricate a sturdy chastity belt for Her Ladyship, and the armourer's wife would go up to the castle to take her measurements."

The photo of Lili was now being passed around the table, moving rather slowly as the committeemen noted the historical inaccuracy of her belt.

"A few more questions," Father Prud'Homme said, turning to the detective. "At the performance you saw, were there many French in the audience?"

"Yes, *mon père*, about 40 per cent French, 60 per cent English. Among the French there was a busload of men from St. Remi de Shefford, who had told their wives they were going to a baseball game in Montreal. The night before there was a busload from St. Chrysostome."

"Disgusting," the priest muttered. "This will be noted in my article." But in a way, he reflected, the effect of this lewd dancer was not entirely evil. The bus going back to St. Remi de Shefford after the show would be filled with men with stiffened penises. At home, they would wake up their wives, and as a result, some babies might be born – helping to keep the French-Canadian population high in the face of English encroachment.

But regardless of this positive contribution, Mademoiselle Lili L'Amour must be banished from Montreal forever. The

Public Morality Committee would thus be placated, for the time being, providing time for men of greater wisdom to work out a sensible way to deal with the ongoing problem. The priest smiled to himself as he gestured to the waiter with his empty cognac snifter.

4

For his historic lunch with Lili L'Amour, Richard chose his best silk tie, the one with the regimental stripes of the Royal Northumberland Fusiliers. He tied and untied it three times before he got the big Windsor knot exactly right, with the tie hanging down not too long and not too short. The knot sat snugly in the starchy collar of his best white shirt, and the whole thing was neatly framed by the lapels of his grey worsted suit. Looking down at his shoes, he was pleased to see that the shine he had achieved last night, in half an hour of buffing, was still dazzling this morning.

On his way out of the house, in the hall, he ran into his mother. "Where on earth are you going?" she asked, "all dressed up on a Saturday morning."

"I'm having lunch with the prime minister," Richard said. "He wants my advice."

"All right, all right," Mrs. Lippman said, with a great show of resignation. By now she had learned to accept this kind of answer. Richard was grown up now, he kept reminding her, and he was entitled to a private life.

With a jaunty goodbye wave to her, he stepped out onto the street, into the bright September sunlight. As he walked down toward the bus stop, he realized he could have given her a much better answer than the one about the prime minister. "I'm off to the Ritz-Carlton Hotel," he should have said, "to have lunch with one of the most beautiful women in the world, who happens to be a striptease dancer." That would have been an even more satisfyingly ridiculous answer.

Arriving at the Ritz twenty minutes early, Richard went straight across the lobby to the men's room. Here, amid the sumptuous brass fittings, he made a final check of his appearance. To his dismay, the mirror told him that that stubborn tuft of hair toward the back of his skull was sticking up again. With his comb, he worked to subdue it, all the while studying himself in the mirror. The pimples of yore were all gone, thank God, but his general appearance still wasn't good. Too much forehead and not enough chin, he told himself, as he invariably did when confronted by a mirror. But the sight of his shoulders cheered him up a bit: the very generous padding, almost to zoot-suit dimensions, broadened him to the point where Lili would probably not notice his narrowness. Standing on tiptoe, he once again considered getting a pair of those elevator shoes from New York, to give himself a bit more height.

With a final tug against his tuft, Richard pocketed his comb and went out into the lobby and across to the Palm Court, where he was to meet Lili. He sat down in a deep leather chair facing the entrance, so he could see her as soon as she came in. *If* she came in. Had she really arranged this tryst with him, or was it only a dream? His morning elation turned to sudden gloom. What if he sat there for an hour and still no Lili? Would he have lunch at the Ritz alone, downcast, ashamed?

There was only one other person in the Palm Court, a middle-aged man with a very red face who was sitting on the other side of the room. "Good morning, Stephen, m'lad," he called across to Richard. "How are we today?"

"We're fine, sir," Richard replied. "And how are you?"

"Flourishing," said the man, who seemed to be already drunk at noon. This, Richard realized, must be Cedric Lambert, a legend in Montreal. Lambert was the black-sheep scion of one of the city's oldest and wealthiest families. He spent almost every day quietly drinking in the Palm Court, or in the Maritime Bar downstairs. Whenever a member of high society came by, old Cedric would greet them by name, almost always getting the name wrong. At five o'clock, two of the hotel's bell-boys would help him stagger across Sherbrooke Street, to the mansion where he lived.

"How're your daddy's horses doing, Stephen?" Lambert was now calling across to Richard.

"They're doing fine, sir," Richard called back.

How would Lambert greet Lili when she came in? – if she came in – Richard wondered. She would, of course, be stark naked, without even the regulation pasties up top and with no G-string to conceal the mystery down below. Lambert would not notice these details, but would simply say, "Good morning, Margaret. How's your mother today? Is she any better?"

And here she was now! Lili! Sailing through the doorway, long-limbed and ravishingly beautiful under those extravagantly arched eyebrows. She was, of course, fully dressed, in a rather severe grey linen suit that was as chaste as it was elegant. Only her hat was flamboyant, a black straw hat with an enormous brim, lacquered to make it shine in the sun.

"I'm not talking to you any more, Deirdre," Lambert called out to her as she entered. "Not after what you said about me to Hannah."

Lili looked startled, but managed a sweet "Good morning" for Richard.

"Good morning," said Richard, hoping his voice wouldn't tremble. "Great to see you."

"What's with him?" Lili asked, nodding toward Lambert.

"Don't take it personally," Richard whispered. "He's sloshed. His father owns lots of shares in the hotel."

Lunch was to be in the garden, and after the maître d' led them to their table, Lili ordered two champagne cocktails. If only Stanley and Martin could see me now, Richard thought, as he fumbled in his pocket for a match to light her cigarette.

"Look – ducks," said Lili, gesturing at the pond, where a mother duck was swimming haughtily, followed by her squadron of ducklings.

"It's beautiful here, isn't it?" said Richard. "So many flowers." He lit his own cigarette, the gold-tipped black Sobranie she had given him. The perfumed Turkish tobacco was unfamiliar, and he struggled to suppress a cough.

"Yes, beautiful," said Lili, "but it's a bit dead, don't you think?"

Richard had to agree that it was a bit dead, all the other tables being occupied by diners who were eating and conversing very quietly and sedately. The Ritz was very much the domain of Montreal's upper crust, and these were all people with English or Scottish names, people who abhorred mealtime noise or display. Very few Tremblays ate here, and even fewer Cohens, so there were no sudden outbursts of loud laughter, no hands gesturing in the air, no boisterous table-hopping.

"I usually like Dinty Moore's for lunch, or the Indian Room," Lili was saying, "but they're so noisy. And we need to talk, don't we?"

"Uh, yes, I guess we do," Richard said, wondering if he had heard her correctly over the thunder of his heartbeat.

A waiter brought the champagne cocktails and Lili raised her glass. "A toast," she said, and Richard, hoping his hand would be steady enough, followed suit, positioning his glass so that it could clink against hers, when the time came.

"Here's to Richard and Lili working together," she said. "Happily and profitably."

He managed the clink, but in getting the glass to his lips he spilled some of the wine down onto the table.

"If you don't mind, let's talk business right away," Lili said. "I want you to write beautiful poetry for me, Richard. I'll have it set to music so I can dance to it. While I dance, while I slowly slip out of my costume, your poetry will be read in the background, by a great voice, like Milton Cross. You know, the guy on the radio on Saturday afternoon, the opera. And don't worry, you'll be well paid for your work."

Stunned at the prospect of this, Richard could think of nothing to say. To give himself some time, he started to nod his head up and down, very slowly, as though pondering the pros and cons of the project.

"You look doubtful," Lili said. "You don't think it would work."

"No, no. I just need a minute to think about it."

"I'm not changing the subject," Lili said, "but did you happen to see last Wednesday's *Herald*?"

"No, I missed Wednesday's," said Richard, not bothering to point out that Westmount people never read this sleazy downtown tabloid.

"Then look at this, will you?" Lili said, reaching into her black crocodile handbag and producing a newspaper clipping, which was encased in celluloid to survive much handling. It was Vincent Geraghty's column, "Lights and Shadows of Montreal." The column was headed "It's Much More Than

Striptease." Geraghty, the paper's entertainment editor, wrote with little restraint:

Do you believe in reincarnation? If you don't, then go to the Gayety Theatre this week and study the dancing of the remarkable – no, the phenomenal – Lili L'Amour. Is she not the reincarnation of the late great Isadora Duncan?

As every schoolboy knows – or should know – Isadora Duncan invented – yes, invented – what we've come to call Modern Dance. It was she who first took the dance beyond – yes, far beyond – the prancing puppetry of the ballet. It was she who first astonished audiences by showing them how a woman's body could flow, could drift, could soar – to create poetic visual music. Her art made her the toast of Europe.

Perceptive members of the Gayety audience will, if they look carefully, see how the glorious Miss L'Amour is really Isadora Duncan reborn. Isadora was, of course, clad in the flowing vestments of ancient Greece, while Miss L'Amour offers much of her art in the nude. The debased audiences of the Gayety insist on seeing female flesh, and Miss L'Amour must make a living. But were she clad in ancient Greek raiment, Lili could be Isadora – yes, Isadora.

Geraghty's column went on to burble about how Lili – yes, Lili – could go far beyond the burlesque theatres of North America if she were properly attired. Like Isadora, she could grace the concert stages of London, Paris, and New York. Lili could be Gluck's Iphigenia in Aulis, a bacchant in Wagner's *Tannhäuser*, a flower maiden in *Parsifal*. Anyone who had seen Lili at the Gayety in her Jungle Goddess dance, in which she made love to a giant parrot, would be sure to agree, Geraghty said. Anyone who had seen Lili in Wrongly Convicted –

pursued by heartless police and shivering because of lack of clothing – would be bound to agree. These near-mythological pieces, Geraghty argued, were in the liberated idiom of 1948, but if Isadora Duncan were alive today she too might well divest herself of her gown and, naked, throw her divinely undulating body into Trapeze Girl.

"This is wonderful," said Richard, when he finished reading.

"Isn't it?" said Lili, who had ordered two more champagne cocktails. "Isadora sometimes danced to poetry," she said. There was a dramatic pause. "And now Lili L'Amour needs a poet. But is it going to be Richard Lippman?"

"Well, uh, I don't know whether I'm good enough," Richard said. "I've only been a poet for a year or so. Maybe you need stuff that's more professional."

"Like what?" said Lili.

"Something like:

She walks in beauty like the night
Of cloudless climes and starry skies;
And all that's best of dark and bright
Meet in her aspect and her eyes."

He went on, through the "one shade the more, one ray the less" bit, happy that he had not long ago memorized it, the idea being that he might recite it some day to impress the right girl at the right time. And now, here was the right girl! He carried on into the third stanza – "on that cheek and o'er that brow" – but as he orated he wondered whether she wasn't getting a bit bored. Still, he plunged on until the very end, with its "heart whose love is innocent."

"And that's professional?" she asked when he finished.

"Yes, it's by Lord Byron," he said.

"Well, I don't like it," she said. "All he's saying is that she's kind of cute, because he wants to get her into bed. But nothing happens, Richard. He just goes on and on, how cute she is. To dance to something I need a story, something that moves, something with a beginning, a middle, and an end – as old Professor Klugman used to say."

"You went to college?" Richard asked.

"Only for a year," Lili said. "Then my father died and I had to go to work."

"I could look through my Byron book again," Richard said. "I could probably find you something with a story."

"Look, Richard," she said, "you've got to have more confidence in yourself. Your poems are much better than this Byron's, even if he is a lord. Like the poem you mailed to me, 'When Danty does sweet Lili espy.' Is that how you pronounce it – 'Danty,' like 'panty'?"

"No, it's 'Dante,'" said Richard.

"I adored it," Lili said. "Especially when Beatrice hears Dante say, 'Alas, my former love, your star is faint, eclipsed by Lili's radiant moon.' And then old Bea's pathetic speech when she breaks the wine bottle in the bathtub and cuts both her wrists – 'making crimson the soapy water.' Now that's telling a story, which I love. When I read your Beatrice speech, Richard, I cried, it was so beautifully tragic. I actually choreographed the Beatrice part this morning and danced it right into the bathtub."

Richard took a gulp of his champagne as he imagined her sinking down into her bathtub, making little hot-water waves, her glorious breasts afloat at high tide. What he could not possibly imagine was what had actually transpired that morning at the LaSalle Hotel, where she was staying. Vincent Geraghty, entertainment editor of the *Herald*, had been standing beside her bathtub, his shirt sleeves rolled up as he scrubbed her back with the loofah she always travelled with. It was a big, rough loofah, and Vince wasn't afraid to administer the merciless kind of scrubbing she craved. Then, when she stepped out of the tub, he towelled her dry, exactly the way she liked. In the brief eight days since they had met, Vince had quickly learned how to do the things that pleased her.

"As a dancer, my body is my instrument," Lili had told Vince. "When you do it right, darling, my instrument is being tuned. I need a lot of that." Now, with her after-bath skin warm and glowing, she had led him out of the bathroom into the bedroom, happy to know that he would do it right.

"Maybe you could rise from the water like Aphrodite," Richard was saying, still visualizing her in the bathtub. "I could write something about the crystalline droplets falling from your, uh, from your arms. As you rise from the foam."

"Come on, Richard," she said, "I can't rise from the water, can I? I'm Beatrice, remember? I've just cut my wrists. I'm dying tragically in the soapy, crimson water. The curtain is coming down." There was a new sharpness in her voice that made him realize that working with her might not always be smooth sailing. But still –

"You're right," Richard said. "We'll let you die in the tub."

"I like it that you said 'we,'" Lili said. "That means you're going to be my poet, doesn't it?"

"Yes, I'm going to be your poet."

"Great," Lili said, and she leaned toward him to shake his hand, giving him an intoxicating whiff of her perfume. "You'll be well paid for your work, Richard," she said. "My agent will call you from New York about that on Monday. But right now, I'm starving. Let's have a look at these little old menus. And don't worry, I'm paying. This is strictly a business lunch and I'm paying."

As Richard opened the big, leather-bound menu, the familiar "older woman" thought kept bumping back into his head.

He and his friends often discussed how an "older woman" might invite a fellow into her bed if she took a shine to him. They had heard stories about this, incredible stories. And now could the fabulous Lili L'Amour be Richard Lippman's older woman?

Forcing himself to concentrate on the menu, he shuddered at the prices. Lunch at the Ritz was strictly à la carte and could set you back more than two dollars. And many of the dishes had exotic, mystifying names. What, for instance, was steak tartare? What was *coulibiac de saumon*? Lili ordered the *tournedos Rossini*, whatever that was, and he ordered the steak tartare. At the $1.25 they were asking for it, it must be even more sublime than the juicy rib steak that he had once enjoyed at Moishe's.

"You're very sophisticated, Richard, eating raw meat," Lili said, as the waiter put the steak tartare down in front of him.

"They say it's very good for you," Richard managed to say, as he looked down at the repulsive plate. He would have to eat it. He would gladly walk barefoot across blazing coals for Lili L'Amour, so the least he could do was to try to attack this mess she was buying for him. Attack it without throwing up. And it was then that he realized that he wanted much more from Lili than for her to relieve him of his despicable virginity. No, he was irrevocably, positively, and confusedly in love with her.

As he poked his fork into the carrots that sat beside the raw hamburger, Lili started talking about this Isadora Duncan that they had read about in Vincent Geraghty's column. With Richard's poetry in the background, she said, she could make a dream come true – to dance, like Isadora, in concert halls and not in burlesque theatres, and to dance with her clothes on. "It's much more classy if you don't have to take them off," she explained.

For a moment Richard was taken aback by her use of the word *classy*. Not long ago, in one of their ice-cream parlour seminars, he and his friends had been discussing semantics and had decided that people who used words like *classy* and *class* were themselves definitely not classy. These were words used only by the hoi polloi. But Stanley and Martin must have been wrong; Lili L'Amour had used the word and this was definitely one classy woman, especially with her appreciation of fine poetry.

"It would be strictly Modern Dance," she was saying. "I would wear gorgeous flowing robes, probably in earth colours." Again Richard was taken aback, this time by the thought that his poetry would make it possible for her to drape herself in earth colours and thus deprive a million men of what they wanted to see. But then it occurred to him that if he was truly in love with her, he didn't want a million men ogling those phenomenal breasts. No, he most definitely did not want that. Yes, he would dress her. Her nakedness would be for his eyes alone.

While she was talking about Isadora, he managed to get almost half of the steak tartare down before pushing his plate away, protesting that he had eaten a big breakfast and didn't have room for much more. But there was room for dessert, and the spectacular *bombe Nesselrode* with chestnuts that the waiter urged on them promised to compensate for the torture of the tartare. With the *bombe* the waiter brought a half-bottle of golden wine. "Château d'Yquem 1934," he said. "As you know, it's the greatest of the dessert wines. With the compliments of a gentleman over there." He nodded at a table at the other side of the duck pond, where four distinguished-looking men were having lunch.

"Tell him thanks, whoever he is," said Lili, who seemed to be accustomed to tributes of this sort.

"He says he is a fan, Miss L'Amour," the waiter said. "He asks whether you would do him the honour of allowing him to come over and exchange a few words with you." The waiter handed Lili the man's calling card, which described him as "Sir Charles Hammond, K.C.M.G., President, Canadian Pacific Railway Company."

"If he's a fan, send him over," Lili told the waiter. "We can give him a minute or two, can't we?" she asked Richard.

As he watched the man get up from his table and start across the garden, Richard concluded that this was the British Empire personified: in his beautifully cut Savile Row suit, Sir Charles exuded quiet authority, and there was even quieter arrogance in his large, square jaw. But as soon as he greeted Lili, it was evident from his accent that he was Canadian and not British. He was, as Richard was to learn later, the last Montrealer to be knighted by the king, before Ottawa decreed that Canadian citizens could no longer accept this kind of foreign honour. But Charles Hammond had gotten in under the wire and was now entitled to put the letters K.C.M.G after his name. This meant that he was a Knight Commander of the Order of St. Michael and St. George, although his envious friends in the Mount Royal Club said the K.C.M.G. really stood for Kindly Call Me God.

Lili introduced Richard – "my poet" – and the knight commander favoured him with the briefest of nods and total lack of interest.

"What I wanted to tell you, Miss L'Amour," said Sir Charles, "is that I have seen your magnificent performance at the Gayety. And then the other day, I read that article in the *Herald* that compared you with Isadora Duncan. I want to assure you that the article was absolutely correct. You see, I used to know Isadora years ago, in Paris, before her tragic death. You may well be her reincarnation."

Sir Charles had said all this while standing beside their table, and Lili, obviously entranced, now said, "Won't you sit down and join us?"

"I would love to," said Sir Charles, "but I have to get back to those three Greek fellows over there. You see, I'm in the process of selling them one of our surplus steamships, and they'd be offended if I left them for too long."

"I'd love to hear more about Isadora," Lili said.

"And I'd love to tell you," said Sir Charles. "Why don't I call you and we could have lunch some time. Are you staying here at the Ritz?"

"No, I'm at the LaSalle," said Lili.

"I shall call you soon," he said and, with a bow, went back to his table.

"The crummy old LaSalle," Lili said to Richard. "The Ritz is where an artist like me should be staying, don't you think?"

"Absolutely," said Richard fervently.

"And I definitely will be staying at hotels like this, when I start doing Modern Dance to your poetry. And making big money."

"Definitely," said Richard, but suddenly he felt down in the dumps. What chance did a seventeen-year-old schoolboy have in competition with a knight commander who owned a railroad and several steamships?

He watched glumly as Lili paid the bill. "Look," she said, as they left the garden, "I've got a matinee this afternoon. Why don't you come down with me now and see me do my Little Red Riding Hood number. It's a new one I'm developing. In her fight with the big bad wolf, Little Red Riding loses all her clothes and is left wearing only her hood. I'd like to know what you think of it."

"Yes, I'd love to see it," said Richard, suddenly cheerful again.

"Maybe you'll be able to poetize it for me," said Lili, as they got into a taxi.

5

"*Mais où est-il donc?*" asked Claudette, exasperated. "*Il est déjà cinq heures et demi.*"

"*Un peu de patience,*" said Galipeau, the private detective. "*N'oublie pas que tu seras très bien payée.*"

"I have to make supper for my children," said Claudette, looking at her watch once again. "They get very hungry."

Claudette was very good at her work, but she was so damned impatient. She always wanted to get it over with. Galipeau rumpled the pillows beside her as she sat up in the bed, fully dressed from the waist down but with only a brassiere up top. "You'll take off the brassiere when he arrives," Galipeau said. "Yes, of course," said Claudette, irritably.

They were in the usual room in the Ford Hotel, which Galipeau always got at a very good rate, seeing that he needed it only for an hour or two. Claudette – or Monique if Claudette was unavailable – would sit up in the bed, bare-breasted, and when the gentleman climbed in beside her Galipeau would quickly take a few photographs. This would be all the evidence needed to get a divorce.

"I found them in room 415 of the Ford Hotel, 1425 Dorchester Street West, Montreal, at 5:36 p.m. on September 10, 1948," Galipeau would testify.

"Were the sheets in the bed rumpled?" he might be asked.

"Yes, sir, they were very badly rumpled," Galipeau would say.

Adultery was the only grounds for divorce, and it had to be proven. After the battling parties agreed on the financial terms of the split, the lawyers would dispatch the husband to the Ford Hotel, to be caught by Galipeau with Claudette – or Monique or Marie or Linda.

"It's now a quarter to six," said Claudette.

"Please relax," said Galipeau. "I'm going to give you an extra five dollars."

For a moment he thought he might calm her down by telling her that they were waiting for a very important client, in fact the president of the Canadian Pacific Railway, but he decided to abide by his policy of never introducing the client to the woman he was going to get into bed with. There was no need for them to know anything about each other.

Sir Charles arrived at five to six, with no apologies for being late. "Please take off your jacket and your shirt," Galipeau told him, in the manner of a doctor about to examine a patient. "But keep your trousers on. You will be under the covers from the waist down."

"Do I keep my shoes on in bed?" Sir Charles asked.

"If you wish," said Galipeau, feeling that one of the richest men in Canada should be allowed a bit of discretion.

"My name is Emery Richardson," Sir Charles said to Claudette, extending his hand to her as he climbed into bed beside her.

"Claudette," she replied, shaking his hand and taking off her brassiere.

Sir Charles was starting to enjoy this. It amused him, as

head of the Canadian Pacific, to give the name of the president of the competition, the Canadian National Railways.

Galipeau was now getting his camera ready. As he focused it, he was pleased to note that Claudette was really quite homely, with a very saggy bosom. He had long ago learned not to hire good-looking girls for this work; after the picture was taken, the client sometimes felt that the amount of money he was paying for this service entitled him to a brief roll in the hay, something that Galipeau viewed with distaste; he was a detective, not a procurer.

"Are you ready?" asked Galipeau, looking through the viewfinder of his big Speed Graphic camera.

"Do I touch her in any way?" asked Sir Charles.

"No, just look very surprised," said Galipeau. "Remember, I have just burst in through the door."

The flashbulb bathed the dingy room in sudden light, as Galipeau took his first picture. He repeated the process twice more, and then it was all over.

Claudette was into her brassiere and blouse in five seconds and was immediately out the door, pausing only to collect her fifteen dollars from Galipeau. But Sir Charles, thoughtful in front of the mirror, was taking his time putting his necktie on. "Mr. Galipeau," he said, "you seem to know what you're doing. You seem efficient."

"I try my best, sir," said Galipeau.

"Would your services be available to me for other matters, perhaps delicate matters?"

"What would those be, sir?"

"Well," said Sir Charles, "I am interested in finding out whatever I can about Miss Lili L'Amour, the striptease dancer. For instance, has she been sleeping with a young boy called Lipsky, or Lipper, or something like that? Possibly Jewish."

"I can find that out for you, sir," said Galipeau.

Sir Charles snapped his cufflinks shut and put on his jacket. He handed Galipeau his calling card. "My private phone number," he said. "I would like to have an answer as soon as possible."

"Sir Charles," said Galipeau, "by chance I have been investigating Miss L'Amour for another client. I know something about her that is perhaps more interesting than who she happens to be sleeping with."

"What would that be?" Sir Charles asked.

Galipeau hesitated, as though pondering, as he fingered Sir Charles's calling card. "I don't know, sir," he said. "If I told you I might be in a conflict of interest."

"There are ways to settle such conflicts," said Sir Charles, reaching into his billfold. He extracted a fifty-dollar bill and held it out to the detective.

"I shall tell you, sir, in the strictest confidence," said Galipeau. "Because I think you and I may be working together quite a bit in the future." He took the fifty-dollar bill and handed Sir Charles his card, with his unlisted phone number on it. But still he seemed to hesitate.

"Look, Mr. Galipeau, I'm in a hurry," said Sir Charles. "What's the big secret?"

"You must not tell anyone," said Galipeau. "But tomorrow night, at the Gayety Theatre, Miss L'Amour will be performing her very popular Little Red Riding Hood dance. As soon as she achieves nudity, except for the hood, of course, the police will storm into the theatre and arrest her on the grounds of gross indecency. She will spend the night in jail, and God help her in the morning if she doesn't have an excellent lawyer."

"And how do you know all this, Mr. Galipeau?" Sir Charles asked.

"I am working for a group of important men who are devoted to protecting the morals of our city. I shall be in the theatre tomorrow night for two reasons. First to testify at Miss L'Amour's trial as to the filthiness of her performance, and secondly to quickly get the names of several others in the audience who can be persuaded to testify similarly." When he said "persuaded," he winked and waved the fifty-dollar bill that Sir Charles had given him.

"You are a good man, Mr. Galipeau," said Sir Charles. "You know, we have a few detectives on our staff at the railroad, but they are rather crude fellows. They are not nearly as articulate as you are."

"Thank you, sir," said Galipeau. "I am fortunate in having had a good education." He neglected to mention that he had once been a lawyer but had been disbarred after a scandal involving the funds of some widows and orphans.

"Yes, we will be doing business together," said Sir Charles, shaking the detective's hand and leaving the dingy, adulterous room. Going down in the elevator, he rejoiced in the fact that Galipeau's news would be immensely useful in his plans for the luscious Lili.

Outside the Ford Hotel, Sir Charles's chauffeur was waiting for him in the big black Cadillac, ready to drive him to the Mount Royal Club, for drinks, dinner, and perhaps a game of bridge with some other tycoons.

"Divorce," Sir Charles said, as they drove off. "It's a beautiful word, isn't it, Hugo?"

"If you say so, sir," said Hugo.

"At fifty-five years of age I suddenly feel reborn," said Sir Charles. "Do I look reborn to you, Hugo?"

"You do, sir, you do," said Hugo.

"Do you remember, Hugo, that night back in February when you were waiting for me outside that apartment house on Stanley Street?" said Sir Charles. "When I took a piss into the snowbank before getting into the car?"

"I remember that, sir," said Hugo.

"I didn't realize it at the time," said Sir Charles, "but that piss was the beginning of my rebirth."

Lighting his pipe and inhaling the fragrant tobacco, Sir Charles let his mind go back to that cold, moonlit night. He'd been in the apartment of Miss Dorothy Hayes, one of the CPR's most attractive and capable young stenographers, a girl who was anxious to demonstrate to the exalted big boss that her capabilities went far beyond shorthand and typing. In fact, for a girl who was not even French, she was phenomenal.

Emerging from the apartment building that night, feeling very good indeed, Sir Charles decided to recapture a moment from his boyhood in Saskatchewan. In those days, like every Canadian boy, he had delighted in urinating into the snow, pleased by the distinctive gurgle made by the hot pee as it hit the cold snow, and by the nice yellowish pattern that could be made against the pristine whiteness, if you waved it around a bit.

He was in the midst of doing just this when Donald McLeod, trudging up the street from the club at the corner, confronted him.

"Is that you, Charlie?" McLeod had said, in disbelief.

"It is truly me," said Sir Charles, shaking off the last few drops. "Nothing like a good piss after a good screw, is there?"

McLeod had been the wrong man to say this to. Or perhaps the right man. As an important elder of the A&P – the Church of St. Andrew and St. Paul – McLeod had been deeply shocked by Sir Charles's remark. When he got home, he related the episode to his wife, substituting, of course, the word *urination* for the word *piss* and the word *intercourse* for *screw*. At lunch the next day, right after the concert of the Ladies' Morning Musical Club, Mrs. McLeod had related the story, in the greatest confidence, to three of her friends, substituting the phrase *doing number one* for *urination*. Within hours the tale was all over the Square Mile and was seeping into Westmount. Within days it became clear to Lady Hammond that she must ask for a divorce. She had long suspected Sir Charles, fearing that his private railway car was nothing more than a travelling brothel, as it rolled across Canada with the engine's plaintive whistle going *hoo-hoo-hoo* in the night. She had learned to live with these private suspicions, but now, with the Stanley Street urination-after-copulation out in the open, eliciting chuckles all over the city, divorce was the only option.

The divorce idea struck Sir Charles as being the most brilliant ever voiced by his wife. Thirty years of marriage was quite enough, especially now that the children were grown up and Rosemary was becoming more cuckoo by the day. Dear Rosemary was now in touch regularly with the dead and with other worlds. She was filling the house with more and more spiritualists, mediums, telepathists, yogis, fakirs, gurus, sages, astrologers, and spoon-benders. Those who weren't in a trance were guzzling from the best bottles in Sir Charles's cellar, the wine serving to lubricate the transmigration of souls. The big granite house up on the hill, built by the great architect Findlay in the age of the Edwardian robber barons, now reeked of incense and tinkled with Tibetan bells. Lady Rosemary Hammond drifted through all this attired in the robes of a Sumerian princess, announcing after her trance that she had been in touch with Jacques Cartier and Tecumseh. But fortunately for Sir Charles, she was not so unhinged that she couldn't take proper umbrage upon learning that her husband was frequently having himself a wee piece of tail. And so, on the advice of Tecumseh, she demanded a divorce.

In the weeks that followed, Rosemary, loyally drinking a potion given to her by one of her fakirs, was the picture of serenity. But her lawyers fought like hyenas. In the end, she would have the house and an enormous financial settlement. Sir Charles, reeling after signing the papers, took comfort in the fact that it was she, as plaintiff, and not he as the supposed defendant, who would have to make that unpleasant trip to Ottawa.

Unlike the other eight provinces, Catholic Quebec had no courts that dealt with divorce, so the only way a Quebec marriage could be dissolved was by act of Parliament. Thus Rosemary, accompanied by her lawyer and her detective, would appear before a committee of the Senate. Aggrieved by Sir Charles's filthy adultery – with Claudette in the Ford Hotel – she would testify that she could never forgive him, that there was no hope of reconciliation. She would reply to a few routine questions, and perhaps the odd salacious one if an old senator felt frisky that morning. It was all a charade, and all the players knew it, but it was probably no more of a charade than the way in which several other aspects of the nation's laws were interpreted. The Senate would pass an act "for the relief of Rosemary Hammond" that would dissolve the marriage, after the automatic approval of the House of Commons and the representative of His Majesty the King. Lady Rosemary and Sir Charles, through their lawyers, would get handsome documents detailing the act of Parliament that had cast them asunder. Galipeau would get 250 dollars, Claudette would get fifteen dollars, and the lawyers would get much more.

As he contemplated the beautiful simplicity of this arrangement, with Rosemary having to endure the grimy ordeal in Ottawa, Sir Charles noticed that Hugo, as instructed, was now driving up Drummond Street. They would pass the unfamiliar LaSalle Hotel, where Lili was staying, and Sir Charles wanted to have a look at it.

"What kind of a hotel is this, Hugo?" he asked, as the Cadillac paused in front of it.

"It's not first-rate, sir," said Hugo. "Theatrical people stay here."

Was she in there now? Sir Charles wondered. Was that young Jew-boy in there with her, defiling that body of hers? And probably filling her head with more nonsense about Isadora Duncan? Well, no matter. Once she was under the tutelage of Charlie Hammond she would learn to be more choosy. Surely she would see that the Crillon in Paris was more comfortable than this seedy LaSalle in Montreal.

"On to the club, Hugo," Sir Charles said, and they drove up toward Sherbrooke Street. As for Lili being arrested for gross indecency, that was all to the good. Sir Charles would put the best lawyers of the CPR at her disposal, and they in turn would arrange for the best witnesses money could buy. Representatives of the Montreal Museum of Fine Arts would testify that Miss L'Amour's dance was high art, not obscenity, and they would display nudes by Renoir and Goya. Representatives of the symphony would agree, invoking the name of Isadora Duncan. From the classics department of McGill University would come professors to affirm that nudity was *de rigeur* on the stages of ancient Greece. All these institutions received handsome contributions every year from the Canadian Pacific Railway and from Sir Charles personally. They were all immensely grateful, and would act accordingly. Lili L'Amour, speedily acquitted of any crime, would also be immensely grateful – and would act accordingly.

"It's that female again," Mrs. Lippman said, calling Richard to the phone, her hand not quite covering the receiver.

It was Lili, after three days of silence, during which he had agonized over the thought that she might have hated the latest poem he had sent her. But no, to the contrary, she wanted to see him. "Can you come right now?" she said. "Down to the hotel? I'm in room 618."

"I'll be right down," said Richard, preparing for the worst. She had surely found his Orpheus and Eurydice theme too obscure. He was going to be dismissed as staff poet.

"Who *is* that female?" Mrs. Lippman asked, yet again.

"She's Lili L'Amour, the striptease queen," said Richard.

"Can't you ever be serious?" said Mrs. Lippman.

On his way downtown, in the gathering dusk, he reviewed his Orpheus and Eurydice piece. Perhaps he had gone too far by putting in stage directions suggesting which piece of clothing she should take off with which line. And perhaps he shouldn't have suggested that when the bodice came off, the pasties should be square rather than round, in keeping with the ancient-Greece theme. Perhaps this was choreography, and none of his business. He would have to learn to write more dispassionately, not letting the lines be dictated by the tingle in his pants.

But suddenly it occurred to him that his poem might have caused a tingle in *her* pants. Richard had heard that there were women who wanted it just as badly as men did. He found this difficult to believe, but Lili had sounded somewhat agitated on the phone, hadn't she? Could this possibly be it? Could today be the day? As he got off the number 83 streetcar at Mountain Street and started toward the hotel, his elation gave way to disquiet. Would she quickly realize that this was his first time? Would he make a hash of the whole thing? he wondered, reviewing in his mind what he visualized as being the mechanics of the procedure. Should he ask for her indulgence? Should he say, "Lili, please be gentle with me"? Or was that what the girl was supposed to say?

She greeted him at the door to her room in her bathrobe. "Come in, come in," she said. "Sorry I'm not dressed yet, but I'm in a panic." She gestured at the bed and the chairs, which were littered with clothes and underclothes. There were two large suitcases open on the bed, each of them half-filled with clothes, handbags, and shoes.

"What's going on?" asked Richard.

"I'm leaving town," said Lili, "but I wanted to see you before I go."

"But you've still got two more weeks at the Gayety."

"They're going to have to do without me," she said. She started clearing things off the dresser and putting them into a leather case – hair curlers, jars of creams and powders, perfumes, lipsticks. Grimacing, she told him how the police were coming to arrest her, during her show, for gross indecency and worse. Sir Charles Hammond, the man Richard had met at their Ritz luncheon, had tipped her off. Sir Charles knew everybody and everything. He had offered to get her great lawyers to take her case, but she had refused.

"When the police come for me tonight," she said, "I just won't be there. But I want us to stay in touch, Richard. That's why I asked you to come down here before I go. I want more poems. I loved that Orpheus and What's Her Name. It was beautiful, especially that bit when she descends into the infernal regions and has to take off her vestments because the fires are so hot down there."

"Where are you going?" Richard asked.

"To New York," she said. "I'll see my agent there and he'll get me a new gig somewhere. They always want me in Boston. And Baltimore and St. Louis."

"We want you in Montreal, Lili," he said, wondering whether there was a tear forming in his eye.

"No, you don't," she said grimly. "Have you seen this?" she asked, handing him a newspaper.

It was that morning's *Le Devoir*. A headline on the front page proclaimed L'OBSCÉNITÉ RÉPUGNANTE DE LILI L'AMOUR and the article, by Father André Prud'Homme, occupying four columns, denounced her for the corruption of youth and her offence to Christian values. There were many closely reasoned paragraphs defining what constituted obscenity – and Lili personified it. Father Prud'Homme quoted witnesses who reported that when she danced "*un relent de frénésie sexuelle empeste le théâtre*" – the stink of sexual frenzy filled the theatre. The article concluded by demanding that this disgusting woman – who had the effrontery to use a French name when she wasn't French – be arrested immediately and be driven out of Montreal – forever.

"I got one of the waiters downstairs to translate it for me," Lili said.

Her eyes were brimming with tears, and Richard awkwardly put his arm around her shoulders. "You're an artist, Lili," he said. "Never forget that. Artists are always getting into trouble with the authorities."

She smiled sadly and gave him a little kiss on the cheek. "You're a lovely person, Richard," she said. "Now would you mind turning around while I get dressed?

He turned his back to her. Obviously it was okay to see her naked on the stage, but not in her bedroom. And that phrase "You're a lovely person . . ." That, of course, killed all hope. It was something his aunt might say. Why couldn't she have said, "You're a dangerous man, Richard Lippman. I'll have to watch myself when you're around." Dangerous, not lovely. Man, not person.

"Okay, the coast is clear," she said, and he turned around to see her dressed now and flinging more things into her suitcases.

"Look," he said, suddenly inspired, "why don't you let yourself be arrested and spend a night in jail. My uncle Morty will get you out fast. He knows all the police and judges. But if you've been in jail, think of the publicity. And I could poetize it. You could start your dance in a costume with jailhouse stripes. And this time the poem could be by Lord Byron, 'Eternal Spirit of the chainless Mind / Brightest in dungeons, Liberty thou art.'"

"Sorry, darling," she said, cheerful now, "but I don't want any jail, never. And I want Lord Richard, not Lord Byron."

There was a knock on the door, and she opened it for a man wearing knee breeches and a chauffeur's cap. "Ah, Hugo," she said. "I'll be ready in a minute." She introduced Richard and Hugo.

"Sir Charles sends his apologies," said Hugo. "But he had some last-minute business at the office. He will join you on the train, just before it leaves."

"Oh, didn't I tell you?" Lili asked Richard, who was taken aback. "I'll be going to New York in Sir Charles's private railway car. Quite by coincidence he has to go to New York too, on business, so he's had his car hitched onto the regular Delaware and Hudson night train."

"You'll be interested to know, madam," said Hugo, "that I've just put Armand aboard the train."

"Who's Armand?" asked Lili.

"He's Sir Charles's chef," said Hugo. "You'll be having braised saddle of lamb for dinner tonight and nougatine pudding with mocha sauce for dessert. For breakfast there will be finnan haddie and blueberry pancakes. And Armand told me to tell you that if you don't like blueberries he has raspberries too."

"It's an incredible railway car," said Lili. "Sir Charles tells me it has a kitchen, a dining room, a library, and even a shower in each of the two main bedrooms."

After going down in the elevator with Lili and Hugo, Richard watched Hugo stow her suitcases in the trunk of the big Cadillac.

"Now, we're going to stay in touch, aren't we?" she asked Richard as they stood beside the car.

"Yes," he said.

"You'll write me lots of letters, won't you?" she said.

"Yes, I will," he said.

There was no kiss on the cheek as she got into the car, just a handshake.

He watched as the Cadillac, black as a hearse, drove off slowly down Drummond Street toward Windsor Station, where the magical train awaited, with a shower in each of the two – repeat, two – bedrooms. There's a poem in all this, he thought bitterly – and perhaps even sardonically. If only he were Lord Byron, he could get at least three cantos out of the two and a half weeks since he had first met Lili.

6

When Richard arrived at Gagnon's Ice Cream Parlour for the regular Friday night seminar, he found his friends already seated in their usual booth. They had ordered their sundaes, and when Odette brought them to the table it was obvious that they were exploring new territory. Abandoning his usual Pistachio Surprise, Martin had ordered the Aloha Hawaiian Delight, which seemed to Richard to be marred by a garnish of crushed pineapple that was oppressively large. Instead of his habitual Banana Split Royale, Stanley was experimenting with a Mint Madness, which the menu promised would be seated on a seductive peppermint pattie. As for Harold, he was pushing to the outer limits of chocolatism with the Triple Double-Chocolate Indulgence, which was crowned with Paradise Fudge.

"We are on the verge of new things," Martin said portentously, pointing out that next week they would be leaving high school behind them, to embark on higher education. Martin, Stanley, and Richard would be going to McGill and overweight Harold, having just announced his bizarre choice, would be trundling his great bulk over to the University of Toronto.

"Poor old Harold," Stanley said. "He's not going to get laid in Toronto, is he?"

"Definitely not," said Martin. "It's forbidden there."

"It's forbidden here too," said Harold. "Or haven't you noticed?"

If the group was venturing into new areas of ice-cream gastronomy, its seminar's intellectual agenda was unchanged. As always the topic was sexual starvation.

Harold might have more luck with girls, Richard decided, if he weren't so fat, with his belly subjecting his shirt buttons to such alarming pressure. By contrast, scrawny Stanley was Laurel to Harold's Hardy. Even when smiling, Stanley looked woebegone, and girls who didn't know that he came from a wealthy family might conclude that he was impoverished, with no access to an automobile. As for Martin, Richard envied his movie-star good looks but couldn't understand why girls weren't repelled by his incurable sloppiness, his rumpled suit, and his always stained necktie. Today his tie bore evidence of at least two different meals, as well as a pineapple stain from the Aloha Hawaiian Delight that he was gobbling.

"Did you hear about that bastard Gregory?" Stanley asked Richard.

But Richard hadn't heard, and they told him how Gregory, the high-school football star, had just visited their booth long enough to tell them how he had taken Sex Bomb Patricia, from Miss McMonagle's class, up to the Summit in his father's car. There they had gone all the way.

"We asked him what it was like," Stanley said, "and do you know what he said?"

"No, what?" asked Richard.

"He said he was too much of a gentleman to discuss it. And he got up and left, the bastard."

"We should have beat the shit out of him," Martin said. "The three of us together could have done it."

"But there's a lesson to be learned here," said Stanley. "Everybody knows that Sex Bomb Patricia will never go out with high-school guys. Gregory was the exception that proves the rule. What little Patsy wants, and what all girls who are ready for it want, is older men. That means guys who go to college. They're called 'college men.' And as of next week, we'll all be college men. We'll be in the running."

"I personally am going to start smoking a pipe, which is very sophisticated," said Harold. "I shall be looking for girls who go all the way."

"Smoking a pipe is forbidden in Toronto," said Martin.

Odette came to the booth to ask Richard what he wanted, and Richard, entering into the seminar's spirit of adventure, ordered a Tutti-Frutti Dreamboat Special. Waiting for it, he was tempted to tell them about Lili, to show them her letter, which was in his pocket. But that wouldn't do, would it? Lili had to remain secret, or the magic would be gone. If he told them, it would only give rise to crude, vulgar jokes.

He wished these morons weren't here in the booth, feeding their ugly faces, so he could take this sweet letter out of his pocket and read it again, for the seventh time.

Mayfair Hotel,
Boston, Mass.
September 22, 1948.

Dear Richard,

Well here I am in dear old Boston and believe me it is boring. How I miss Montreal, with its gaiety (Gayety, eh?) and its lively atmusphere and its great big Mount Royal up there. The niteclubs (or is it better to write "nightclubs") here are nothing like your El Morocco, your Chez Paree, your Samovar. And of course I miss you, too, dear Richard. You really are a very nice poet.

I am performing at the Howard Athenaeum Theater here, which is not as grandioze as it sounds but is O.K. I am the headliner and we are getting good crowds, but still, I am always on edge and irespective of where I am in my performanse I have to keep glancing to my left, into the wings. If I see the red light suddenly go on there it means the police have just come in the front door and I have to cover up ye olde body very fast. Dear old Boston.

The trip to New York in Sir Charles' private raillway car was fabullous. Talk about luxury! Braysed saddle of lamb for dinner! Over Irish coffee he told me all about this Isadora Duncan, who he met in Paris 25 years ago. Do you know how she died? She was on the French Riveira and was going for a ride in an open sports car. She was wearing this beautiful silk scarf, five feet long, and it was trailing over the side of the car and as soon as the car started it got caught in the spokes of one of the back wheels and it tightened when the wheel went round and it choked her to death!

Isn't that beautiful (by that I mean tragic, of course)? Could you poetize that for me, Richard? With the right words, I can just see it. I can do wonderfull things dancing with a scarf, although getting a car onto the stage might be difficult.

While I was in New York, I showed Lenny your Orpheus and What's Her Name – I must learn how to spell it and how to pronounce it – poem and he thought it was great. He will set it to music and I will try it out here in Boston, which is a real intellectual city. Lenny is a fine musician, and I was once married to him. We are still friends, which is more than I can say about my other former husbands, sons of bitches all of them – if you will pardon the expression.

Now I must hurry up and get dressed, because Sammy the Sequin Man is coming to see me. Sammy is a very ammusing little fellow, who lugs around a big black valise on wheels that's almost as big as he is. From it he sells us girls everything we need – pasties, G-strings, boas, 7-veil outfits, garter belts, break-away bras, negligees, etc., etc. He also carries a fantastic line of perfumes, lotions, creams, powders, lipsticks – all imported from France and very expensive. Dear old Sammy, he pops up wherever you are – at the Follies in Los Angeles, at the Star & Garter in Chicago, at the Bijou in Philly.

Please write soon.

Love,
Lili.

September 23.
P.S.: Richard, dear, can I ask a favor of you (or should I say "from you?") I hesitate, but I ask. First, I should confess (or should I say "must confess?)" that I have always wanted to be a writer, ever since I was a little girl reading books and my daddy told me that books were made by people called writers. I think I told you I went to college for a year before I had to quit for financial reasons. But while I was there, Professor Klugman gave me very good marks for my English compositions. He was real helpful, old Klugman, although I sometimes had to discourage him from becoming too friendly, if you know what I mean.

Anyway, I want eventualy to write my memmoirs, a book I will entitle *Dancing Exoticaly*. To learn what I need to know for this project, I have been taking a corespondence course – "How to Become a Highly Paid Author" – from the O. Henry Institute of Des Moines, Iowa. The course is fairly helpful, but sometimes they get mixed up at the Institute and last week they sent me a criticism of an essay entitled "Our Old Mule Daisy," which was obviously written by some other student.

I need help, Richard, so if I write to you now and then, would you be a dear and point out where I go wrong in spelling, grammer, choice of words, sintax, etc. I would be lovingly grateful.

L.

Richard tuned out of his friends' smutty conversation as he slowly ate his Tutti-Frutti Dreamboat Special and once again let his mind roam over the letter, which by now he knew by heart. So she wanted to be a writer and he would be her teacher! It was a thrilling thought. But again he was struck by the fact that he really knew very little about this Lili. For instance, she seemed familiar with all the Montreal nightclubs – the Chez Paree, the Samovar, etcetera – that to Richard were only famous names. And she'd had an unspecified number of husbands, something she had never mentioned before. And most disturbing, there was that trip to New York in that bastard's private railway car, chugging through the scenic Adirondack Mountains in the moonlit night. Snug inside one of the two – repeat, two – lavish bedrooms. Could that digni-fied, false-British Sir Charles be a gash-hound like everybody else? Probably. Did she resist? Did she yield? He forced his mind off this subject and tuned in to Martin, who was talking about The Project.

"Before you came in, Dicky-boy," Martin was saying, "we decided on Thursday night. Is that okay with you?"

"I'll have to check my agenda," Richard said.

"What do you mean, agenda?" Stanley said. "What could be more important than The Project?"

They had been planning this venture for a month – a rite of passage between the childishness of high school and the manhood of university. They would start out at about seven o'clock on the great night and would go downtown to the Taverne des Sports for a beer to calm their nerves. Then they would go straight across the street to the legendary whorehouse at 312 Ontario Street East. They would ring the bell and the madam would open the door. They would tell her they had come to see a show. They would each give her five dollars and they would be shown upstairs to a bedroom. They would stand around the bed and after a few minutes two naked girls would enter and would sink down onto the bed and would start pleasuring each other with massive dildos. Many of the mysteries of the female anatomy would finally be cleared up.

"Something I just heard," Harold said. "If you give one of them an extra five dollars, she will light a cigarette, put it into her snatch, and smoke it that way."

"I find that hard to believe," said Martin.

"My brother's friend Larry saw it with his own eyes," said Harold.

"But is it anatomically possible?" said Stanley. "I mean, there's no physiological connection between the lungs and the pussy, is there? And she can't smoke without using her lungs, can she?"

"Maybe she doesn't inhale," said Harold.

As this sordid discussion went on and on, Richard tuned out again. He had decided he wasn't going to go to 312. No, the whole thing was disgusting. That was no longer the way he wanted to think of sex. Now that high school was over he wanted something else. Perhaps something called love. He thought of his beloved Lili dancing to his poetry. That was what he wanted – love. And if it was tragic love, so much the better – for a poet.

When he got to McGill he would have to get rid of these coarse, grubby friends and find new ones. For Martin, Stanley, and Harold, life's only tragedy was not getting laid. They knew nothing about poetry, the idiots, and would only make fun of him if they knew how deeply poetic he was. Yes, new friends. Or perhaps no friends at all. A poet didn't need friends, did he? All he needed was a Lili, and maybe nothing more.

Put on your red-and-white sweater
For you'll have none better,
And we'll open up another keg of beer,
For it's not for knowledge that we go to college,
But to raise hell all the year.

They sang it on the second day of Freshman Week, assembled in the ballroom of the Students' Union. They were there to be bombarded with vital information about the labyrinth of student activities, as well as to learn the words of the university hymns. For Richard, the event was another disappointment. Despite the solemnity of the grey Victorian buildings that ringed the campus, Freshman Week so far seemed designed to promote frivolity rather than studiousness. Still, there were a few songs that had some nobility about them, like:

Hail, Alma Mater, we sing to thy praise.
Great our affection, though feeble our lays,
Nestling so peaceful and calm 'neath the hill,
Fondly we love thee, Our Dear Old McGill.

But even this was not enough to raise the minds of Richard's friends out of the gutter.

"My lays ain't going to be feeble," Stanley whispered.

"No, ma'am, I'm a-goin' to lay you so as you'll stay laid," said Martin.

Richard couldn't be bothered to point out to these ignoramuses what they probably didn't know: that a lay was a song, a poetic song. Obviously they had forgotten old Sir Walter Scott's "Lay of the Last Minstrel," which they had been supposed to study in high school – a refrain with beautiful lines like "That if she loved the harp to hear / He could make music to her ear."

On the stage of the ballroom, the master of ceremonies – a fourth-year student in the hallowed red-and-white sweater of the Scarlet Key Society – was now addressing the first-year rabble. "I want you to get on your feet and stop talking and be respectful," he said. "Look at number four on your song sheets, which pays tribute to our founder, the dear old gent who left enough money in his will, back in 1813, to start the university that bears his name. Let us sing:

James McGill, James McGill,
Peacefully he slumbers there,
Blissful though we're on the tear,
James McGill, James McGill,
He's our father, oh yes, rather,
James McGill."

But if old James were alive now, Richard reflected, and if he could hear the conversation of Martin and Stanley, he might have second thoughts about founding a university that attracted this kind of mentality.

"Are you checking out the stock?" Stanley was whispering, nodding toward a group of girls who were sitting near the windows.

"What about that big redhead?" Martin asked. "I'd sure like to cut that one out of the herd."

When the singing was over, the freshmen and freshettes started wandering around the ballroom, looking into booths where representatives of various campus clubs were anxious to recruit new members. "Let's join everything," said Stanley, carried away by the glamour of it all. "Don't be silly," said Martin. "What we're looking for is a little hanky-panky, and you're going to find it in some clubs and not in others. That Philosophical Society over there looks like a dead loss, but will you look at that slick little chick in La Société Française? That's for me, *oh là là*."

The Players' Club was attracting a lot of attention. This year they were going to do *Dear Ruth*, by Norman Krasna, and they would need not only actors and actresses but also stage-hands and costume people. But it was the Red and White Revue that had Stanley and Martin signing up immediately. The Revue's booth was decorated with photos of last year's production, with lots of girl dancers in very short skirts. There was a gramophone playing a record of last year's original hit song, "It's the Psychological Way to Look at Love."

"Come on, Richard," said Stanley, thrusting an application form at him. "They're going to need skits and songs. Right up your alley." But Richard said he would have to think about all this before making any extracurricular choices. Actually, he had already decided to have nothing to do with any of these clubs. The scene here in the ballroom seemed distressingly like an extension of high school, where he had always been an avid joiner of any kind of club. Even back in elementary school he had been in the Stamp Club and the Boy Scouts. Now, embarking on manhood, surely all this clubbery should be left behind. Especially for a poet. Could you see Shelley signing up for the Duplicate Bridge Club? Or Keats choosing the Radio Workshop?

As for that Red and White Revue, the idea was beneath contempt. To think that they wanted Richard Lippman to write songs and skits for a tacky little college musical. He, Richard Lippman, author of the great Lili L'Amour's acclaimed, ground-breaking Orpheus and Eurydice dance, soon to have its premiere in Boston. The same day he had received her letter, he had answered her by saying that he would come to Boston to see that dance performed. Would she let him know as soon as she received Lenny's music and started rehearsing? He would take the train down on a Friday night and come back on Monday morning, thus not missing any lectures. He would pay for the train ticket, and a lavish hotel room and lavish lunches and lavish after-theatre suppers, by cashing in the hundred-dollar Victory Bond his mother had bought for him during the war.

Now, as he wandered past the Sociological Society's booth in the ballroom, he was starting to see himself travelling with Lili – to Los Angeles, Philadelphia, Chicago, everywhere – constantly writing new and more exciting material to inspire her divine undulations.

7

Richard's parents had been delighted, a year ago, when he told them he had finally made a decision: he was going into law; like his father, he was going to be a great lawyer. They had celebrated this momentous decision by taking him to dinner at Ruby Foo's. Here, as he ate his *moo goo guy pan*, he congratulated himself on the success of his lie. Becoming a lawyer was, of course, out of the question. What could be more boring than a life spent drawing up contracts for his father's boring businessmen friends, or helping them sue each other. But by telling his parents that he was dreaming of sitting behind a desk in a law office down on St. James Street, he was finally able to put an end to his mother's nagging, to his father's repeated question: "What, if anything, Richard, do you plan to do with your life?"

At McGill, he could look forward to four stimulating years without having to decide what, if anything, he was going to do with his life. Here he would be learning how to think and, of course, he would be honing his poetical skills. Now, sitting in the afternoon sun on the steps of the Arts Building, he was leafing through the textbook he had just bought for Latin 1A, and he was happy to see that he would soon be learning how

Virgil did it. He would become a master of scansion, deftly marking elisions and caesurae. Verses like *"Ergo etiam cum me supremus adederit ignis"* would yield the secrets of their rhythms, and stringing spondees and dactyls together would become child's play. For a moment he wondered whether Lili might do a classical kind of dance to one of Ovid's very sexy stories, read in Latin, of course. But even if that was a bit impractical, he could learn a lot from Ovid and Livy. Yes, his poetry needed a bit more discipline and a bit less of the wild inspiration that was generated so often from the crotch. Yes, McGill was the place to bathe yourself in classicism, what with the Grecian pillars of the Arts Building and the elegant statuary of the Three Graces, so vulgarly described as the Three Bares by the campus tour guide during Freshman Week.

Closing his Latin 1A textbook, Richard summoned up his courage and headed over to the Students' Union. In the basement he found the offices of the *McGill Daily*, the student newspaper. The room was loud with the clatter of typewriters and the air was blue with cigarette smoke. In a far corner Richard found the desk of the feature editor, an angry-looking, bushy-haired fellow – probably a fourth-year student – who was shouting into his telephone. "For Christ's sake, I told you I wanted it pungent," he was saying. "What you've given me is flatter than piss on a platter." He was waving a sheet of paper as he spoke, finally slamming it down on the desk, almost knocking over a half-empty coffee cup that had a cigarette butt floating in it.

"I have to deal with idiots," he said to Richard, putting down the phone. "And what, sir, can I do for you?"

"I notice that you sometimes run a poem," said Richard, "so I brought you a few." And he handed the editor the half-dozen he had selected from his recent output, including two of the Lili poems.

"Christ, not more poems," said the editor. "Can you please tell me what's happening this year? The campus is crawling with poets. I'm suffocating in poetry." He took Richard's offering and, without looking at it, put it down on a pile of papers.

"Look, uh, I'm sorry," said Richard, reaching out to retrieve his poems. But the editor put his hand down on the pile of papers, to keep them where they were.

"I've got a fireplace at home and we always need kindling," said the editor. "But seriously, if you're a writer, maybe you can give me some prose, some zippy prose. What we're looking for is short essays – say, seven hundred words – denouncing something. You're a freshman, aren't you? Haven't you noticed anything about McGill that you hate?"

"Well, I could look," said Richard.

"Make it pungent, make it pithy," said the editor, reaching for his ringing phone.

On the way home, hanging from a strap in the crowded bus, Richard felt the high spirits of the afternoon draining out of him. He was just another crawler in a campus that was crawling with poets. He saw himself as a slimy worm, burrowing through black earth, bumping into other blind worms, getting entangled with them, slithering hordes of them.

When he got home, there was a letter from Lili waiting for him, waiting to depress him even more.

Mayfair Hotel
Boston, Mass.
October 6, 1948.

Dear Richard,

How are you? I trust you are learning great things at the university. As for me, what I am learning here is mighty disapointing. I will not be dancing your beautiful Orpheus and

Eurydice – there, I now know how to spell her name! But I can't dance her, at least not in stupid Boston.

Last week Lenny sent me terrific music that he composed for this dance, fitting in perfectly with your words. I got a very nice anouncer from the radio station here to read it, off-stage, in his rich voice. I got the orchestra into the theater in the morning for rehearsal.

It was going beautifully, especially after the snake bites Eurydice's foot and she dies and descends into the infernall regions. Lenny made the violins go very sad at this point and Albert, the radio anouncer, spoke that wonderful line of yours – "Too hot to bear are the fires of hell." This, of course, is the signal for me to start taking my clothes off, to cool down. Roasting, I start by taking off my bodice and that little Greek apron thing.

It is at this point that Mr. Schemmerhorn comes into the theater, of which he is the manager. He stands at the back, as Albert booms out your immortal "Flames so red, thighs so white" line. But before I can go down to the G-string – as you suggest in your excellent coreography suggestions – Mr. Schemmerhorn yells, "What in hell is going on here?" The violins screech to a halt, Albert stops reading and I freeze, right there amid the flames of hell (imaginary flames, of course, but the set designer told me he could make very realistic flames for me when we get to mount the show).

But we are not going to mount the show. To make a long story short, Mr. Schemmerhorn, marching up from the back of the theater and talking in his loud voice, forbids me to do poetry and points out that my contract says he must aprove my act. He says that the audience here is lo-brow and would not put up with poetry. Mr. Schemmerhorn is a vulgar man and you would not believe his language. He asked me didn't

I ever notice that most of the men in the audience, especially at matinees, wear raincoats, even in dry, warm weather. Yes, I'm afraid I have noticed this. He starts making jokes about the raincoat brigade, which makes Albert, the radio announcer, and the whole orchestra crack up laughing, but which makes me blush.

I tell him that I know that there are also intelectuals in the audience, boys from Harvard, which is the big university here, who come to see me dance, and they would love Richard Lippman's poetry. But Mr. Schemmerhorn says those boys get enough poetry at college and they come here for something else. He starts making vulgar jokes about what they are here for and again the orchestra and Albert are doubled over with laughter. But this makes me so mad that I walk off the stage and go to my dressing room. I am boiling. I think seriously about quitting and telling that bastard what he can do with his contract. I would tell him in his own kind of language, if you know what I mean.

But I am not quitting, Richard, because – to put it simply – I need the money. I know you have high principals, Richard, and hope you will not think less of me for this.

Quite by coincidence, that very night, right after the show, three Harvard boys were waiting for me at the stage door. I went to dinner with them at a lovely fish restaurant and learned that they were from the Beacon Hill district, which is where the aristocracy here lives. Their names – Lowell, Cabot, Winthrop – are those of people who came to Masachusets three hundred years ago. These very nice boys said they would love to see me dance to your poetry. So there, Schemmerhorn!

The boys seemed to know a lot about my profession, and asked many questions about other artists they had seen, and who of course I know, like Peaches and Ann Corio.

They wanted to know how Rosita Royce trained her doves to perch in exactly the right places. They wanted to know the exact dimensions of Evelyn West's famous Treasure Chest (naughty boys!).

They were very mature boys and I was able, without blushing too much, to answer their technical questions about G-strings and pasties. (They serve very great whisky sours at this fish restaurant, and that makes the conversation flow pretty good.) But I had to draw the line when they wanted to know about Noel Toy, the Chinese stripper who also sings. She plays the Gayety in Montreal from time to time. Have you ever seen her? Well, the Harvard boys, who are really quite innocent, wanted to know what the hidden meaning is in her song "Is it true what they say about American women?" I told them that I too didn't know, because the mere thought of it is so embarasing. I used to tell Noel that she shouldn't be singing that kind of song.

Why am I telling you all this? Just to get it off my chest, how complicated life is when you can't decide who to trust. This question arose just after we finished our fish and were starting in on our dessert – delicious coconut cream pie. It was then that the boys invited me to a big party they will be having on Saturday night up at the university. I said I would have to think about it, and right then who comes into the restaurant but Mr. Schemmerhorn. I introduce him to the boys and he gives with one of his big, oily grins. The next day Mr. Schemmerhorn tells me these boys are all big liars. The one who calls himself Lowell is really Jack Ginsberg. The Winthrop is really a Weintraub. When I said I doubted this, Mr. Schemmerhorn said he knows their fathers. I hate liars, Richard, so I don't think I'll be going to their party on Saturday night. On the other hand, maybe it's Mr. Schemmerhorn who is the liar. Maybe I will go to that party.

In closing, let me say I'm sorry I've had to give you this bad news about our Orpheus and Eurydice. But the good news is that we are not going to quit trying, are we? The theater manager in Cincinnati, where I go next, is a very cultured man and I know he will love the poetry. Meanwhile, are you poetizing anything these days? I hope so. Please write.

Love
Lili

When he finished reading the letter, Richard decided that it was the boys who were the liars, not Mr. Schemmerhorn. But that was irrelevant, wasn't it? The main lesson of today was that nobody wanted Richard Lippman's poetry – not in Montreal, where McGill was crawling with poets, and not in Boston, where even the most beautiful naked woman in the world couldn't promote it.

Slinking into the kitchen to prepare himself a strong cup of Ovaltine, Richard realized that maybe he ought to sober up, get rid of his Smith-Corona poetry typewriter, and prepare for a sombre life behind a desk in a law office down on St. James Street, probably his father's office.

8

"What's bothering you, laddie?" asked Stanley.

"Nothing," said Richard. "Nothing at all."

They were having lunch in the Union cafeteria. Martin and Stanley were devouring their chicken pot pie while Richard was staring glumly down at his soup, stirring it listlessly with his spoon and not eating. He could only think of his future, poring over contracts in that gloomy law office.

"You've got to cheer up, young fellow," Martin said, hungrily spearing the last piece of gelatinous crust from his pot pie and managing to deposit a bit of it on his necktie.

"If it would help to talk about it, whatever it is, let's talk," said Stanley.

"Look, I'm perfectly all right," said Richard.

"If you've got a dose of the clap, this new penicillin stuff they've discovered will fix you up right away," said Martin. "It's a wonder drug."

"I told you, I'm okay," said Richard.

"You had your poem in the *Daily*," said Stanley. "Wasn't that good?"

"Yeah, that was good," said Richard. But it wasn't good. In fact it was contributing to his gloom. He had, of course, been surprised and thrilled to see that one of his poems had been accepted and printed the very day after he had taken it down to the *Daily* office. It was great to see his name in print, his byline. But after a few minutes he realized that "Ode to Zero" was probably the worst poem he had ever written. It was nothing more than a futile effort to sum up the futility of life. He had written it in the middle of the night, just after Lili had taken off for New York in that accursed private railway car. He had meant to throw it away, but somehow it got mixed into the sheaf of poems he had given that bushy-haired feature editor. That bastard probably ran it as a kind of joke.

"You look so down you'd think your best friend died," Stanley said.

"But remember, laddie, we're your best friends," Martin said.

It was true, but Richard wished it wasn't so. Ever since they arrived at McGill, these two boring lummoxes had attached themselves to him like barnacles to the bottom of a ship. For them, it was high school all over again. Wherever he went on the campus, they were there – sitting beside him in the English 2 lecture, milling around with him at the Men's Smoker, getting genned up with him at the Gen Session, squeezing onto a sofa with him at Professor Tolhurst's compulsory tea party. And now they were trying to drag him to a dance.

"Look at this," Martin was saying, pointing to a notice in the *Daily*. "It's tonight. The Freshman Get-Acquainted Dance. Members of the Big Sisters' Club will introduce the girls to the men."

"We're men now," said Stanley. "Doesn't that make you feel good?"

"Yeah, I guess so," said Richard.

"Everybody will be wearing a name tag," said Martin. "Which means you'll be able to pretend you're nearsighted and get real close to the girl's chest as you try to read her name on her tag."

That night, when the three of them entered the Union ballroom, Johnny Holmes's orchestra was playing "Chattanooga Choo Choo," but only two couples were dancing, while the freshman hordes stood by, watching.

"Good," said Martin. "They haven't done the introductions yet."

But now the music came to an end, and a muscular, fourth-year girl in a Big Sisters sweater stepped up to the microphone. "Because you're all so painfully, ridiculously shy," she said, "I guess we're going to have to do something about it. So let's go, sisters."

As the orchestra obliged with a fanfare of trumpets, a platoon of Big Sisters came marching into the ballroom and launched into a frenzy of introductions, dragging boys and girls together and announcing their names to each other after reading the names from their name tags. It was all done in loud voices, in rapid-fire volleys. And it was all over in a few minutes, a ritual designed to "break the ice" and which, even if nobody remembered anybody else's name, made it possible for a boy to approach a girl and ask her to dance.

Even before the introductions were over, the orchestra launched into "The Hut Sut Song." Richard found a vacant chair in the wallflowers' row and sat down, watching as Martin and Stanley each found a girl to join them in the frenetic jitterbugging. Glumly, he wondered what the scene was right now in Boston. Did Lili eventually go to some wild party with those three Harvard boys, those despicable imposters? Were they filling her with gin and running their horny hands all over her?

Did she ever give a thought to her poet, languishing in Montreal? Tomorrow he would answer her letter and tell her he was starting a new poem for her, about Diana the Huntress, although the whole effort now seemed pointless.

There were still only a few dancers on the floor, and when the song came to an end the obnoxious chief Big Sister was at the microphone again. "Let's see if we can't get some life into this morgue," she said. "The next number will be a Ladies' Choice."

As the band struck up Glenn Miller's "Moonlight Cocktail," girls all over the room were asking boys to dance. Out of nowhere, it seemed, a tall brunette appeared in front of the chair where Richard was sitting. Without a word, she imperiously held out her right hand, and Richard had no choice but to take the hand and lead her out onto the floor. As they started dancing, the band's vocalist was singing Kim Gannon's immortal words:

"A couple of jiggers of moonlight and add a star,
Pour in the blue of a June night and one guitar,
Mix in a couple of dreamers and there you are:
Lovers hail the Moonlight Cocktail."

As they danced slowly, still without exchanging a word, Richard realized that this girl was, in a word, gorgeous. And from a bit of pressure from her hand on his shoulder, he realized that she wanted to be held more firmly. He pulled her closer and became aware of the contours of her body, astonishingly both soft and firm at the same time. Fortunately he had remembered to prepare for this kind of dancing and had put on his jockstrap, to hold down the inevitable disturbance in his trousers.

"'Stir for a couple of hours, until dreams come true / As

for the number of kisses, it's up to you,'" the singer continued.

And now she was talking! "I loved your poem," she said. "It was superb."

"You saw it in the *Daily*?"

"I read it six times," she said. "It made me cry."

"Oh," said Richard, wondering how to deal with all this. "I'm sorry if it made you cry."

"'Ode to Zero,'" she said. "It was so wonderfully bleak. So magnificently hopeless."

"Well, I was trying for futility," Richard said. "I mean to show how futile everything is, and so on."

"'Broken limbs of trees / Moaning in distress,'" she said, quoting from the poem. "'Near an empty cave, in clotted darkness.'"

"It took me a while to make up my mind about that," he said. "Whether the darkness should be clotted or spotted."

"'The blackened wind that murders hope,'" she said, quoting further. "'Cold and wet and choking.'"

Elation was what he felt now, the very special elation that comes to a poet when he hears a stranger recite his lines. He drew her closer as they danced on, to Glenn Miller's intoxicating melody:

"Follow the simple directions
And they will bring
Life of another complexion where you'll be king.
You will awake in the morning and start to sing
Moonlight Cocktails are the thing."

The music came to its end and, unwillingly, he released her from his embrace. He wondered how to further the conversation as he stood awkwardly, studying her long black eyelashes. But this heavenly apparition was at no loss for words.

"I'd like to talk to you about poetry," she said. "Could we do that?"

"Oh, sure," he said. "Of course."

"But not here. It's too noisy, isn't it?"

"Yes, far too noisy," he said, after quickly searching for a fast, witty rejoinder and failing to find one.

"How about a coffee tomorrow," she said. "Five o'clock? In the cafeteria?"

"You weren't wearing a name tag," he said, as he brought the two cups of coffee to the table. "I really don't know your name."

"I'm Sophia Bruce," she said, reaching over to shake his hand. "That's Sophia, eh? Soph-eye-a, not Soph-ee-a. And please don't call me Sophie. I hate Sophie."

"I will never call you that," he said, suddenly realizing that he couldn't remember ever addressing a girl by her name. If he addressed her at all, it was as "you." One probably only uttered the name itself in the heat of passion, breaking away from the kissing for a moment to pant, "Soph-eye-a, Soph-eye-a, Soph-eye-a." Would he ever have occasion to pant that? he wondered, as he drank in the lustrous jet-black hair that framed her face.

"Do you have to rush home for dinner?" she was saying. "Or do you have ninety minutes to spare?"

"I have 216 minutes to spare," he said, happy that the old noggin, the old wit, was finally starting to work.

"Good," she said. "There's something I want to show you." She stood up abruptly, leaving her coffee untouched, took hold of his elbow with her lovely hand, and led him to the door.

Her car was parked directly in front of a big curbside horse trough, under a no-parking sign that warned motorists that they must not block access to the trough. But obviously this

Sophia was not concerned about the law or about the thirst of the milk-wagon horses that wouldn't be able to get at their water. The car was a 1934 Airflow Chrysler, the first streamlined car ever built, a beautiful machine. But this one was much scratched and dented, and its thick coating of grime suggested that it hadn't been washed since before the war.

"I bought it last week," she said. "It was very cheap because the guy said it has a few mechanical problems." Inside, clumps of stuffing were sticking up through tears in the leather of the front seat.

She pressed the starter a few times but got only a few coughs from the engine. She looked perplexed and Richard suggested she pull the choke. She immediately grabbed at the throttle, but of course nothing happened. "That's the throttle," Richard said. "This is the choke." He took her hand and guided it across the dashboard to the choke, which immediately got the car going.

"You'll have to be patient with me," she said, with a weak smile. "I'm just learning how to drive."

"You're doing just fine," he said, as the car leapt away in a series of violent jerks and headed toward Peel Street. Outside the Montreal Amateur Athletic Association she almost killed two amateur athletes whose quick reactions saved them. They brandished their squash racquets and shouted obscenities after her. By now Richard was terrified, but at the same time was pleased that the choke-throttle thing had helped him establish a bit of authority in their budding relationship. At the dance, it was definitely she who had been in control, imperiously leading him out onto the floor. At the cafeteria, she had again been in control, forcing him to abandon his coffee and leave the building with her, to be taken somewhere to see something – all unspecified. But now, driving the car, she was not particularly in control, and he could assert himself. He could point out, for instance, that one should not attempt to shift gears without first depressing the clutch.

"Don't be alarmed," she said, as they headed down the Windsor Street hill. "The guy who sold me the car told me the brakes aren't perfect, but they work most of the time."

They made it alive to the bottom of the hill and, after an interesting left turn, with lots of horns blaring, headed east along Notre Dame Street. They went past the criminal courts, past the city hall, past the Château de Ramezay, and then far into the east end, a mysterious part of the city where Richard had never been. They were near railway tracks and could hear the crashing noise of locomotives shunting. The air was heavy with soot. They went past Bercy Street, past Marlborough, past Rodier – each street more shabby than the last.

Finally they turned south, into a garbage-strewn alley. Here, at the waterfront, was a row of jerry-built wood- and tarpaper shacks. There were grimy children running around, kicking a tin can. They stopped and stood staring at the car as Sophia parked it.

"Welcome to Shack Town," she said. "Big families live here. There's no indoor toilets. Those children are probably hungry."

"This is awful," said Richard.

"There are pockets of slums like this all over town," Sophia said. "I'll show them to you when we've got more time."

After a long silence, he said, "Why are you showing me this?"

"You can't guess?"

"No, I can't."

"I thought you might like to write some poems about it."

As he pondered this, a gaunt woman wearing what looked like a nightgown came out of one of the shacks and up to the car.

"Qu'est-ce que vous voulez ici?" she said to Sophia.

"*Excusez-nous, madame*," said Sophia. "*Nous partons.*" And she started the car and drove away, heading back along Notre Dame Street.

"That was really awful," said Richard, who could think of nothing else to say.

"Did you see that little girl's teeth?" she said. "I thought of that great line in your poem: 'From decaying teeth, a feeble, crumbling bite.'"

"Do you think the *McGill Daily* would like more of that 'Ode to Zero' kind of stuff?" he asked.

"Not the *Daily*, silly," she said. "I want you to write for *Vanguard*. I'm going to be the literary editor."

"What's *Vanguard*?"

"It's going to be a terrific magazine," she said. "Founded by me and some friends."

"What kind of a magazine?"

"Let's not beat around the bush," she said. "Are you afraid of the word *communist*?"

"No, of course not," he said, although he was indeed afraid of the word.

"We'll have great articles from the Soviet Union," she said. "How they've done away with poverty, and so on. But we also want hard-hitting stuff from right here, bitter stuff, black stuff. From writers like you. And now I'm going to shut up, because I can see that you're already thinking." To verify that he was already thinking, she turned her gorgeous head toward him, taking her eyes off the road and again almost drawing blood from some pedestrians.

They were in Westmount now, going up Mount Pleasant to The Boulevard. As they climbed the hill, the big houses became bigger and richer, Italianate became Scottish Baronial, and then houses became mansions as they went up Belvedere Road. Finally they turned into Sunnyside, near the very top of the mountain, from where you could look down on the city and the river and, on a clear day, all the way across to the Green Mountains of Vermont.

"From up here you can get a great view of the slums," she said. "Slums east, slums west, slums south. You can't see slums north because they're behind the mountain."

"And you've brought me up here to see the contrast," he said. "For the Communist poems."

"Of course," she said.

She had parked her battered Airflow Chrysler in front of what seemed to be the biggest mansion of them all; in fact it was more of a castle than a mere mansion, a castle inspired by the chateaux of the Loire and Canada's great railway hotels.

"Just a minute," she said, getting out of the car. She went over to the castle's huge wrought-iron gate, unlatched it, and threw it open. Gunning the car, she sent it hurtling through the gate and down the long driveway.

"Hey, what are you doing?" Richard shouted in alarm.

"I live here," she said. "Isn't it disgusting?"

Without hitting anything, she brought the car to a halt inside the *porte cochère*. The ornate front door of the castle opened and a butler appeared.

"Ah, Miss Sophia," he said, in a British accent. "I thought I heard the car."

"We'll have some tea, Phillip," she said.

"In the sunroom or in the garden?" the butler asked.

"In the garden," she said. "Cucumber sandwiches and cherry tomatoes. And ask Maggie if she's made any more of those little shortbread cookies."

9

After they finished their tea in the garden, Sophia led Richard into the house, to introduce him to her ancestors. The first of these, whose large portrait hung in the library, was the heavily bearded patriarch, Alexander Bruce (1770–1838). "My great-great-great-grandfather," Sophia said. "He came over from Scotland when he was eighteen years old, speaking Gaelic and wearing a kilt. Became a fur trader, became a partner in the North West Company, and became very rich robbing the Indians blind. Basically he was a thief sitting in the back of a big canoe, with a big pile of furs, while his French-Canadian crew paddled up front. Had a meek little wife in Montreal, Elsie, and had a different Indian wife every winter, out in the West. Alexander was a very nasty piece of work, trading rotgut liquor to the Indians. But his son was even worse."

She led Richard to another portrait, this one of a man resplendent in an army officer's dress uniform. "This is Hector, his son," Sophia said. "He was a Sunday soldier, a member of the militia. He said he helped put down the Rebellion of 1837, and in the family we're not allowed to say that he never went anywhere near the front lines. But he was right up front in the cheering section when they publicly hanged those French-Canadian freedom fighters. The thought that there might ever be democracy in Canada made my illustrious ancestors very nervous."

Richard was tempted to tell her that he too had an ancestor who was involved in the Rebellion of 1837. But far from being a coward, Captain Horace Lippman had taken a bullet in the shoulder in the Battle of St. Eustache. But of course old Horace, like Hector Bruce, had been on the government side, not on the rebel side, and this would not endear him in the eyes of radical Sophia.

Sophia was now taking Richard by the hand, a gesture that thrilled him, to lead him down a long hallway, past a suit of armour standing ready with a mace, to the drawing room, where there were more portraits of ancestors to be denounced. Sir Rupert Bruce (1836–1904) was a builder of railways, a corrupter of governments, a cooker of the books, a conniver in the great Pacific Scandal of 1873 that brought down Sir John A. Macdonald.

As Richard admired Sir Rupert's magnificent mutton chop whiskers, Sophia told him how the Chinese coolies that built the railway for him and for his fellow capitalists kept falling off the trestles and down into the canyons, dying like flies. And nobody gave a damn.

"You know why I'm telling you all this," she said.

"You want me to write an epic poem," he said.

"Yes," she said, giving his hand a little squeeze, which made him wonder whether he shouldn't consider the idea. Why not paint on a larger, more ambitious canvas? Why not let these Bruces illuminate the Canadian story, to show its dark and sinister colours? Why not win her love by telling the world how rotten her family was?

"And this is my grandfather," she said, pointing to another portrait. "He built this house we're in, and the crummy little houses in Griffintown for the workers in his factories. No indoor plumbing and lots of rats. Starvation Jack, they used to call him, because of the generous wages he paid."

"And this is your father?" Richard asked, looking up at the last of the portraits, suddenly nervous that this beardless, modern-looking man might come striding into the room at any minute.

"Yes, that's Daddy," she said. "He's into everything, but mostly insurance. The less said about him the better. Right now he's off with Mummy in England, shooting pheasants – or peasants – or some damn thing."

Sophia drove him home in the Airflow Chrysler. There wasn't far to go, as the Lippman house was halfway down the hill, between the aristocracy at the top and the proletariat at the bottom; it wasn't quite a mansion, but it was a very big house, in the middle of a very big lawn, with many trees all round.

"I'm going to give you lots of notes about the nasty Bruces, for your poem," Sophia said, as they parked in front of the house. As she said it, she gave his hand another little squeeze.

"Yes, that'll be terrific," he said, as the electricity of the squeeze penetrated to the furthest reaches of his body. He wondered whether this was an invitation to attempt a light kiss, but he decided against it. Free love, he had heard, was one of the most attractive aspects of communism, but perhaps now was too soon to try to get the ball rolling.

"I've often thought I ought to write about the Bruces myself," Sophia said, "as an essay, or even a book. But the fact is, Richard, I just can't write. If I have anything at all to offer, it's that I'm a good organizer. I know how to organize people. I know how to push projects. I don't want to sound conceited, but in the class struggle that's very important."

Of course she didn't say it, but Richard realized that he himself was now in the process of being organized. He at once resented it and loved it.

The meeting of the editorial staff of *Vanguard* was taking place in the editor's shabby basement apartment on St. Famille Street. There were eight staffers there plus one newcomer, Richard Lippman. The editor, Sam Rudner, had objected when Sophia told him she was bringing this brilliant young poet, but Sophia had been insistent.

"I'm the only Communist he's ever met," she had said. "We have to educate him."

"How do we know he doesn't work for the police?" Rudner asked.

"He doesn't," Sophia said. "Trust me."

Reluctantly Rudner realized that he would have to trust her – for two reasons. First, most of the money to pay the printers for the first issue of *Vanguard* was coming from this poor little rich girl, who had devised some complicated scheme to get it out of her father. And secondly, Rudner was determined, despite an initial failed attempt, to get her into bed.

"This is Richard Lippman," Sophia announced, taking him around the room to introduce him to the others. "He's going to make a huge cultural contribution to the magazine." As he watched this, Rudner decided that this was surely an uptown Jew. His sports jacket looked like real Harris tweed and his tie was surely one of those handwoven woolen ones that could set you back two dollars. And the way he said "How do you do?" and not just "Hi" branded him as being as being a Westmounter, about as far away as you could get from the St. Dominique Street ghetto. Rudner, thirty-five years old, meat and fish manager at a Steinberg groceria, was an uncompromising son of that ghetto, and he despised the uptowners, who were basically Jewish fascists driving flashy Buicks.

But now here was one of them, right in the middle of things. And, damn it, was he sleeping with Sophia? Had he surmounted the barrier she had erected against Rudner and, it seemed, against any other comrade who would like to get into her? Rudner knew something of the status of Sophia's love life, she having confided in Molly, *Vanguard*'s copy editor, and Molly having passed on the essentials to Rudner. Sophia, it seemed, had spent the summer between high school and university in Switzerland, at some fancy girls' finishing school. And while there she had become involved with an older fellow called Renato, from the other side of the tracks. Renato had relieved her of her virginity – thank God for that – and had opened her eyes to the beauties of marxism. But suddenly one day this Renato had vamoosed to Paris, leaving nothing but the briefest of goodbye notes for Sophia. Heartbroken, Sophia swore off men forever. Henceforth all her energies would be devoted to The Cause. But now had this poet, this uptown jerk, managed to melt the ice? It seemed to Rudner, watching her introduce this Richard around the room, that she was very proud of him – and possessive. This was extremely irritating.

Sophia and Richard had arrived late at the meeting, in the midst of a heated debate about Sergei Eisenstein. The first issue of *Vanguard* was going to pay tribute to the glories of the Soviet cinema of the 1920s, during the years right after the revolution, and one of the comrades was defending the article he had written about Eisenstein. "Are you telling me that *Potemkin* is not one of the greatest films of all time?" he said, indignantly.

"That's exactly what I'm telling you," an angry-looking woman said. "When you watch Eisenstein you're watching formalism, that's what you're watching."

"Why aren't we talking about Pudovkin?" a man beside her said. "Which of us didn't cry when we saw *Storm Over Asia*, that scene where the socialist hero refuses the cigarette that's offered to him by the capitalist firing squad? That, comrades, is cinema."

"Bullshit," said a man at the back of the room. "That's bourgeois soap opera. Anything for a bit of cheap drama. But just what does it do for the revolution?"

Listening to all this, Richard marvelled at the passions that were being voiced, about movies he had never heard of. What a contrast to the discussions about movies he and Martin and Stanley used to have over ice-cream sundaes at Gagnon's on Friday night. The most intellectual discussion he could recall was about *Slave Girl*, with the alluring Yvonne de Carlo. Besides the improbability of the talking camel, there was that idiotic scene in which five hundred warriors all fell dead in about one second. The most recent film they had analyzed was *Mother Wore Tights*, where their discussion had revolved around Betty Grable's legs and the phenomenal way in which she could fill a sweater. But here, he realized, in this stuffy little basement apartment on St. Famille Street, he was among adults, now talking about some Russian director called Dovzhenko and his film *Earth*, which celebrated the determination of the socialist worker.

"What about that scene in the drought?" somebody was saying. "When the tractor's radiator boils over and the peasants keep the machine going by filling the radiator with their urine. That is cinema."

That sounded pretty good to Richard, but here was that woman again, shouting "Formalism!" And again there was an uproar.

But now the voice of Sam Rudner rose about the tumult.

"Will you all shut up!" he yelled. And when they did, he started pacing up and down the room, declaiming.

"What is this I am hearing?" he said. "Is this a Marxist study group or is it a little bourgeois debating society? Is it a parade of half-baked egos? Am I hearing the voice of Trotsky? What am I hearing? Please tell me."

There was no response from the others, some of them fidgeting uncomfortably in their rickety folding chairs.

"Eisenstein, Pudovkin, Dovzhenko," he said. "Which was the greatest? Well, let me tell you, comrades, none of them was great. That word *great* belongs in Hollywood fan magazines. Eisenstein and the others were simply Stakhanovite workers in their respective cinema collectives. They were submerging their egos to produce collective art that would further the goals of the revolution. In *Vanguard* we want articles about all three of those collectives, pointing out the lessons we can draw from their work, how filmmakers here in Canada, thirty years after the great Soviet Revolution, can find ways to inspire our own revolution. Is that clear?"

Heads nodded everywhere in the room and there were mutters of "Yes," "Of course," and "Absolutely right, Sam." Listening to him, Richard realized that this man was indeed very good, the way he started his oration by shouting and then gradually lowered his voice until he almost whispered its climax, forcing his audience to strain to listen to the depth of his passion. But now, to Richard's alarm, he had turned his head toward Richard and was fixing him with a long stare.

"Tell me, Comrade Lippman," he finally said. "Are you by any chance related to Gerald R. Lippman?"

"Yes," said Richard uneasily. "He's my father."

"The big lawyer?" asked Rudner. "Who represented the Lady Anne Dress Company in its fight with the union?"

"Yes, I guess so," said Richard, now extremely uncomfortable.

"You must have been proud of your father, back in 1934," Rudner said. "How his clients paid the girls in their factory six dollars a week, for seventy hours of work. A filthy sweatshop crawling with cockroaches. With one filthy toilet, always blocked, for four hundred girls. How they hired goons to attack the girls during the Dressmakers' Strike. Do you remember all that?"

"Nineteen thirty-four?" said Richard. "I was three years old."

"Take it easy, Sam," Sophia said. "We all have families. We all have to deal with that."

"I remember that strike like yesterday," a hefty middle-aged woman said. "Lady Anne Dress and all the other factories. There were thousands of us, marching down St. Catherine Street. There were policemen on horseback, flicking whips at us. And we stuck hatpins into the sides of the horses."

"Maybe you'd like to write something for *Vanguard* about that strike," Rudner said to Richard.

"Well, I could think about it," said Richard glumly.

"Great idea," said Sophia. "I'll help you with the research."

It was Tuesday morning and he should have been in Moyse Hall, at the English 2 lecture, learning exactly what John Bunyan had in mind when he wrote *The Pilgrim's Progress*. But Sophia had persuaded him to skip the lecture and do something much more important, something that would further his socialist education. So here he was, on the waterfront, marching up and down and carrying a placard that said "No Bullets for Dictators." Sophia's sign said "Send Bread, Not Guns." As they marched, they and the dozen or so other picketers chanted, "Peace in China, Peace in China."

They were picketing the SS *Cliffside*, a cargo ship that was being loaded with guns and ammunition for Chiang Kai-shek's

Nationalist Army, locked in battle with Mao Tse-tung's Communists. "Makes you ashamed to be Canadian, doesn't it?" Sophia said as the police arrived to disperse the picketers. But if Richard was ashamed of anything it was of the fact that he knew nothing about the civil war in China; he always skipped newspaper stories about that conflict, just as he skipped other boring stories, like the city council's debates about tax rates.

"We absolutely have to win in China," Sophia said, as they drove off in her Airflow Chrysler.

"Absolutely," said Richard, ashamed now of both his ignorance and his new-found phoniness.

His education continued that night in the Students' Union ballroom, where Sophia brought him to listen to a speech by Tim Buck, leader of the Labour Progressive Party, which was the recently sanitized name of the Communist Party of Canada. The big room was filled to overflowing as Buck denounced the United States and its grandiose Marshall Plan. "It's nothing more than an American plot to dominate the economy of Western Europe!" he thundered. "It's all to protect the capitalist system!"

There was sporadic heckling as Buck outlined the reasons why all of Europe would soon be Communist. "And Canada, too," he said, "will eventually be Communist. And then the working class will come into its own."

"The working class can kiss my ass!" somebody at the back of the hall shouted, and Richard turned to see that it was his skinny friend Stanley, who was standing there with sloppy Martin.

"You see what we're up against," Sophia said.

"Disgusting," Richard said, feeling double guilt for his sense that Tim Buck's droning on about the steel industry in the Ruhr Valley would have been intolerably boring without the lively catcalls from the floor that punctuated it.

As they left the ballroom, with Sophia talking to him animatedly about post-war Europe, Martin and Stanley confronted them. "Hey, Richard," Stanley said, "aren't you going to introduce us?"

But Richard averted his eyes and ignored him.

"Was that you, yelling like that?" Sophia said to Stanley.

"Yes, ma'am," Stanley said, with a broad grin.

"Do you know this person?" Sophia asked Richard.

"Not really."

"I should hope not," said Sophia, taking his arm and marching him away. Much later, as he reflected on that evening's events, it occurred to Richard that his snubbing of Stanley and Martin was a turning point in his life. He had finally climbed out of the childish wading pool and had ventured into the deep, dangerous waters of maturity. But would he have to prove himself by denouncing his father and the Lady Anne Dress Company?

"'The dead eye sees naught but cracked and jagged shards of life,'" Sophia said. "That's beautiful, Richard, really beautiful."

"And this," she continued. "'Wounded faces on a wounded street.'" Her voice was trembling now as she continued reading Richard's poem, the long poem inspired by their visit to the slums. It was almost midnight, after an agitprop meeting they had attended downtown, and they were now parked in her car in front of Richard's house. He had decided that this was the time to give her the poem, and she had turned on the overhead light in the car to read it. Uneasily Richard wondered what his mother might make of this scene, if she glanced out of her bedroom window and kept on glancing until he got out of the car.

"We're going to print this in the magazine with lots of white space around it, so it will stand out," she said, and continued reading the pages he had given her.

"Is it maybe too long?" he asked.

"No, no," she said. "It's perfect. And this: 'The child that knows the acid taste of hunger's grip.'"

Looking at her, Richard was elated to see that tears were forming in her eyes. Could a poet hope for anything more than to make a reader cry? And yes, she was now openly weeping, and he hastily gave her his handkerchief, happy that it was pristine and newly laundered. She smiled at him wanly, apologetically, as she mopped her eyes. It occurred to him that as soon as she finished reading the heart-rending couplet that concluded the poem, on page five, it would be the right moment for him to inaugurate the first kiss.

"Oh, Richard," she said, as she put the sheaf of paper down on the dashboard. She was still dabbing her eyes as he leaned over and approached her lips. Dropping the handkerchief, she threw her arms around him and they kissed vigorously. But after a while she pulled away and looked at him mournfully. "No, Richard, no," she said. "We can't. Or at least I can't. Not now. I just can't get involved."

She turned off the car's overhead light and they sat silently in the darkness. He wondered what to say. Perhaps he ought to say a polite and unemotional "Good night," and put his hand on the door handle, in the hope that she would reach out to detain him. Then they could spend hours discussing just why the kissing had to stop. To make the threat of his exit more real, perhaps he should ask her to give him back his handkerchief. After all, it was one of his best handkerchiefs, a birthday gift from one of his aunts, pure Egyptian cotton with hand-rolled edges and his initials gracefully embroidered on it. But then he decided to do exactly the opposite. He would leave the handkerchief in her possession. Looking at it in the morning, she would remember the tears it had absorbed; and the initials R.L. – in Old English lettering – would remind her of who it was that could awaken such strong emotions in her.

When he got home, there was a letter from Lili waiting for him. It was enough to propel him down into new, uncharted depths of gloom.

Cincinnati, Ohio.
November 7, 1948.

Dear Richard,

Great news! Orpheus and Eurydice, with dance stylings by Lili L'Amour and poetry by Richard Lippman, is now in rehearsal and will have its daybue five days from now on the stage of the Alhambra Theater! It would be great if you could get down here to see it, but I guess Cincinnati is pretty far from Montreal. And you are probably too imersed in your studies, which explains why I have not recieved a letter from you in some time. And as you know, my dear, I am counting on you to correct my grammer and spelling.

As I think I mentioned in a previous letter, the manager of the Alhambra here loves Culture, with a capital *C*, and although I have been hired, as what I like to call an exotic dancer, which I just invented, he is encouraging me to try blending your culture into my exoticry. Is that a word, exoticry?

Mr. Barstow, that manager, has got an announcer from the local radio station to read your poetry offstage, while I dance. He's a very nice young man called Alan Germain. Alan turns out to be much more than just a radio news reader. Besides having a beautiful deep voice, he also has much dramatic experience, in the amateur theater here.

Going over your poem, he is making some changes in the wording, to make it, as he says, "more understandible in Cincinnati." I know you won't mind, but some of it is now really different, but it sounds great in that voice of his.

Besides his literary ability, Alan also knows a lot about choreography. You will remember when you first gave me the Orpheus and Eurydice script you put in some stage directions, like when she descends down into the underworld at which point she takes off this part of her costume and at which point she takes off that part, to cool off in the increasing heat of hell. Well, that worked beautifully back then. But with the new rhythms in the text – Alan's contributions – it just doesn't work. So we need new choreography.

So Alan has volunteered to help me with this, and not just in theory. He has been coming in in the morning, when the theatre is dark and empty, and he works with me on stage, with music from a little gramophone he brings. His sense of timing is uncanny, as he makes good suggestions about my movements, and like he says, "I think we're going to have a work of art."

I'm writing this in my dressing room – it's nine o'clock in the morning – and there's a knock on the door. It's Alan. So I'll simply say

Love,
Lili

How could she do this to him? Was she completely insensitive? Or was she doing it on purpose – a sadist revelling in his agony? First it was that bastard with the private railway car to New York, that total luxury with *two bedrooms*, ha, ha. And now it was a radio-station jerk "who makes good suggestions about my movements." Did he make his suggestions more vivid by laying hands on her? Grimly Richard visualized the scene on the stage of the empty theatre, at ten in the morning. She was down to pasties and G-string, pausing and asking for advice, when this Alan bastard went up to her and . . . And finally, at eleven o'clock, after her convulsions in the coitus scene, they would go back to her dressing room, where he would help her wipe the glistening perspiration off her lovely body. And then . . .

To drive this horrendous scene from his mind, Richard forced himself to try to think logically. Lili was, after all, a mature woman, more than just a girl, like Sophia. She had been married an unspecified number of times and probably had no problem hopping into bed with a man without actually being in love with him. Richard had heard of such women. And if Richard had not managed to hop in with her he had only himself to blame. Why had he been such a coward? Why, when they had been together in Montreal, had he not made a move? Why had he not declared himself? Why, why, why? Lili, if she had given the matter any thought, had probably concluded that young Richard wanted to keep things platonic, or that he wasn't really physically attracted to her. In those poems he had written for her he had compared her with Helen of Troy and other beauties of yore, but she had probably thought that these were just poetic exercises, not groans of longing and lust.

The thought of his poetry jabbed another spear into his flesh. That son-of-a-bitch radio announcer with the deep voice was rewriting his Orpheus and Eurydice masterpiece to make it "more understandible in Cincinnati." Richard shuddered to think how his lines might be violated. His

In thy resolve be firm, O Orpheus
Be forward in thy gaze
Turn not thy head

Lest all be lost
And thy love be snatched
Back to the flames of hell.

How would the radio bastard rewrite this for Cincinnati? Would it be "Don't look back, Orphy-boy, or we'll all be in deep shit"?

Feeding a sheet of paper into his typewriter – his cheap, first-draft paper this time – he resolved not to censor his fury.

> 9 Murray Avenue
> Westmount, Quebec
> November 10, 1948.

Dear Lili,

Please be advised that I will not allow my poetry to be corrupted by any ignorant jerk who happens to come by. What you told me in your letter about some radio announcer rewriting my work has left me feeling violated. Has it ever occurred to you that –

He paused in his typing and studied what he had written. Then he slowly pulled the paper from the Smith-Corona, tore it in pieces, and threw the pieces into the wastepaper basket. This approach was wrong, wrong, wrong. The true meaning of love had suddenly revealed itself to him at 2:25 a.m. on October 23, during his acute suffering following Lili's decamping to New York. Yes, Love Means That You Have To Put Up With A Lot. That was the essence of it, pure and simple. Just grit your teeth and put up with it, Richard.

So, instead of sounding angry in his letter he would ignore the horrors of Cincinnati and write something sweet to Lili. He would tell her how to spell *debut* and *understandable*. He would speak blithely about the good progress he was making with his Diana the Huntress poem. He would resist the temptation to tell her that the first thing Diana should do with her bow and arrow would be to shoot that radio announcer, Sir Charles Hammond, and God knows how many others.

Two days later, the sight of Sophia lifted his spirits a bit, especially as she had been waiting for him outside the Arts Building when he came out of Latin 1A. "Coffee," she said. "We have things to talk about."

She didn't seem to want to talk just yet, and as they walked silently down the campus, Richard tried hard to keep looking steadfastly ahead, without turning to stare at her, so beautiful this morning with her dark hair spilling out from under her perky tam-o'-shanter, with its black pompom on top.

In the coffee shop, after he brought the cups to the table, she said, "We had a meeting of the editorial board last night. And I read them your wonderful poem." She paused, pouring more sugar into her cup and gazing at him, as though unwilling to go on.

"How did it go?" he asked.

"Well," she said, "I got into trouble when I got to that part about that poor man Mathieu, how he committed suicide when he couldn't find a job, how he threw himself under the wheels of the train. 'The scream of the wheels as they sliced, the head rolling down toward the factory gates.'" There was a tear in her eye and she paused, reaching into her purse for a handkerchief. And he was elated to see that it was *his* handkerchief, the one he had given to her in the car. Happy day, she was keeping it!

"Well, when I read that I started to cry," she said. "And I noticed that Molly and Barbara were also crying. And do you know what happened?"

"No, what?"

"Sam Rudner yelled at me and told me to stop reading," she said. "He said we sounded like a bunch of rich bitches from Westmount, at a meeting of Federated Charities. He said that to be effective in the class struggle we have to suppress sentimental bourgeois emotions that can be a substitute for action. We have to be cold and disciplined. And he told me to read that part again without crying."

"Jesus," said Richard, "did you do that?"

"I did," said Sophia. "It wasn't easy."

"But what about the poem?" he asked. "Did they like the poem?"

"They all loved it," said Sophia. She hesitated, putting still more sugar into her coffee. And then she said, "Sam said it was very good, but it was only half there, or maybe a bit less than half."

"What does that mean?"

"He said that you've stated the effects of the situation, but not the cause of the situation and how the problem could be solved."

"I don't get it," said Richard.

"He says you have to do some more work on it," she said. "You can keep the beautiful parts, of course, but you should intersperse some lines that point the way to action."

"Lines?" he said. "What lines?"

"Lines that you can select from the material we're studying. *The Communist Manifesto*, the works of Marx and Lenin and Stalin."

"I just lift out some lines and stick them in?" said Richard. "Is that it?"

"If the lines don't fit nicely," said Sophia, "you could paraphrase."

"I would have the freedom to paraphrase Lenin?"

"Within reason," said Sophia. "Sam says he hopes you'll understand that *Vanguard* is not a vehicle for the egos of authors, but a writers' collective. And the key word in the party is *discipline*. Do you have any trouble with that, Richard?"

"No, none at all," he said, wondering whether he should ask for his handkerchief back. First there was that rewrite down in Cincinnati and now there was this. If it was his turn to start to cry, he would need that handkerchief.

10

"It's for you," his mother said, after answering the phone. "It's a female."

Richard took the phone from her and waited for her to leave the room. She was by now well trained to respect his need for privacy, but she was taking her time actually leaving. "Who are all these females?" Mrs. Lippman asked, pausing in the doorway.

It was probably Sophia, and Richard didn't mind keeping her waiting while his mother made her slow exit. This would be the third time Sophia had called him in recent days to discuss what the magazine wanted to do with his poetry, and again he would have to put her off, explaining that he was still reading the book she had given him, to see how he could incorporate some of its activist ideas into the passivity of his verses. But *The State and Revolution: How to Change the Social Order*, by V.I. Lenin, was so agonizingly boring.

But it wasn't Sophia on the phone, it was a new female, speaking in an American accent.

"This is Joyce Jaworski," she said. "I'm a friend of Lili L'Amour. I've just arrived in town."

"Oh, hi," said Richard. "How's Lili?"

"She's great," Joyce said. "She gave me a letter for you. Could we meet for a coffee or something?"

The prospect of getting the letter made him decide to skip his three o'clock lecture – Chemistry 16 – and meet this Joyce instead, right away.

"How about the Honey Dew, at three o'clock?" he said, and he instructed her how to find his favourite coffee shop, at the corner of Burnside and Mansfield.

As he went out the door, Mrs. Lippman said, "How come you're not wearing your alpaca? It's cold out."

"It's not cold enough for that," said Richard, although it was indeed cold enough today, what with the sharp November wind. But his beige Alpacama overcoat – the Tudor model, with extra wide lapels – would have to stay in the cupboard if he was going to be a Communist. How could he let himself be seen by the comrades wearing a forty-two-dollar coat, made of luxurious fabric woven by starving peasants in the high Andes of Bolivia. No, a simple cloth coat, like the one Lenin was reputed to have worn, would have to do. Thinking back to the dreadful slums Sophia had shown him, he could never parade around in a soft Alpacama, that super-capitalist garment that his mother had bought for him; he felt guilty enough as it was, what with his doubts about that all-important discipline that Communists had to exercise.

Joyce Jaworski had arrived at the Honey Dew before Richard, and he found her sitting in a booth, sipping coffee and reading the *Herald*. She had told him on the phone that he would recognize her because she had red hair, and she indeed had hair that was very red, and done up in a big bun. To go with the hair, she had abundant freckles and pouty cherry lips. If it weren't for the most dazzlingly scarlet fingernails Richard had ever seen, this Joyce could be the girl next door in an Andy Hardy movie.

"From dear old Lili," she said, handing him one of Lili's familiar perfumed mauve envelopes. He wanted to open it immediately, but realized that this would be impolite. He would have to make a bit of conversation first.

"What brings you to Montreal?" he asked.

"This," she said, pushing the *Herald* across the table. With one of those red fingernails she pointed to an ad on the entertainment page. It was for the Roxy, a second-rate burlesque theatre on St. Lawrence Main. "The Newest Sensation!" the ad said. "WHIRLWIND WANDA! Come see her take it off!"

"I'm Whirlwind Wanda," Joyce said, with a small smile that seemed apologetic. "I start tonight."

"So you're what Lili calls an exotic dancer," said Richard.

"Thank you," she said, "but I'm really just a stripper. I'm not like Lili – at least not yet. But why don't you open that envelope? I can see you're dying to do that."

Lili's letter was a short one:

New York,
November 22nd, 1948.

Dearest Richard,

As you will see, Joyce is a lovely girl, but very nervous. She's new to the business and very unsure of herself. Montreal will be especially hard for her as some idiot told her they will hate her because she doesn't speak French. Any advice or reassurance you can give her will be much appreciated. Could you find time in your busy schedule to show her around town a bit? As you see, I have enclosed a money order for fifteen dollars. Maybe you could take her to lunch in the Ritz Garden (remember?).

As for me, things have taken a surprising (and very good) turn. Thus I am off to Europe tomorrow. I must rush now but will write more fully from the boat.

> Much love
> Lili

"She's going to Europe," Richard said. "Did you know that?"

"Oh, sure," Joyce said. "I went shopping with her on Fifth Avenue. She bought some really fancy travel stuff. Including one of those portable boudoirs."

"Do you know why she's going to Europe?" Richard asked.

"Well, she was a bit mysterious about that," Joyce said. "But I think there's a gentleman involved, if you know what I mean."

"Yes, I know what you mean," Richard said, glumly.

To get his mind off Lili in Europe, he asked Joyce how she became an exotic dancer – he persisted in calling her that – and she obliged by telling him her life story in detail. She grew up just down the street from where Lili had lived, in that small town in Minnesota. She had always wanted to be a dancer, and when she finally broke free from her family and made it to New York, she looked up Lili, who had taken her under her wing and had found her an agent. Her first job was as a Rockette in the chorus line at the Radio City Music Hall.

"After a year it became so damn boring," Joyce said. "Thirty-six puppets in a line. Lift, kick, lift, kick. I was going crazy until Lili steered me into stripping."

"I was in New York last summer," Richard said. "I saw the Rockettes. Were you there then?"

"Yes, I was number fifteen, counting from the left."

"Then I saw you," Richard said. "As I said to my friend, 'Look at number fifteen. Doesn't she stand out from the rest?'"

"Are you kidding?" she said. "If I stood out from the rest I would have been fired right away. Like I told you, we were dancing puppets. But it was sweet of you to say that." And she favoured him with a warm, girl-next-door smile.

"How long have you been exotic dancing?" he asked.

"Stripping," she said. "I'm very new at it. This is only my second gig. My first was in Philadelphia, where I was not very good."

"Oh, I'm sure you were good," Richard said. That smile of hers had started him thinking that perhaps Lili had sent him a birthday present, in the form of this Joyce Jaworski. That red hair made her quite sexy, didn't it? And she was emitting a perfume with a hint of cinnamon in it, a perfume that seemed to beckon. Maybe . . .

"Look," she was now saying, "Lili told me you had some good ideas about choreography and stuff like that. Would it be too much to ask you to come and see my show? And tell me frankly what you think of it? And maybe give me some ideas how I could improve?"

"Yes, I'd be willing to do that," said Richard, hoping that it sounded as though he'd be making something of a sacrifice to do it.

"You're very sweet," said Joyce. "Here's a free pass to the crummy old Roxy Theatre, so you won't have to pay."

The Roxy was on St. Lawrence Main, below St. Catherine Street, a stone's throw from the busy brothels of the red-light district. It was considered to be a second-rate burlesque house, but to Richard it seemed that third-rate might be a more accurate label. The first thing that struck him when he entered was the odour – that of some kind of acrid disinfectant, as though the management wanted to mask some more sinister smell.

The seat that he found for himself seemed to have a broken spring somewhere under its scuffed leatherette surface. The heavy curtain that concealed the stage had probably once belonged to a more important theatre; now it was shabby and wrinkled. Compared with this flea pit, Lili's Gayety Theatre was the Royal Opera House. And the atmosphere here was further degraded by a boy who was marching up and down the aisle before the show started, shouting "Peanuts, popcorn, Cracker Jack!" As Richard would learn, when he became more familiar with the traditions of burlesque, this boy was known as a "candy butcher."

Now, from the orchestra pit, if you could call four musicians an orchestra, came the strains of "God Save the King," and the audience stood up reluctantly. Finally they could sit down when the anthem came to a wheezing halt and the music segued into a spirited fanfare. The house lights dimmed as the old curtain creaked its way open. During the fanfare, the master of ceremonies came onto the stage, but instead of trotting briskly, as he should have done, he was limping painfully.

"Sorry about this, folks," he announced, pointing to his left knee, "but I had a terrible accident last night. You see, I had to get out of bed real fast and jump out the window when the lady's husband came home unexpectedly. The old bugger was supposed to be in Toronto. Ha, ha, ha. Ow, ow, ow."

But the response from the audience was weak, nothing more than a few snickers.

"Where's Whirlwind Wanda?" a man in the front row shouted.

"Yeah, will ya hurry up?" another man called out.

"Yes, we have a star-studded show for you tonight, ladies and gentlemen," the master of ceremonies went on, ignoring the fact that there were no women in the audience. So let's get started with the Amazing Edgar, direct from Chicago, the Windy City, who will astonish you with what he can do with his balls."

As the orchestra broke into, incongruously, "She'll Be Coming Round the Mountain When She Comes," the Amazing Edgar came trotting out, dressed in the piebald costume of a medieval court jester. He was juggling not with balls but with three Indian clubs. He was obviously a beginner, and it wasn't long before he managed to drop one of the clubs. His career, like that of many other artists, was getting its start at the Roxy, which was known for giving a chance to youngsters who were on their way up in the world of show business and were willing to work for a pittance. Always humane, the theatre would also book seasoned performers who were on their way down, thanks to old age or alcohol. The audience had no right to complain, what with admission to a two-hour show costing only thirty-five cents.

But still, dissatisfaction was beginning to ripple through the room as the Amazing Edgar started trying to juggle four balls. "Where's Wanda?" the loudmouth in the front row now called out.

"Yeah, bring her on!" another man shouted.

These two louts, who were frequent patrons of the Roxy, surely knew that the stripper would not come on until the end of the show, as its climax; leading up to that moment, for the delectation of that element in the audience with more aesthetic tastes, there was always a procession of acts like that of Flam-o the Fire-eater, Beppo the Clown, and Gaylord Updike, the crooner.

"Ain't he great?" the master of ceremonies was asking, as the Amazing Edgar brought his act to a stumbling halt. "Ain't he great? One of the stars of tomorrow, although not necessarily today. Let's give him a big hand!"

After Edgar, several acts followed one another, some limping, some staggering, and a few, like Mahatma the Magician, surprisingly good. After Mahatma sawed his girl assistant into three pieces, there was finally an ovation from the audience, perhaps because she emerged from her ordeal so lightly clad.

As the applause and whistles died down, the master of ceremonies was back on the stage. "And now, ladies and gentlemen," he proclaimed, "the highlight of this cultural evening. You've seen them all – Gypsy Rose Lee, Rosita Royce, Lois DeFee – but you've never seen anything like the one and only, the incomparable, the *ne plus ultra* Whirlwind Wanda! So here she is, directly from her triumph in Tennessee, her victory in Virginia, her ovation in Ohio, our new sweetheart, Whirlwind Wanda!"

The orchestra produced a fanfare and Joyce Jaworski came tripping onto the stage, dressed as a French maid in black stockings and a tiny skirt. As the spotlight followed her, Richard realized again that she was indeed truly gorgeous. And, as she went into her dance, he realized, after about fifty seconds, that in the whole history of stripteasery, this must surely be the worst act ever.

"You see that big, fat building down there?" Richard said. "That's the Sun Life Building, the biggest office building in the whole British Empire."

They were looking down at the city, from the lookout on top of Mount Royal. It was morning and Richard was doing what Lili had instructed him to do, in her letter: he was showing Joyce around town. But Joyce was in a low mood and was showing little interest in the touristic glories of Montreal. All she wanted to talk about was her performance at the Roxy.

"Please be truthful, Richard," she was saying. "I was really, really, really awful, wasn't I?"

"Look," he said, "you weren't awful. Like I said, you're new to the game and you've got a few rough edges, which you will eventually iron out."

"Rough edges?" she said. "Are you kidding? I was a total disaster, total."

"That's not true," he said, lying patiently. "I tell you what, let's go into the Chalet and have ourselves a spruce beer."

"Good," she said. "Let's get drunk."

"It's not alcoholic," he said. "But it'll cheer you up."

But the spruce beer – the best kind, made by the Indians in Caughnawaga – did nothing to lift her mood, so Richard decided to take her to Montreal's greatest tourist attraction, St. Joseph's Oratory, where she could mingle with people in much more miserable circumstances than her own. These were supplicants who came to the famous shrine to pray for deliverance from every imaginable disease and affliction.

"Look," he said, pointing to the forest of abandoned canes and crutches hanging from the ceiling. "Those are from people who were cured."

"I don't know what was worse," Joyce said, "my dancing or the way I stripped."

Still trying to cheer her up, Richard led her over to the glass reliquary that housed the pickled heart of Brother André, the founder of the shrine.

"They cut it out of his body right after he died," Richard explained. "It's responsible for the miracles that take place here every day."

"The audience hated me," Joyce said. "I could tell they hated me."

"They applauded, didn't they?" said Richard. "And some of them whistled, didn't they?"

"Only at the end," she said. "Only because I was naked, the dirty pigs."

They left the shrine, high on its hill, passing the pilgrims who were struggling up the one hundred stairs on their knees, as they prayed. Still determined to make her appreciate the wonders of Montreal, Richard led her across Queen Mary Road to the wax museum. Here they could appreciate a vivid tableau in which a very lifelike Father Jogues, the missionary priest, was being burned at the stake by the Hurons in 1683. And in the next room they could almost smell the searing flesh as the tormentors of Saint Lawrence roasted him on a huge iron grill.

"Isn't that horrible?" Richard said.

"Why am I kidding myself?" Joyce said. "I have no future in the theatre. I should do the smart thing and go back to being a waitress."

"How about some lunch?" Richard said. "Doesn't that make you hungry?" He gestured at the realistic flames that were treating Saint Lawrence like a huge tenderloin steak.

Lunch was to be at the Ritz, sponsored by that big fifteen-dollar money order that Lili had sent him. The Garden, where Lili had suggested he entertain Joyce, was, of course, closed for the winter, so Richard had made a reservation in the Oval Room. Now, as they entered the hotel lobby, Joyce finally stopped criticizing herself long enough to take some interest in her surroundings.

"This is the sort of hotel I should be staying in," she said. "You should see the dump where I'm staying, where the Roxy puts you."

"I'm sure some day you'll be staying right here," Richard said.

"Yeah, when I make my fortune as a waitress."

As they entered the dining room and sat down at their table, heads turned to scrutinize them. All the ladies and gentlemen at the other tables were clad in the statutory muted greys and browns and blacks of Montreal high society; amid this expensive drabness, Joyce's tight-fitting, bright-green dress, Christmas-like in combination with her flaming red hair, made for a violent visual intrusion. The lady diners exchanged glances of disapproval, while the gentlemen were, of course, intrigued.

"Will you look at these prices?" Joyce was saying, as she examined the menu.

"Don't worry about it," Richard said. "Order anything you like."

As most of the menu was too French for her, she asked Richard to order for both of them. So he asked the waiter to bring them a glass of wine, and then the *mousse de foie gras*, the *canard à l'orange* and the profiteroles.

The wine seemed to do more for her than the spruce beer had, and soon she was gazing intently across the table, into Richard's eyes. "Is there any hope for me, Richard?" she asked. "If I could get a new act?"

"The answer is yes," said Richard. "Definitely yes."

"Lili tells me you're a genius when it comes to choreography," she said. "You know all about stagecraft, and you write brilliant poetry. Do you think . . ." She paused and reached across the table to touch his hand lightly. "Do you think you could help little old me?"

"I've already been thinking about that," he said, untruthfully. "I'm sure we'll be able to come up with something."

"Lili showed me a wonderful poem you wrote for her dance," she said. "Maybe you could write a poem for me."

"Joyce," he said, "please believe me, you're not ready for poetry yet. That might come later." Suddenly he realized he had called her "Joyce," and not "you." Somehow this gave him a feeling of power, especially as it was combined with his denying her what she wanted – his poetry. Denying her this made him feel tall. He would not allow himself to be pushed around by this Joyce, the way Sophia and the Communists were trying to push him around.

"Lili said you were sweet," she was saying, "and that's so true."

The *mousse de foie gras* arrived and she started eating it ravenously. There was no need for more conversation at that moment, so Richard started thinking about just what kind of an act could be concocted for this redhead. He felt he was becoming knowledgeable about the art of the striptease, having visited the Gayety for three Saturday matinees since Lili's departure. He wanted to see how other headliners compared with Lili, and he had been pleased to note that none of them could come anywhere near his heartthrob's artistry. Perhaps he could get Joyce to borrow some bits from these three. Perhaps from Ann Corio, who was summa cum laude when it came to the classic bump and grind; but as he recalled, Joyce had done a bit of that on the Roxy stage, without much distinction. Perhaps she could add a bit of tassel-twirling, the way Evelyn West and Her Treasure Chest did it, but Joyce's chest, while delightful, was perhaps not gigantic enough. As for Ginger Snapp, there was nothing in her routine that could be of any use. Ginger was what they called in the trade a "chatterbox": she spoke to the audience. After prancing around the stage a bit, she and the music would stop. She would gesture out at the audience and shout, "Okay, boys, I'm about to start taking it off, so you too can get started and slip your hands under your raincoats." After taking off a few items of her costume, she would point toward one unfortunate man in the audience and shout, "What? Are you finished so soon? Your wife must be real proud of you, eh?" No, Richard thought, Ginger Snapp's concept was far too vulgar for Joyce.

"What do you think of my stage name?" Joyce was asking,

as the *canard à l'orange* arrived. "Whirlwind Wanda," she said. "That's not very good, is it?"

"No, it isn't," Richard said. "Part of the problem, if I may say so, is that you're moving too fast, all the time. It makes it hard for the audience to have a, uh, have a good look and, uh, appreciate the details."

"I'm glad you say that," Joyce said. "The whirlwind routine is my agent's idea. He made me study Georgia Sothern, who is also a redhead. She rushes around the stage like a maniac while the band plays 'Hold That Tiger.' For Georgia it works, but for me I don't think it does."

"No, it doesn't," said Richard. "But didn't you ever create a routine of your own?"

"Yes, I did," she said. "I was always inspired by Lili, and I wanted to do something classy, like her, with a strong narrative. But they didn't want that, the bastards. Like I told you, Montreal is only my second gig. My first one was in Philadelphia, at a dump called the Grenada. The manager wanted to see what I was going to do, so I did what I invented, called Mystery Girl. It was very slow and spooky. I was going to have smoke in the background, and a Chinese gong. But the damn manager said it was too intellectual for the Grenada."

"So what did you do instead?" Richard asked.

"I'm ashamed to tell you," said Joyce.

"If I'm going to help you, Joyce," he said, "I have to know everything."

She seemed depressed again as she jabbed her fork listlessly at the profiteroles.

"They gave me the name Cutesie Pie," she finally said. "I came on as a big baby. I stripped down to a diaper. Instead of pasties, I had two little baby's bibs, which flapped up and down when I moved, if you know what I mean."

"Yes, I think I know what you mean," said Richard. "How did it go over with the audience?"

"They loved it," she said. "But I hated it."

"I don't blame you."

"It's these damn freckles," she said, gesturing at her face. "A girl with freckles is always a child. She can never be taken seriously."

"But your freckles are cute."

"You see what I mean?" she said. "In high school, when we did plays, I could only get small comedy parts. I could never be the heroine."

"But comedy is important," Richard said. "People love comedy."

"I need a routine that's completely new," she said. "I need a new name, a new identity."

"Well," he said, "I have the beginnings of an idea."

"Oh, what is it?" she said, eagerly.

"I'm going to have to think about it," he said. "It might take a few days."

11

"I had lunch at the Ritz yesterday," Richard said, trying to sound worldly.

"The Ritz?" said Uncle Morty. "That's the worst food in town. What did they give you, an English muffin?"

"We had *canard à l'orange*," said Richard.

"Garbage," said Uncle Morty. "If you want to be physically strong and mentally sharp, this is what you eat." He pointed to the chopped liver topped with fried onions that the waiter was putting down in front of them. "This is the food," he said, "that has sustained our people in our darkest days."

They were, of course, at Freda's Restaurant. To Richard's happy amazement, Uncle Morty had phoned him, out of the blue, and had invited him to lunch. He had something to discuss with Richard. But they couldn't seem to get down to it, what with the frequent visits from other diners, who came over to the table to say hello to Morty Mintz, and to have a word with him, this renowned boss of Montreal's biggest illegal gambling operations. The town's most important magnates were paying homage to him, men like Liebowitz of Well-Bilt Clothes, Kaplansky of Peerless Dress, Garber of Acme

Sponging and Pressing. Finally, by the time the waiter brought the dessert, the procession came to an end and Uncle Morty could reveal the purpose of this lunch.

"Okay," he said, "let's plunge right in. Tell me, Ricky-boy, why have you become a Communist?"

"What?" said Richard, almost choking on his strudel.

"Let's not beat around the bush," said Uncle Morty. "I happen to know that you're writing something for this *Vanguard* magazine, and that you were down on the waterfront picketing a ship."

"How do you know that?" asked Richard, amazed.

"Come on, Ricky-boy," said Uncle Morty. "You know I have connections in this town. With the police, it's mostly the Morality Squad, but they're in touch with other outfits, like the Red Squad, the anti-subversive boys. Things I might be interested in get passed along to me."

Richard sipped his tea nervously, at a loss for words.

"Believe me," said Uncle Morty, "at every commie meeting there's at least one informer. The police know what's going on and who's who."

"So what's wrong with me attending a meeting?" said Richard.

"What's wrong?" said Uncle Morty. "Christ, boy, just how wet behind the ears are you? As a favour to me, the anti-subversive boys haven't put your name on the list – not yet. Captain Boisclair owes me one, if you know what I mean. But if you keep on with this nonsense, even Morty Mintz won't be able to keep you off that little old list."

"So what if I am on this list, whatever it is?" said Richard. "Who cares?"

"Oy vey," said Uncle Morty. "Don't you know anything? Don't you know that if they have a file on you as a Communist that file follows you for the rest of your life? To start with, they give it to the FBI and you will never again get into the United States. And this is Quebec, eh. Do you realize we're living in Quebec? Do you realize we have something here called the Padlock Law? If they raided your father's house and found Communist literature in your bedroom they could padlock the house and your family wouldn't be able to live there any more."

"They'd never do that, would they?" asked Richard.

"Probably not," said Uncle Morty. "But it might cost your father a pretty penny to buy them off. And with our dear old premier, Maurice Duplessis, even a payola might not work. Your father, remember, went around telling everybody he contributed big to the Liberals in the last election. I sometimes think he's as ignorant as you."

In response to this, Richard felt a sudden surge of indignation – and courage. "Did it ever occur to you, Uncle Morty," he said, "that the Communist way might be the way to end some of the misery in the world? Did it ever occur to you that there are people who are starving? That not everybody is having chopped liver for lunch?"

"And about this Sophia Bruce," said Uncle Morty, consulting a piece of paper that he took from his pocket. "So she's a looker, but do you have to sell your soul to Joseph Stalin just to get laid? If you want girls, why don't you ask your old uncle? I can fix you up."

"How do you know about Sophia?" asked Richard.

"Like I told you, there's a police informer at every meeting," said Morty.

That night, in bed, Richard was still wrestling with the problem. Could he really say goodbye to communism, giving up all hope of ever doing anything decent with his life, to alleviate the misery of mankind, to fight the hideous monster that was capitalism? To give it up, without properly exploring it, would be sheer cowardice. But then again, what about that file the FBI would have, that would keep him forever out of the United States? There would be no more trips to New York, like the one last summer, when he had driven down with Stanley and Martin in Stanley's father's big DeSoto.

What a splendid adventure it had been, driving down the romantic Route 9 and, halfway down, camping out for the night in their tent on the shore of Lake George. Camping out in the fragrant piney woods, roasting hot dogs on the campfire. In the morning, driving on southward again, and not going too fast, so they could appreciate the little wooden signs at the side of the road that advertised a shaving cream called Burma-Shave. The signs came at seventy-foot intervals, each sign bearing one line from a nifty little quatrain. "His cheek was rough," the first sign would say, and the second sign would say, "His chick vamoosed." Then, third: "And now she won't," and fourth: "Come home to roost."

"Now if Milton wrote poetry like that," Martin said, "they wouldn't have to force us to read it."

There were many different stanzas along the road, but they decided that their favourite one was "She eyed his beard / And said, 'No dice, / The wedding's off / I'll COOK the rice.'" Martin and Stanley set this one to music and sang it repeatedly, in various operatic modes, all the way down to Poughkeepsie.

As for the city itself, the three of them agreed that life offered nothing better than a long weekend in New York, zooming up to the top of the Empire State Building and then eating lunch on Times Square at Horn and Hardart's Automat, where putting two nickels into a slot let you open a little glass door and take out your bacon-and-tomato sandwich.

After lunch you could go up the street and take in a musical like *Oklahoma!* or *Brigadoon* – without buying a ticket. You'd simply hang around on the sidewalk outside the theatre and wait for the crowd to come out for a smoke at intermission. When the bell rang, you'd march right in with the paying customers and quickly find your way into any empty seat. Or, if the theatre was full, you'd stand at the back with the standees. You'd only see the second half of the show, but with a musical that didn't matter too much.

For dinner you'd splurge on Lindy's, where you'd hope to see some characters from Damon Runyon's short stories, characters like Harry the Horse or Liver Lips Levine. You might sit at the very table where Arnold Rothstein, the gambler, had eaten his last cheesecake – Lindy's world-renowned cherry cheesecake – before going out onto Broadway to be shot dead by one of his creditors. It was all very thrilling. And late at night, for the price of a beer, you could sit at the bar in one of those smoky little places on Fifty-second Street and listen to Fats Waller's piano or Dizzy Gillespie's trumpet. No, there would be no more of that, no more New York, if Richard did what Nicolai Lenin – and Sophia Bruce – wanted him to do.

He needed more time to think all this over, to make a decision that would have to be final, from now until the end of his life. But one thing was urgent: until he made that decision, his poem must not appear in *Vanguard*, which would be closely scrutinized by the FBI. But how to make sure that the poem would at least stay out of the first issue of the magazine? He would phone Sophia and arrange a meeting to tell her that he wanted to improve the poem. He would tell her he had some radical new ideas that, among other things, would include some of the maxims of Maxim Gorky. So would she please temporarily withdraw the poem that they had now? The pages he had given her were just a feeble bleat compared with the powerhouse blast that he could produce, if only he could have a bit more time, enough time to get the poem ready for the second issue, not the first one.

But as soon as he formulated this approach, and mentally rehearsed his conversation with her, he knew that she would try to talk him out of it. She would want to know just what he planned to do with his text. She would tell him that he had already achieved perfection; she would flatter him, she would cajole him; she would put her hand on his arm and would gaze into his eyes. There might even be the offer of a kiss.

No, he would not phone her, he would write her a letter, an immensely persuasive letter. It was now three o'clock in the morning and he got out of bed, took his pen and his yellow legal-size pad from his desk, and went downstairs to the kitchen, to brew himself a cup of Ovaltine and to write.

"Dear Sophia," he wrote. "I am at this moment in the throes of artistic creation. I am in a ferment of ideological inspiration. I am, for the first time, seeing things agonizingly illuminated by a light coming from the East, by an incandescent sun rising from the horizon of Moscow and Leningrad . . ." He paused to take the bubbling Ovaltine off the stove. Yes, this was going to be one hell of a letter, good enough to cause her to take his present masterpiece from the hands of the *Vanguard* editors and wait for the improved masterpiece – which might never come. And perhaps as she waited, in eager anticipation, the "Not now" that she had voiced after their one-and-only kiss might slowly be transformed into a "Yes, now."

As he sipped his Ovaltine, he visualized the gorgeous Sophia, those excitingly quizzical eyebrows, those black tresses under that jaunty tam-o'-shanter. But then something strange happened to that vision: Sophia's face was slowly fading out and, just like in a movie, was dissolving into the face of Joyce Jaworski. The black tresses were being chased off the screen by a glorious abundance of red hair. Joyce was coming forth very strongly, and was taking charge of his fantasy.

And then the idea suddenly came to him, in a flash – the new identity he would concoct for the gorgeous Joycie. She would no longer have to be Cutesie Pie or Whirlwind Wanda; she would have a new name that was arrestingly sublime. Tearing the Sophia letter off his yellow pad, he poised his pen over a blank page. He would unveil the new name in the form of a press release that would go into her press kit, with her photos. When she arrived in a new town with her new act, this press kit could be sent to the newspapers and the radio stations, and it would certainly intrigue them.

He started to write, slowly and unpoetically this time. He felt he could produce good journalese, having been the editor of his high school's monthly newspaper. And he had recently read, in *Liberty* magazine, a fascinating article about the great New York show-business press agents, men like Harry Grundman and "Daddy" Elliott. These men, the article explained, often stretched the truth in their press releases and sometimes, in sketching the biographies of their clients, produced brilliantly colourful fiction.

As he started to write, Richard realized that a press release, unlike a poem, didn't have to be absolutely true, but also unlike a poem, it always had to make sense for the reader.

12

When Richard had phoned Joyce to tell her that he had devised a new identity for her, she had insisted on inviting him to a lunch that she would pay for. So now they were sitting at a table in the raffish American Spaghetti House, around the corner from the Roxy Theatre. It was, she said, her favourite restaurant.

"You see that fat man over there in the corner?" she whispered. "That's Angelo Moreno, a very big gangster. And you see those two men with him? They're his hoodlums. We could see some shooting any minute."

She was excited and sparkling today, a far cry from the dejected Whirlwind Wanda of the other morning. "And you see those girls over there?" she said. "They're working girls, if you know what I mean."

"Yes, I know what you mean," he said. Why were people always asking him if he knew what they meant? He always said that he knew, although in this case he wasn't sure that he did.

"They work for Madame Bizanti, who is a very big madam," Joyce was saying.

Some of the girls at the long table, Richard noted, were

quite young and quite slim, while others were middle-aged and fattish. All were brightly rouged and painted, and all were wolfing down their fettuccine and meatballs ravenously.

"They're on their lunch break now," Joyce said. "They only get forty-five minutes for lunch, the poor things, and that includes the walk up from De Bullion Street and back. They say lunchtime on Friday is very busy in their business, if you know what I mean."

"Yes, I know what you mean," Richard said. In her five days in Montreal, Joyce seemed to have learned more important things about the city than he had learned in a lifetime.

As the waitress brought their scaloppines, Joyce's mood changed from frivolity to lip-biting nervousness. "Okay," she said, "I'm ready. What's my new name?"

"Your new name," Richard said, having rehearsed the line carefully, "is Freckles."

"What?"

"Freckles."

"Seriously, what's my new name?"

"Read the press release," said Richard, handing her what he had typed on a sheet of the expensive pink paper that he used for love poems. It came right to the point:

MEET FRECKLES, THE GIRL NEXT DOOR
Will She Take It Off?

Because her father is a world-famous neurosurgeon, she can't use her real name. But audiences who have seen her perform agree that Freckles is a very appropriate stage name, especially if you wonder whether the freckles on a girl's face extend all the way down her lovely body.

Since childhood, Freckles has suffered from shyness, an overwhelming shyness. When her parents' friends came to the house, she would run out of the room. At school, she could never read aloud, as requested by the teacher. As a teenager, because of her beauty, she was often asked to go to dances, but the idea of dancing with a boy was out of the question.

By the time she was eighteen, her shyness had become such a handicap that her parents sent her to New York to be treated by Dr. Gregory Zilboorg, the world-famous psycho-analyst. After spending eighteen months on his couch, Freckles learned from Dr. Zilboorg that she suffered from sangrosophobia, a rare malady first identified by Sigmund Freud in 1908. It all arises from the unconscious mind. Girls suffering from sangrosophobia are so inhibited that they cannot take off their clothes on their honeymoon.

Dr. Zilboorg's prescription was a bold one. He took Freckles to Minsky's burlesque theatre to see the strip-teasers. "This is what you must do, my child," he told her. "You must plunge in, you must force yourself to do this in public. You will cease being ashamed of your body when you learn how much gentlemen appreciate it."

Since then, Freckles has been trying to follow Dr. Zilboorg's prescription, with the cooperation of sympa-thetic theatre managers across North America. Audiences have been cooperative too, watching with patience as, in the words of Dr. Zilboorg, her id struggles with her superego as she tries to remove each item of clothing.

Freckles grew up in a small town in the Midwest, which cannot be identified. Her family lives in a house with a white picket fence. And not long ago, when she performed in Los Angeles, a Hollywood producer blurted out, "Why, she's the girl next door!" This led to a screen test and yes, she will indeed play the sweet, freckle-faced girl next door in the next Andy Hardy movie.

Joyce read this document twice and then said, "Is it all right to say my father is a neurosurgeon? Actually he's a mailman. He delivers letters."

"It's perfectly all right to say he's a neurosurgeon," said Richard.

Joyce slowly got to her feet, walked around the table, and kissed Richard on the forehead. "You're a genius," she said. "A very sweet genius."

Back in her chair, she read the press release a third time, and as she read, Richard saw tears forming in her eyes.

"Do you know what you've done?" she asked.

"No, what?" Richard said, uneasily.

"You've made me love my mother," she said. "That's what you've done."

"I don't get it."

"My mother is Irish," she said. "That's where I get the red hair and the freckles. I used to hate her for that, especially when I used to put chalk on my face to hide the freckles. But now, Richard, I love my freckles and I love my mother."

"Great, great," said Richard. "But you know, Freckles is going to have a whole new routine. Whirlwind Wanda was fast, but the Girl Next Door has to be slow. The guys – I mean the audience – has to be able to have a good look."

"I know, I know," she said. "Lili told me you have great choreography ideas. Like exactly when to remove the blouse, when to remove the bra, etcetera, etcetera. Can you help me with that, Richard?"

"I will help you," he said, nervously twirling his forkful of linguine.

"I will need new music," she said.

"Yes," he said. "Chopin, not 'Hold That Tiger.'"

"My father will like that," she said. "He's Polish."

"You'll need a white picket fence on the stage and a girl-next-door costume," he said.

"Yes, yes," she said, excitedly. "You don't know what this means to me, Richard, to get such a great press release. When I was becoming Whirlwind Wanda my agent in New York got a newspaper guy to work with me on a press release, but I just couldn't work with him. The dirty pig was only interested in one thing, if you know what I mean."

"Yes, I know what you mean," he said, suddenly dejected.

"Lili told me you're not like that," she said. "You're not just another wolf."

"No," he said glumly, "I guess I'm not."

"We'll need pictures of me for the press kit, won't we?" she asked.

"Of course," he said.

"Well, I've got some pictures," she said. "Shall we go up to my room and pick some out?"

"Great idea," he said, his spirits now lifting.

"But I hope you won't be embarrassed," she said. "Most of the pictures are of me in the nude."

"Uh, oh, that'll be all right," he said.

"I mean, we're both professionals, aren't we?" she said. "It's like you're the doctor and I'm the patient."

"That's exactly right," he said, hoping his voice wouldn't tremble.

The Roxy Theatre put up most of its performers in the Broadway Hotel, a small, ancient, cheap, and musty establishment just a few doors down the street from the American Spaghetti House. Rooms on the first floor of the Broadway were rented by the hour, but those on the four floors above were available for longer-term occupancy.

"Flam-o the Fire-eater is next door," Joyce said, as she unlocked the door to room 306. "Gaylord Updike, that lousy crooner, is down the hall. He's always trying to visit me, the dirty pig. That's why I have to keep this door double-locked."

Her room was tiny and drab, with just a narrow bed, a night table, a small dresser, a kitchen chair painted green, and a wash basin. The bath and the toilet were down the hall.

"Isn't this awful?" she said. "To think that my father is a world-famous neurosurgeon."

"And that you got straightened out by Doctor Gregory Zilboorg, who doesn't come cheap," Richard said.

"Let's have some music," she said, pointing to a small pile of records on the dresser. "Pick something nice."

As he started looking through the records, she went over to the night table, where there was a small portable Victrola. "Let's hope it's going to work," she said, as she turned the crank handle vigorously. "I had to have the spring replaced last week."

Richard had chosen *That Old Black Magic* and he handed her the record. He sat down on the green kitchen chair and she perched on the edge of the bed as they listened to Glenn Miller's immortal rendition, with Skip Nelson and the Modernaires singing, "Icy fingers up and down my spine, / That same old witchcraft when your eyes meet mine."

"Okay, let's get down to business," she said, as the music came to a scratchy end. "Let's look at the pictures." She reached under the bed and produced a shabby suitcase. Opening it, she took out a large brown envelope. Meanwhile, Richard had chosen a Sammy Kaye record and she put it on the turntable.

As the Three Kadets sang, "Here I go again / All aglow again / Taking a chance on love," Joyce patted the bed beside her and said, "Come sit here, so we can look together." When he sat down, she inched toward him, so the flanks of their thighs were touching.

The first glossy photo, eight by ten inches, showed her standing up, stark naked, holding something above her head that might be a beach ball. Richard was studying this carefully when she took it from him and handed him another picture. This one was taken from behind, with artistic lighting that brought out the glorious sculpting of her back and the saucy hemispheres of her buttocks.

"Who took these pictures?" Richard asked.

"They're by the famous Marco of Manhattan," she said. "Most of the girls have their nudies done by Marco. He's a pansy, so he doesn't bother us, if you know what I mean."

"I know what you mean," he said, although he wasn't absolutely sure. Only recently he and his friends had heard rumours about the existence of men who would rather sleep with other men than with girls. Martin said that there really were such men. They were very secretive and were called pansies or fruits. But Richard found the whole idea very hard to believe.

He examined more photos. In one she was writing on a stenographer's pad, a naked secretary taking dictation. In another she was hanging washing on a clothesline, the perfect housewife. In another, taken from behind, she was bending over to pick something up from the floor and to provide an intriguing perspective of those rear hemispheres and adjacent features.

"Of course newspapers would never print these pictures," he said.

"Of course not, silly," she said. "But our agents tell us that if we enclose a few with our press releases the editors will pass them around the office and they'll make the reporters so happy that we might get a bit of publicity."

"The reporters will be very happy," said Richard. The more discerning among them would be much taken by her areolae, which he now noted were darker and, in circumference, considerably larger than those Richard had studied in the Swedish nudist magazines that Stanley kept under his mattress. As for the breasts themselves, they seemed about 18 per cent perkier than those of Lili, but perhaps for this reason they lacked the patrician dignity and authority of Lili's.

"Oh damn," Joyce was saying. "That damn needle again." The record on the Victrola, Charlie Barnet's *I Hear a Rhapsody*, was sounding very sour and scratchy. "Let's put in a new one," she said, opening a little tin of cactus-spine needles. Was she so poor that she had to use cactus, Richard wondered. Couldn't she afford steel needles?

"Do you like Larry Clinton?" she asked, putting another record on the turntable.

"Love him," said Richard.

They looked at more pictures as the vocalist sang, "It's not the pale moon that excites me, that thrills and delights me / Oh no, it's just the nearness of you."

Picking up the last of the pictures, she grimaced. "That part's ugly, isn't it?" she said, pointing to the generous thatch of dark hair that adorned her mons Veneris. "I should have had it airbrushed out, like they did in the other pictures, but Marco gets four dollars for every airbrushing and at that point I ran out of money."

"It's not ugly, it's beautiful," Richard said, taking the photo from her to examine the thatch more closely. "It's really beautiful."

"Oh, come on," she said. "You're kidding."

"No, I'm serious," he said. "It's very beautiful. In fact everything about you is beautiful." He blurted it out, without his usual writer's forethought and rehearsal. "You're very, very, very beautiful, Joyce."

"Am I?" she said.

"Yes," he said.

"You're beautiful too, Richard," she said.

"It isn't your sweet conversation / That brings this sensation," the vocalist sang, "Oh no, it's just the nearness of you."

Her face was now tilted up toward him and Richard, figuring that this new angle might mean that she wouldn't mind being kissed, lurched forward and threw his arms around her, and their lips began kissing.

After quite a bit of this, he felt her hand opening his collar button and loosening his necktie. In the confused writhing and legerdemain that followed, he realized that like one of those oriental goddesses, she didn't have two hands but four, managing at the same time to do most of his undressing as well as her own. He helped where he could, but was hindered by his ignorance of the function of various female buttons, clasps, elastics, and so on.

"When you're in my arms / And I feel you're so close to me," the song continued,

All my wildest dreams come true.
I need no soft lights to enchant me
If only you grant me
The right to hold you ever so tight
And feel in the night
The nearness of you.

By now all their clothes had been ripped away and things had reached a frenzied pitch. But suddenly Richard paused, uncertain of the next move. In the past, when trying to imagine the mechanics of the procedure, he had often wondered whether there might be a problem if the angle of his erection turned out to be too acute, or not acute enough, to effect a smooth entrance into the Garden of Eden. Much would depend, of course, on the degree of slant at the lady's point of entry, but none of the anatomy textbooks he had consulted had been very precise about this. Now, despite the excitement of the moment, this geometrical conundrum was coming to mind again, and was making him hesitate. But Joyce, disturbed by this loss of momentum, took hold of his member with one of her four hands and guided it deftly into its destination. And so – lo and behold! – Richard Lippman, formerly virginal, at long last gained admittance to the Garden and – glory be! – he and the Girl Next Door actually began *doing it*!

13

Did girls compare notes the way boys did? Would Joyce tell Lili what had happened, perhaps just by hinting at it? Richard had mixed feelings about this possibility. On the one hand, he would like Lili to think that he had become a suave and skill-ful cocksman, an accomplished thruster. On the other hand, was it not better to be seen as he really was – a tormented poet, suffering the ravages of hopeless love? Yes, he was definitely Sir Philip Sidney and not Lord Byron.

But the question was, in more ways than one, academic, because Joyce and Lili were surely not in touch with one another at the moment. Lili's letter, just arrived, made this quite clear.

Middle of the Ocean
November 25, 1948

Dear Richard,

I am writing this on board a magnificent big ship called the *Ile de France*. We are half way across the Atlantic Ocean. I write this in my private sitting room in my private de luxe suite called the Chateau d'Estaing. This is one notch up from First Class. All the suites on the ship are named after great French chateaus – or is that chateaux?

Last night I had dinner – *Jambonneau de Poulet Montglas Dauphine* (I wrote it down for you) – at the Captain's Table. You should see that Captain, he is more handsome than Gary Cooper. There was a Countess de Something and a Lord Somebody at the table. We were all dressed up for dinner, of course, the gents in tuxedos and the ladies in evening gowns. Fortunately I was able to do a wirlwind shopping at Bergdorf Goodman in New York just before we sailed and at dinner I was wearing my Schiaparelli. Have you ever heard of Schiaparelli? It's the tops. Believe me, this dress was a great success. "Your gown does admirible justice to your contours," Sumner Welles, who was sitting next to me at dinner, said. That's the way Sumner talks – "your contours." Do you know who he is? He used to be Secretary of State in the United States government, President Roosevelt's right-hand man. At one point he was trying to hold my hand, the old dog, and I'm going to have to watch him.

By now you are asking yourself, "What is Lili L'Amour doing in the middle of the ocean?" Well, this is a working holiday. I am being employed by Sir Charles Hammond, president of the Canadian Pacific Railway. You remember Sir Charlie – you met him when we had lunch at the Ritz. He is here too, in the suite next door to mine, the Chateau de Frontignan. He is on board to study how the *Ile de France* does things, and pick up some ideas that he could apply to his Canadian Pacific ships, like the *Empress of Canada*, the *Empress of Britain*, etc. The Empress ships, he has been told, are downright dowdy and could never compete with the very sophistacated French Line ships. So, frankly, we are looking for ideas to steal.

For instance, it is I (just a silly girl) who collects the menu after every meal, as a souvenir, something Charlie, as the president of a competing steamship company, cannot do. Thus, some day, the chefs on the *Empress of Canada* will be asked to whip up a *Chaudfroid of Partridge Cherville*, rather than their favorite Irish Stew. More important, I am to scout out the facilities that are of special interest to the ladies, like the vanities in the cabins, the complementary eau de toilette, the beauty salon, the boutiques. The Canadian Pacific ships have "shops," where they sell heavy Scotch plaid skirts and miniature bagpipes for your grandchildren. But the *Ile de France* has "boutiques," where they sell gorgeous Hermes scarves. To earn my keep, I make notes about all this.

But it's not all work. After dinner, we adjourn to the Salon de Conversation, for coffee, cognac and conversation. You mingle with famous passengers in the Salon, like Duke Ellington and Fred Astaire. Prince Albert of Belgium is also aboard, but we don't see him very much. Sir Charlie generally has more than one cognac and gets into heated arguments about politics, which makes me nervous, especially when he tries to tell Sumner Welles why Canada is better than the United States.

The Salon de Conversation gets boring after a while. Much more fun downstairs in the ballroom. There was a gala there Tuesday night, to raise money for sailors' charities. The ladies were told to charge one hundred dollars for a dance and two hundred dollars for a kiss. Sumner Welles bought my first dance, but I told him the kiss would cost him four hundred, not two. He agreed, but the old fool must have thought that the extra two hundred gave him access to my behind, with one of his busy hands. It was all I could do to break free. Still, we managed to raise a lot of money for those poor retired sailors.

Where is all this leading? you will ask. Well, three days from now we dock at Southampton, England, and take the train to London. There, Sir Charlie assures me, I will surely be able to get a gig as an exotic dancer, a headliner at the Windmill Theater. Sir Charlie knows Mr. Vivian Van Damm, the owner of the Windmill, a world-famous place, you know. Sir Charlie seems to know everybody.

But how are you doing, dear Richard? How are your studies going? When I have an address in London, I hope you will write to me. I very much appreciate your letters and like the way you so gently correct my spelling and grammer. I was happy to learn what a gerund is, and about mettaphors.

But will I ever be a writer? I continue to send exercises to that corespondence course I am taking (in Des Moines, Iowa, remember?) and they write back to tell me that I am doing well. But I wonder. What I write seems to be a bit flat. It doesn't have any sparkle. Thus, when I get going on those memoirs, perhaps you could go over it with me and just touch it up a bit. You know, poetize it. For instance, on this ship I look over the rail and down at the ocean and try to discribe the waves. They are churning, they are lapping, they are heaving. But there is no excitement in those words, is there? If only Richard was here, I keep thinking, he could poetize those waves for me.

I want to discuss all this with you, at length, Richard, but now I have to run. The Passengers' Gala begins in half an hour and I have to go down to the dressing room and get into my toga and put some white powder on my face. They've asked me to be a Living Greek Statue in a tableau. I must stand absolutely still, not move a bit, which won't be easy.

Love,

Lili

P.S. Did Joyce Jaworski show up? She's a nice kid isn't she? Were you able to help her improve that crummy act of hers?

Next morning

P.P.S.: As a Living Greek Statue in the Gala last night I was a success. I found it very difficult to stand absolutely still. So I started to move a bit, just a little bit, just a little shimmy. They started to applaud. The orchestra picked up on it, with just the right jazz, and I began moving quite a lot, and very slinky. Wow, did they ever applaud! I am now big news on this ship, Richard.

L & K
Lili

Oh sure, he'd be delighted. With a few strokes of his genius he'd quickly touch up her shabby prose and make it shine. Yes, in a pig's ass he would. What the hell did she think he was? What did she think poetry was? Something you could squeeze out of a tube like toothpaste? And what was she going to give him in return? A nice picture of that swine Sir Charlie slithering down the corridor in that goddam ship, from his Château de Whoopie to Lili's Château de Nookie? Yes, Lili, thank you very much.

Did all these women think they could ask him to give them his heart and soul and blood, and they would give him what in return – zilch? Lili asking him to poetize her – where the hell did she get that word? – into a new dimension of exotic dance . . . Sophia asking him to help her climb up the political ladder, perhaps to become a Soviet commissar some day . . . And Joyce, to create a new identity for her . . .

But wait, Joyce didn't belong with the other two. Joyce was giving him plenty in return, plenty. Joycie, Joycie . . . What an angel she was! Although perhaps *angel* wasn't exactly the right word. It was hard to imagine an angel doing the things Joycie was teaching him to do, in her bed. No, definitely not an angel, with big white wings flapping around in the bed and getting in the way.

14

One of the great things about McGill, as opposed to high school, was that you could skip classes and nobody cared. With only two weeks left in Joyce's gig in Montreal, Richard was skipping most of his afternoon lectures, so he could spend the time with his Girl Next Door. He even skipped Chemistry 16, missing Professor Heavysedge's annual outburst of advice to the girls. Everybody knew it was coming and there wasn't an empty seat in the big lecture theatre when the old boy let loose. Abandoning his usual topics, like ionization or the properties of magnesium, he devoted most of the hour to a tirade against one of the great evils of the modern age – the bottle-feeding of babies. Mothers must, absolutely must, breastfeed. To do otherwise was to contribute to the degeneration of the human race, to the decline of Western Civilization. Many professors were loony, as everyone knew, but old Heavysedge's obsession was particularly colourful.

Richard had to miss the show, but he knew he would be able to get a good account of it from Martin. "How did the girls take it?" he asked.

"They were blushing," Martin said. "That little Susan was sitting right next to me and she was red as a beet. And Heavysedge kept getting personal about it. You know that Janet, the blonde with the big tits, well, she was sitting in the front row, and he comes up and stands right in front of her while he's yelling about lactose molecules or some damn thing. 'Don't you forget that, young lady,' he says, and he's shaking his finger at her and I swear he's pointing at her left tit."

"And of course the boys were loving it," Richard said.

"We were loving it," said Martin. "And some of us were making funny faces at the girls, which was making them mad as hell. And you know that French guy, Fernand, he was going like this with his lips and making little sucking noises. It was a riot."

But there was one lecture that Richard was determined not to miss. That was English 2, where Associate Professor Jock Ramsay was going to deal with what he billed as "Byron's amatory excesses." This annual event, sophomores advised the new freshmen, was pure sex, and by ten minutes before lecture time there was standing room only in Moyse Hall. There were even representatives from the Faculty of Engineering, louts who were said to be barely able to read and write but who were suddenly interested in the romantic period of English poetry.

Joyce had been asking Richard to show her around the campus, so he brought her to this lecture. As they took their seats, heads turned to take in her red hair and her very tight woollen dress. She obviously didn't belong in English 2, but then again neither did the two waitresses from the Cavendish Restaurant down the street. Professor Jock's good looks, like those of Byron himself, were legendary, and the McGill freshettes were uniformly in love with him. Besides the waitresses, there were three stenographers from the Sun Life

Assurance Company who had gotten wind of the event and were anxious to learn what a bad boy George Gordon, Lord Byron, had been.

No one was disappointed when Professor Jock swept onto the stage, his long black academic gown flowing behind him, much stained with chalk dust. He was a tall, muscular man with a large head of bushy hair. When he reached the centre of the stage he stopped and looked out at the eager audience in front of him. He hesitated, frowning theatrically, as though he wasn't quite sure where he was. And when he finally spoke it was with a thrilling upper-class British accent.

"'So we'll go no more a roving / So late into the night,'" he intoned, starting right in with his famous recital of Byron's poem. "'Though the heart be still as loving, / And the moon be still as bright.'"

He paused in his elocution and went to the blackboard, where he wrote, in large capital letters, HYPOCRISY. Then he resumed:

"For the sword outwears its sheath,
And the soul outwears the breast,
And the heart must pause to breathe,
And love itself have rest."

He went to the blackboard and wrote SWORD and SHEATH on it. "Can anybody tell me what Byron meant by that figure of speech?" He put his hand to his forehead and peered out at the class, like a sailor straining to see a distant shore. The students looked at each other uneasily, but nobody ventured a sound. "Well, I'm glad no one here has a dirty mind," Professor Jock said, and in his rich baritone, he plunged on with the final stanza of the poem:

"Though the night was made for loving,
And the day returns too soon,
Yet we'll go no more a roving
By the light of the moon."

Two or three of the girls started applauding, but Professor Jock held up his hands in a gesture to stop them. "Please, please," he said, in tones of mock protest.

"Isn't he wonderful?" Joyce whispered to Richard. "We could use him in our show at the Roxy."

"Yes," said Richard, "he'd probably add a bit of class."

"Now who can tell me what I mean by that," Jock said, pointing to the word HYPOCRISY on the blackboard.

"He was a liar," a boy at the back of the hall shouted.

"Precisely," the professor said. "One of our greatest poets was an outrageous liar. He had absolutely no intention to go no more a roving. In the days and years to come, he would rove his way into an endless number of ladies' hearts." The students looked at each other expectantly; now he was getting down to the good stuff. They scribbled industriously as Jocko started reeling off a list of Byron's peccadilloes – Lady Caroline Lamb, Lady Frances Webster, Lady Charlotte Harley, several servant girls, Claire Clairemont. "And that, plus many another, was only in England," the professor said. "In sunny Italy there was Marianna, Margherita, and Teresa."

"Wow!" said Joyce.

"Yeah," said Richard. But he noted that the professor was being very careful. It was all innuendo. He said the poet would keep roving his way into ladies' hearts, not their pants. Last year a young associate professor had been abruptly fired for being too graphic and imaginative about Robert Herrick's bedroom adventures. And now Jocko, in talking about Byron's character, was using sanitized words like *concupiscence* and *lubricity*, which the students, making their notes, would have to look up in the dictionary later. But above all, Professor Jocko never stopped scolding Byron for being so concupiscent, wasting so many hours that could have been spent writing poetry. The Dean of Arts might well have been auditing the lecture from the back of the hall, and it was essential for lecturers to adopt the right moral tone. But while Jock was denouncing Byron for being such a cocksman, any student with a bit of an ear could detect that he was really admiring His Lordship.

"From each of these conquests," the professor was saying, "Byron, pretending to be sentimental, collected a lock of the lady's hair. He kept these locks in little envelopes. And his most cherished envelope – can you believe this, ladies and gentlemen? – contained the hair of Augusta Leigh. And who was Augusta? She was his half-sister. Yes, brother and sister had a very close relationship."

As the professor paused to let this enormity sink in, Richard realized how, up to now, it had never occurred to him that, in real life, great historical figures could have been just as anxious to get their ashes hauled as the average man of today. There had certainly been no hint of this in the textbooks you studied in high school. Back then, the notion that Napoleon and Shakespeare might actually have been doing it was as unthinkable as the thought that your own parents must, at some time or other, have done it.

"Byron did not share his era's notions of moral perfectibility," Professor Jock was now saying. "Disillusioned by reality, he longed for an ideal. In his writing, irony came to replace melancholy as he unmasked the self-deceits of mankind."

Quickly Richard started taking notes. This was the sort of thing they could ask you about in the exam. By the end of the hour he had covered several pages. Now, as he and Joyce got up to leave, he noticed Sophia across the room, sitting with – of all people – Stanley. As the room slowly emptied, they remained sitting there, deep in conversation. Now what was that all about?

Richard and Joyce would meet every day at lunchtime, usually at the American Spaghetti House. For Joyce, who slept until noon after her nightly exertions on the stage as Whirlwind Wanda, the meal was breakfast, while for Richard, after his morning's lectures, it was lunch. Occasionally they tried other restaurants in the vicinity, like Le Roi des Chiens Chauds, where you could slather your hot dog with sweet green relish, or the Chung Yung Café, which offered delicious *egg rolls servis avec plum sauce*. But wherever they ate, their conversation was mostly about developing her new routine as Freckles, the Girl Next Door. They drew diagrams of the stage, plotting where she would dance, where she would pause, where she would take off what piece of clothing. But what would her costume be? It wasn't easy to figure this out. For this act, the stripper's usual silks and satins and boas were, of course, not to be considered; Freckles would come onto the stage in very conventional and modest attire. But what should it be? She had obtained an Eaton's mail-order catalogue and they studied it methodically. "This blouse," she would say, "with the dolman sleeve. What do you think?" and "What about this cute skirt? But it looks kind of tight, doesn't it, so I'd have to have one of those spring-loaded releases built into it, so I could snap it off real fast."

"Now wait a minute, Joycie," Richard said. "In your mind you're still Whirlwind Wanda, everything in a big hurry. Never forget that Freckles is very modest. It's a struggle for her to get undressed in front of all those people. She hesitates, she blushes. When she finally decides to take that skirt off, she has to struggle out of it, and the music from the orchestra is appropriate. Remember, your act is tease, tease, tease."

"You're so right. So wise," she said, giving him a little peck on the cheek. And once again this gesture made him feel older and stronger, his lack of confidence now a thing of the past, thanks to this fine girl having become his obedient pupil. And, of course, thanks to his having got rid of the millstone of his virginity.

After lunch, they sometimes went around the corner to explore the sleazy lower reaches of St. Lawrence Boulevard – the Main – the haunt of sailors, bums, and prostitutes. Joyce seemed to take it all for granted, but for Richard it was endlessly exotic, about as far as you could get from the leafy streets of his native Westmount. Where else in the world could you find establishments like the Central Five-Cent Lunch?

The Crystal Gameland was a favourite destination, and they would spend a happy hour there playing the pinball machines and consulting Mysterious Zelda, the automaton fortune teller in her glass case, with her chest heaving, her eyes shifting, and her mechanical hand moving over the fortune cards as she selected one for you. Richard played Skee-Ball while Joyce manipulated the Digger Crane, trying for valuable prizes but in the end having to settle for a few bits of candy. They each grasped a handle of the Love-o-Meter which, after much flashing of lights and ringing of bells, told them that they were "hot stuff."

"Does that mean we're lovers?" Joyce asked, as they left the Crystal Gameland.

"I guess so," Richard said cautiously, hoping that she wasn't about to ask him for some kind of formal declaration of life-long commitment. But to his relief she didn't pursue this dangerous topic, she simply chuckled and said, "Hot stuff," and offered him a stick of chewing gum that she had scooped up with the Digger Crane.

It got dark early these days and by dusk they were cozy in her bed, in her hotel room, with her little Victrola playing Vaughn Monroe as Richard slipped into his safe. It had been an ordeal for him to force himself into a drugstore and sheepishly ask the pharmacist to sell him some. Like all his friends, he'd had one drying out in his wallet for at least a year, bought from Martin's older brother in the hope that one day he might get lucky. But after that venerable rubber had been used up, on that landmark first night, it had to be replaced, lest he suddenly become a father. Now, in the drugstore, when he asked for two dozen, the pharmacist frowned as he reached under the counter for them, saying, "I suppose this is for some joke at school, eh?"

"Yeah," said Richard. "We, uh, use them to, uh, make water bombs."

"Today's kids," the pharmacist said to his assistant. "No discipline at all."

"They get too much spending money," the assistant said.

Occasionally, before their late-afternoon bedtime, Richard and Joyce would take in a matinee at one of the St. Catherine Street movie theatres. At the Palace they saw *Sorry, Wrong Number*, squeezing each other's hand in alarm as Burt Lancaster said to poor Barbara Stanwyck, "Do as I say or you've got only three minutes to live." At the Capitol they saw *When My Baby Smiles at Me*, in Technicolor, with Betty Grable singing "Sweet Georgia Brown." And, on the day before Joyce was due to leave town, they went to Loews to see *Love Finds Andy Hardy*, where Judy Garland sang "Meet the Beat of My Heart." Although the reviewer in the *McGill Daily* had denounced this film as nothing more than an unashamed ode to capitalism, Richard particularly wanted Joyce to see it, as it featured Judy

Garland as Betsy Booth, the prototypical American girl next door. She lived in a small town, in a house with a white picket fence; she was sweet and she was modest, and yet she had lots of spirit, as she tried desperately to catch the attention of Andy Hardy, played by Mickey Rooney.

"I don't know how Judy could say she was so happy in that song, the way Andy was treating her," Joyce said, as they left the theatre.

"It was just a song," Richard said. "She had to sing something, when the band leader asked her to."

They walked east on St. Catherine Street, through the movie-going crowds, stopping at the Liquor Commission store to buy a bottle of wine, to mitigate the sadness of Joyce's last night in town.

"It was hard to understand that Andy Hardy," she was saying, as they entered her hotel room. "I mean, couldn't he see that Betsy Booth was so much better for him than all those other girls? How she kept solving all his problems, while all he wanted to do was kiss that slut Cynthia."

"Andy Hardy was basically an idiot, supposed to be funny," Richard said. "But that Betsy Booth was somebody you could admire, wasn't she? Did you get any ideas from her, like how she would dance, how she would take her clothes off?"

"I sure did," said Joyce. "I was thinking about that all through the movie. For instance, how about this?" She crossed to the far side of the bed and started slowly gyrating her hips. Then she started to undo the first few buttons of her blouse. "Is this the way she would do it?" she asked, vamping around the bed to stand in front of him, swaying. "Like this?" she said, slowly opening two more buttons.

"Yes, that's terrific," he said, putting his arms around her. But she wriggled out of his grasp and retreated toward the door. "Not so fast, mister," she said. "Like you told me, tease, tease, tease."

"Yes, you're right," he said, realizing that he was acting like a member of the audience, an old fart in a raincoat, anxious for her to get on with it. The choreographer in him was pleased with how she was developing her act, but the commotion in his trousers was straining his patience.

"A little music, no?" she said, shimmying over to her little Victrola and putting on Eddie Duchin's *Moonlight and Shadows*. "This is my dress rehearsal," she said. "Or maybe my undress rehearsal."

By now all her buttons were undone and she was peeling off the blouse. She sashayed over to the mirror to examine the effect, and then just stood there, as though undecided about what to do next.

"Shouldn't the brassiere come off now?" Richard said, trying to sound detached and professional.

"Maybe not yet," she said. "Don't forget, I'm the girl next door. Very shy. Notice how I take off my skirt. I do it very carefully and I lay it on the bed. I fold it carefully, to pack in my suitcase. I am going on a trip."

"I hope you'll be back soon," said Richard, by now quite uncomfortable.

"I dunno, I dunno," she said. "Maybe I'll meet somebody on the train."

"Panties next?" he suggested, hopefully.

"Not so fast, mister," she said. "Stockings before panties, don't you know?"

It was taking her an eternity to peel off the stockings, but it was fascinating, the way she was doing it with strange, undulating motions. Watching her, he realized that he had been instrumental in transforming the wretched Whirlwind Wanda, of the sleazy Roxy Theatre, into a potential star, ready for America's most glittering burlesque stages.

"And now, gentlemen," she was saying, "the bra will come off. But please be patient, as it is a much more complicated task than you might think."

"Okay, okay," said Richard, "I've got the idea." He was tearing off his shirt, stepping out of his pants, and wondering how long he could hold out.

"Now don't be crude, Richard," she said. "Like you told me, this is art, remember?"

When they finally got down onto the bed together, she seemed to want to make it a continuation of her act. "We're going to take it very slow this time, darling," she said. "Before we really get started, I'd like you to do a bit of this." She took his hand and put it where she wanted it. "There," she said. "Now I want you to do a bit of that."

Eventually they moved on to the main event, and when they were finished, and lay there recuperating, Richard's old guilty feeling came back. As always, in the midst of it all, he had been thinking of what it would be like if those marvellously vibrating hips belonged to Lili and not Joyce. He always tried, without success, to drive the image out of his head, to deny to himself that he was somehow cheating on sweet Joycie.

And now, in this moment when he wanted only quiet and repose, Joyce was chattering away. "You know," she was saying, "you think of the funniest things at the funniest times. Just now, as we were, er, doing it, I suddenly got a picture of that funny hat Judy Garland was wearing in that scene in the car. I wondered whether in my act I shouldn't be wearing a hat like that. Maybe keep it on as the last thing to take off, when I'm all the way down to pasties and G-string. What do you think? Would the girl next door do that?"

"Maybe," he said. "You should try it out when you start

rehearsing for real, with music and all. Frankly, Joyce, when I was watching your dress rehearsal just now I noticed a few rough edges that need to be smoothed out. You still have work to do, Joyce. I hope you realize that."

"Oh, I do, I do," she said. "And I love how professional you are."

"I try to be," he said.

"Which means you weren't shocked," she said, "to hear that I was thinking of my work back then, during a moment of passion."

"No, these things happen," he said, as she reached over to take hold of his diminished member to get it ready for another bout.

This being Joyce's last night in town, she suggested that Richard have what she called a "sleepover" with her in her hotel room. "It's really special, first thing in the morning, right when you wake up," she whispered into his ear.

"It's a great idea," he said. "Why didn't we think of it before?"

"Yes, why didn't we?" she said.

Leaping out of bed, he got into his clothes and went down onto the street, to catch a number 3 streetcar. At home, he quickly packed pyjamas and his toothbrush into a bag, telling his mother that he was off with some friends to Kingston to watch the McGill-Queen's football game and participate in the riot that would follow it.

"I didn't know you were such a hooligan," she said.

"It's for old McGill – rah, rah, rah," he said, as he sped out the door. And twenty-six minutes later he was back with Joyce.

He had taken some money out of his slim bank account that morning so that he could take her to dinner somewhere nice, somewhere more elegant than the American Spaghetti House, with its low-life clients. They ended up at Chez Son Père, where they ate the renowned *lamb chops Champvallon* and had an *île flottante* for dessert. After dinner they went to the Roxy Theatre, where she made what she swore would be her last performance ever as Whirlwind Wanda. She made it even worse than usual, especially for Richard, watching from his seat in the third row.

Then it was only a hop, skip, and jump to the hotel room, where Richard had the strange experience of getting into his pyjamas and brushing his teeth, all in the presence of a girl, while she took off her makeup and got into her nightgown. This, he realized, was what it must be like to be married.

In the morning, the wake-up exercise was as different and as delightful as she had promised, but there was no time to rest up a bit and have an encore, as she had a train to catch. At Windsor Station, after they checked her bags, they found that the train was going to be leaving half an hour late, so they had time for breakfast in the coffee shop. While they were eating, he gave her the farewell present he had bought for her, a little green-and-gold tin containing two dozen Spearpoint steel gramophone needles, the very best kind. She would no longer have to use those cheapo cactus needles. And she was delighted. The music would sound much less scratchy now.

"Oh, Richard," she said, "every time I listen to Tommy Dorsey I will think of you."

"I will think of you every time I listen to anything at all," he said.

"You know," she said, "you're saying goodbye to Freckles, the Girl Next Door, who didn't even exist a month ago. You did it all."

"I was glad to be able to help," he said, wishing he could think of a more clever remark.

"Of course I'll write and let you know how Freckles makes out," she said.

"I'm counting on that," he said.

The train's departure was announced, and he walked with her to the gate. They said their goodbyes, kissing fervently, and he watched sadly as she went down the platform and onto the train. Then the locomotive snorted and the train started lumbering its way out of the station, on its way to New York.

As he watched it go, he reflected once again on how much he owed to this girl for having initiated him into the rites of the bedchamber. She had helped him up one rung on the steep ladder to maturity. Now if only somebody could help him up the next rung, if only somebody could tell him how to fall out of love with Lili.

15

During the next few weeks, Richard kept seeing Sophia and Stanley together – at lectures, or having lunch in the Students' Union cafeteria, or bent over a chessboard upstairs in the Union games room. If Richard happened to pass them, they either ignored him or favoured him with the briefest of nods. Then, one evening, out of the blue, Stanley phoned Richard at home. Could they meet for lunch? Yes, of course. Could they meet somewhere other than the cafeteria, Stanley asked, so they could have some privacy, without the intrusions of classmates? By all means. Stanley suggested the Pig and Whistle, on McGill College Avenue, and Richard agreed.

Richard had never been to the Pig and Whistle, more formally known as the Prince of Wales Tavern, but he'd heard of it as a dangerous, rowdy place, especially late at night, when it kept selling beer long after the legal closing time. But at lunchtime it was relatively civilized, crowded and noisy but with no really loud shouting and no fistfights in the offing.

Coming in from the street, Richard felt his nostrils assailed by a strong, sour aroma of beer. At their convivial tables, patrons were signalling to the waiters, holding up two or four fingers, indicating whether they wanted two glasses of draft beer or four. Some of the tables were so covered with forests of glasses – some full, some half-full, and some empty – that there was barely room enough for the Pig and Whistle's renowned budget-priced lunches – large, steaming plates of pork and beans or corned beef and cabbage.

Richard found Stanley at a corner table, sipping a glass of beer and eating a bacon-and-tomato sandwich. "Hope you don't mind that I started," Stanley said, "but I was hungry."

"That's all right," said Richard, turning to a waiter who had just arrived to take his order. "I'll have a glass of beer and a sandwich like that one."

"There's no single glasses," the waiter said. "*Tu dois prendre deux ou quatre.*"

"Okay, I'll take two," said Richard.

"We haven't talked for a while," Stanley said. "How have you been?"

"Busy, busy," said Richard. "Filling my brain with knowledge." He had decided not to tell anyone about his adventures with Freckles, the Girl Next Door. Keeping it to himself somehow made the experience much more valuable.

"How do you like this place?" Stanley asked, gesturing out at the room.

"Well, it's sure different from the cafeteria," Richard said. "You come here often?"

"Once in a while," said Stanley. "You can get to learn a lot here."

"Like what?" asked Richard.

"This is a workingman's tavern, as you can see," Stanley said. "You can sit with those guys and listen to what they have to say. The terrible conditions in the factories where they work, the lousy wages, the way the bosses try to break their unions, the way the police break their heads out on the street when they're on strike. If you listen to these guys, Richard, you can learn their language, which is very different from the language we speak in Westmount."

Obviously Sophia had indoctrinated him very thoroughly. This was the party line, in all its purity. Now rich-boy Stanley wanted to learn the workingman's language. Up till now, the only language he'd ever wanted to study was Swedish, so he'd be able to read the captions under the photos in the Swedish nudist magazines that he kept under his mattress at home, rare magazines that somebody had managed to smuggle past the customs inspectors down on the docks. But now Sophia had obviously managed to raise his mind out of the gutter and was taking him into the lofty realms of communism. But was she also taking him into her bed? It was a disturbing thought.

"Does your Sophia come here for lunch too?" Richard asked. "To meet the workingmen?"

"Are you kidding?" said Stanley. "Do you see any women in here? Don't you know that women aren't allowed into taverns in capitalist Canada?"

"Oh, of course, I forgot that," said Richard, who had never been in a tavern before and didn't know what the rules and regulations were.

"That's one of the many things we've got to get changed," said Stanley. "Women workers in this country are even worse slaves than men."

"If I can change the subject," said Richard, "I see you and the beautiful Sophia together quite a bit. Can I ask how all this came about?"

The waiter brought Richard's beer and his sandwich, and Richard started eating, waiting for Stanley's answer.

"It was a turning point, Richard," Stanley finally said. "A turning point in my life."

Richard waited patiently as Stanley embarked on a long pause, sipping his beer with a faraway look in his eye.

"It's a rainy day," Stanley said, putting his glass down. "In fact it's raining very hard. I am hurrying down from the Arts Building to the bus stop on Sherbrooke Street. I don't have a raincoat or an umbrella, and I am running fast, getting soaked to the skin. And suddenly I find Sophia running along beside me."

"'Hello,' she says. 'It's wet, isn't it?'

"'It sure is,' I say. And this is the first time we've ever spoken.

"We reach the bus stop and now there's thunder and lightning, and it's really coming down. Of course there's no bus in sight and I'm preparing to stand there and get really soaked. And then she goes over to a car parked next to the bus stop, opens a door, and gestures for me to get in. She gets in on the driver's side.

"'This is your car?' I say, stupidly.

"'Yes,' she says, and she immediately starts giving me shit, bawling the hell out of me, real mad." Stanley paused for dramatic effect, and for beer. "Do you know why she's doing this?" he asked.

"No, why?" said Richard.

"You remember that big meeting in the ballroom, with the speech by Tim Buck? You were sitting up front with Sophia, and Martin and I were in the back. And I yelled out, 'The working class can kiss my ass!' And there was all that heckling? Well, Sophia remembered that, in fact it made a big impression on her, and as we sit there in the rain in her car she says, 'I've been wanting to talk to you about that ever since.' And she starts giving me a lecture on politics and social justice. This goes on for quite some time and my bus goes by. 'I've made you miss your bus,' she says. 'Can I drive you home?' I say yes, and she says, 'Can we make a small detour? It'll only take half an hour.' And when I say by all means, we drive way out east, out past Rodier Street, down to a terrible slum on a lane near the waterfront."

"I've been there," Richard said.

"I know," said Stanley. "She told me. And we're parked there, in the rain, and a woman comes to the door of a tarpaper shack – it's more of an opening than a door – and a little girl maybe six years old, in a torn, filthy dress, comes and stands behind her. And the woman shoves the little girl out into the pouring rain and she comes up to the car and holds out her hand. Begging, Richard, begging. And this is in Montreal, Canada, in 1948."

"And then Sophia drives you up to Sunnyside, to show you where she lives," Richard said. "In a castle with a butler."

"That's right," said Stanley. "You've been there, too. But here are a few places where you haven't been." He handed Richard some photographs that he took out of a large brown envelope. "I've been taking pictures," he said. "You visited one slum, but I've gone to many. There are pockets of misery all over our beautiful city."

Looking at the pictures, Richard saw decrepit tenements, jerry-built shacks and hovels, crumbling brick dwellings that had been put up for factory workers in the last century. Grimy children played in garbage-strewn back alleys, sad-looking women were hanging washing on backyard clotheslines.

"That's in St. Henry," Stanley said. "Right next to the railway tracks. The black soot from the trains decorates the washing on the clotheslines. And all night long there's the noise of the locomotives shunting back and forth. And this picture is Goose Village, down next to the slaughterhouses. You wouldn't believe the smell. And this is Inspector Street, right downtown, five minutes away from the headquarters of the Royal Bank. In that house a rat bit away a baby's ear. And that's a lane off

De Montigny Street, where there's an epidemic of tuberculosis, the poor man's disease. If you don't die of TB you might die in a fire. These old wooden sheds in the back of the houses are always going up in flames. If the trains don't keep you awake all night, the fire engines will."

"You took all these pictures?" asked Richard.

"Yes, for *Vanguard*."

"*Vanguard*?"

"Yes," said Stanley. "The new socialist magazine. Have you forgotten already?"

"Oh, yes, of course," said Richard. "I know about the magazine, but I guess I forgot the name."

"You wrote a poem for *Vanguard*, didn't you?" said Stanley.

"Yeah, I guess I did," said Richard.

"Well, my friend, that's why we're having this meeting here today," said Stanley. "Sophia thinks that poem is the greatest and she's been begging you to touch it up a bit, put in a bit of a message – like how socialism could clear away these slums, like they've done in the Soviet Union. But you're just sitting on your ass and not writing. Well, buddy, I'm here to twist your arm and get you to work. And to remind you there's a deadline – next Thursday."

"Look," said Richard, "what she's asking for is not easy. I haven't been able to figure out exactly how to do it."

"Frankly, Richard, I personally don't think it's such a great poem, but Sophia's the literary editor and so I guess she knows. But even I can see how it could be improved if you injected a bit of Stalin in it, a bit of Lenin, a bit of Marx. A reference here, a quote there. You don't have to overdo it. It's just a matter of the right word in the right place. And that's what poetry is, isn't it?"

"You know," said Richard, "you're not the Stanley I used to know."

"No, I've got a purpose in life now," Stanley said. He stood up and drank the last bit of beer in his glass. "I've got to run now," he said. "But I'm going to be phoning you, pal, I'm going to be bugging you." He extended his hand to shake Richard's and started for the door.

"Hey, don't forget your pictures," Richard called, starting after him with the brown envelope.

"No, those are duplicates, they're for you," said Stanley. "To inspire you, to remind you that life is not just a bowl of cherries."

That afternoon, during Professor Barr's Modern History lecture, Richard could think only of his lunchtime encounter with Stanley, reviewing it from every angle. Basically he was chastising himself for not having challenged Stanley, for not having accused him of being a fraud, of faking this conversion to communism just to get Sophia into bed. Sophia, beautiful Sophia, the third most gorgeous girl on the campus, right after the traffic-stopping Avril Keaton and the remarkably stacked Georgina Patterson. And there were certain critics who would put Sophia in second place rather than third, slightly ahead of the insufferable Georgina.

Stanley had been lucky, very lucky, right from the start, to have Sophia so angry at him during their very first meeting, that afternoon in the rain. Nothing could be better for a chap than to have the girl furious at you. In their high-school seminars at Gagnon's Ice Cream Parlour, Richard, Stanley, Martin, and Harold had agreed that this was one of the most important things you could learn from the movies. Men and women who screamed at each other in the movies always ended up lovey-dovey, provided of course that it was the female who started the fight. And the more violent the better. Like in *Fools for Scandal*, where Carole Lombard lit into Ralph Bellamy so vigorously. And in *His Girl Friday*, where Rosalind Russell chewed out Cary

Grant, saying, "If I ever lay my two eyes on you again I'm gonna hammer on that skull of yours till it rings like a Chinese gong!"

So Stanley had started his campaign with an advantage, what with having her so pissed off with him from the very start. And, as Richard realized, it would be a piece of cake for Stanley to be convincing as a Communist; in high-school drama productions, he had been a fine actor, and in everyday life a consummate liar.

At lunch, Richard had been on the verge of accusing his friend of this deception, but he had refrained, realizing that he might just sound jealous. And there was nothing more humiliating than that.

But now, driving the Stanley-Sophia problem from his mind, Richard tuned into the lecture, in time to hear Professor Barr launch into ecstatic praise for the outcome of the Congress of Vienna, 1815. From old Barr's tone, Richard sensed that this might well be on the exam, so he quickly started making notes – "Metternich, Castlereigh, Talleyrand. Idealism bad, *realpolitik* good."

As he scribbled his notes, Richard's mind strayed from the machinations of the Holy Alliance to the more complex issue of Stanley's sincerity, or lack of it. What if Stanley had really and truly undergone a conversion, had suddenly found a purpose in life? It was a disturbing thought for a person like Richard who, if asked, wouldn't be able to state what his purpose was – if any. The thought that Stanley might have found belief and commitment was even more envy-making than the thought that he might well have found his way into Sophia's bed.

But then again, Stanley was nothing more than a fraud, wasn't he?

"That's it for today," Professor Barr was saying. "Next time, Napoleon's hundred days, Waterloo, and exile."

That night, at home in his room, Richard spread the slum photos out on his desk to look for inspiration. They were gruesome, especially if you imagined what was going on behind the facades of these crumbling houses, like the tenement out in Hochelaga ward where, Stanley told him, there were five people living in one room, two of them sick and too poor to afford a doctor.

He would have to make one more attempt to fix that poem of his, to inject a message – a glimmer of hope in the darkness. No, not a glimmer, a searchlight. Wearily he opened one of the books that Sophia had given him – *Dialectical and Historical Materialism* by J.V. Stalin. Here, in these closely reasoned pages, he would find his phrases. But after twenty minutes of leafing through the book, he closed it. It was so utterly boring. For respite, he unlocked what he called the "special drawer" in his desk, where he kept, among other things, his poems-in-progress. From under the poems he extracted three eight-by-ten glossy photos of Joyce Jaworski, what she called her "nudies," by the great photographer Marco of Manhattan. Putting away the slum photos, Richard laid the nudies out on the desk. Once again he marvelled at the artistry of Marco's lighting, which made silky sculptures of her splendid flesh. Gazing at the pictures, Richard cursed himself for his shallowness.

But no, he was a poet, wasn't he? A profound poet. In his mind now he was already sketching some lines about Joyce's silky skin. Sharpening his pencil with his penknife, he tried to remember the exact feel of her skin. Yes, silky. Or should it be satin-like? But hadn't he already used the satin metaphor in one of his early poems about Lili? He reached into his drawer to look for that poem. Damn it, why did that wretched Lili have to slink her way into every love poem he tried to write?

16

1949

On the freezing, windy morning of January 1, 1949, Richard woke up with the realization that his muse had abandoned him – forever. For weeks now he had not been able to squeeze a single line of poetry out of his typewriter; all he had managed to do was gaze at the blank page – his reservoir had gone dry. And now, as he greeted the new year by brushing his teeth, he knew that no more poems would ever issue from that typewriter.

But perhaps he wasn't absolutely bone dry; perhaps there was still a tiny spark inside his head that could be fanned into poetic flame. Still in his pyjamas, he went downstairs, put on boots, scarf, and overcoat, and went out the front door to shovel the new snow off the walk. In the past, some of his best ideas had come to him while shovelling snow, or cutting grass. Indeed, the first poem he had ever written had been entitled "Snow."

But now, with the icy wind biting into his face, there was nothing poetic stirring in the old noggin. All that was happening in there was the same painful review of defeats that had been tormenting him for the last few weeks. To start with, his great epic poem would never appear in *Vanguard*; and by now it was certain that Lili would never dance to his inspired verse;

and to cap it all off, there was that vicious rejection letter from that damned magazine.

In November, Richard had sent a dozen of his best poems to *Explorations*, the poetry magazine. On December 22, as a Christmas present, they had come back to him in the mail. Accompanying them was a savage letter from the editor. "Sorry, but these are not for us," the letter said. "If I may offer a word of advice, Mr. Lippman, may I suggest that you stop trying to be Byron or Shelley and write for TODAY. For instance, have a look at Ezra Pound." And that was all there was to the letter, written in a hasty scrawl that made it doubly insulting. Of course Richard had long ago looked at Ezra Pound, and other very modern poets, and had concluded that he too could achieve this degree of incomprehensibility, but he knew he was kidding himself. It wasn't enough to just reel off baffling puzzle-poems; the incomprehensibility had to have that magic, elusive, invisible ingredient that aroused the admiration of professors and critics. Learning how to produce that magic, Richard realized, would be a long and arduous process – and he simply didn't feel up to it.

No, there would be no more poetry. His energies would have to be devoted to other things, like preparation for Life. His daily routine now, like getting educated, certainly didn't have much to do with Life, did it? But what, in essence, *was* Life? Was it more than simple existence? That would be a good subject for a long poem. But of course he was out of the poetry business now, wasn't he?

With these unfruitful thoughts rattling around in his head, he finished shovelling the path from the front door to the street. Going back inside, he took off his overcoat and boots and went to the kitchen to prepare some breakfast. His parents were still asleep upstairs, so he would have to make his own Farina. And as he stood by the stove, wondering how long it ought to boil, he tried to remember what Professor Heavysedge had said in Chemistry 16, in his lecture about the latent heat of fusion at one hundred degrees. Was it 534 calories per gram? And if that was the case, what the hell did it mean?

The Farina was now boiling over, and he grabbed it off the stove. God, he was so ignorant! Education was not irrelevant to Life, as he had decided a few minutes ago, but was absolutely essential. Or was it? Here again was his troubling tendency of being able to believe, at the same time, both sides of an argument, no matter how opposed they were. Maybe that sort of thing would be cleared up next year, when he would be taking Philosophy 2. But right now, as he spooned a great gob of strawberry jam into the Farina, to make it palatable, he realized that he had better buckle down to his studies – immediately.

He had done precious little studying in the fall months, what with all those distractions. There had been Lili, of course, and then Sophia, and then Joyce. And all those hours at the Smith-Corona, tapping out those hopelessly old-fashioned poems, some of which actually rhymed. During those months he had skipped many lectures, and the few essays he had submitted had been hasty and sloppy. It was one hell of a way to spend your first year at university. But now exams were looming. He had better pull up his socks or he could fail his year.

Right now he had better get on with that ordeal that he'd been assigned to suffer during the Christmas break, the five mimeographed pages of Ovid that had to be translated into English for Latin 1A – the *Metamorphoses*, immensely important and immensely tedious. Stuff like "*In nova fert animus mutatas discere formas / Corpora: di, coeptis (nam vos mutastis et illas)*," and so on. Why couldn't Professor Baldwin have assigned something with more zip to it, like "*Tu quoque, materiam longo qui quaeris amori, / Ante frequens quo sit disce puella loco*." That, of course, was from *Ars Amatoria*, The Art of Love, which was so full of practical advice that it got poor old sex-crazed Ovid exiled for life from ancient Rome.

Leafing idly through Ovid, Richard found some advice that seemed tailored to his needs of the moment. It was in *Remedia Amoris*, Remedies for Love: "Love yields to business. If you seek a way out of love, be busy: you'll be safe then."

And so Richard spent the winter trying to bury himself in business, academic business. In English 2 he trudged his way onward as far as Dryden's "Absalom and Achitophel," where he had to master the first hundred lines. In French 3 he learned that there were not one but two *substantifs verbeaux* – the infinitive and the gerundive. In Modern History he immersed himself in the Crimean War.

For Richard that winter, love and/or sex were ever-receding memories. The few co-eds he met, prim in their cashmere twin sets, seemed almost to advertise the fact that they were unseducible. Also, they were basically uninteresting. Each and every one of them, compared with the glowing Lili, was so pallid. Those who weren't Communists, like Stanley's Sophia, were dauntingly intellectual, like Martin's new-found Marjorie.

Martin obviously worshipped the plump and hyperenergetic Marjorie. Introducing her to Richard, in the Union cafeteria, Martin proudly pointed out that she was a student of psychology. "She's researching the question of why we are what we are and why we do what we do," Martin said.

"I've always wondered about that," Richard said, truthfully, but he was still no closer to any answers half an hour later, after Marjorie finished haranguing them about ids, egos, and superegos.

One evening toward the end of March, Richard answered the phone to be greeted by a girlish voice. "Guess who," the voice said.

"Gee, I dunno," said Richard.

"Come on, have a guess."

"Could it be Edith?" he said, thinking of a particularly silly girl who sometimes sat next to him in Chemistry 16 and who kept asking to look at his notes.

"No, it's not Edith," she said. "It's old Freckles."

"Joyce?" he said, astonished. "Is that you, Joyce?"

"It's not Joyce," she said. "It's Freckles, the Girl Next Door."

"All right then, Freckles," he said. "But your voice sounds different."

"It is different," she said. "I'm taking elocution lessons, to speak better."

If the lessons were supposed to make her sound like a very young girl, they were successful. "So what brings you to Montreal?" Richard asked.

"Don't you read the papers?" she said.

"Not lately," he said. "I've been studying for exams."

"I'm opening at the Gayety tomorrow night," she said. "Freckles, the Girl Next Door, is the headliner."

She was staying at the LaSalle Hotel, where Lili used to stay, and not at the sleazy Broadway, where she and Richard had frolicked so energetically on her lumpy mattress back in November. And now she was inviting him to lunch at the LaSalle the next day – in the costly Cavalier Room, with its white tablecloths, and not in the budget-priced Club Room.

He arrived at the restaurant exactly on time, but she was already seated at a table in a corner, waiting for him.

"You look very different," he said, as he sat down.

"But nice?" she asked.

"Extremely nice," he said. But it was weird to find her so different from what she was when he had first taken her to lunch, at the Ritz, when she was Whirlwind Wanda. Then she had worn a tight-fitting, slinky green dress that had attracted much attention; now she was wearing a flowery, billowing gingham dress, a schoolgirl's costume. Her flaming red hair was done up in pigtails, with bright bows. She was a woman of twenty-five trying to look like a young girl, trying to look like Judy Garland.

"You didn't read about me in *Billboard*, did you?" she asked.

"No," he said, "what's *Billboard*?"

"It's the show-business paper," she said, handing him a clipping with a very large headline that said: SHY GIRL NEXT DOOR IS NEW STRIP SENSATION.

Under the headline, a lengthy article told how Arthur Krantz, Freckles's New York agent, was trying to cope with the torrent of requests from burlesque theatres across America for bookings of this new exponent of what H.L. Mencken called "the ecdysiast's art."

After listing seven cities where Freckles had wowed the audience, the article went on to tell how Freckles had come to be a stripper or, as she preferred to be called, an exotic dancer. "Because her father is a prominent neurosurgeon," the article said, "she cannot reveal her real name." From here on, *Billboard*'s article had been lifted, almost word for word, from the press release that Richard had written. It was all there – how she had suffered from agonizing shyness that had virtually incapacitated her; how she had been treated by Dr. Gregory Zilboorg, the famous psychoanalyst; how Dr. Zilboorg had advised her to cure herself by taking off her clothes in public.

"Across America," the article concluded, "people line up to see if this brave girl will succeed in her nightly struggle to overcome her shyness, to reveal whether her charming freckles extend all over her sensational body. Her struggle is epic, and her audiences are never disappointed."

"Without that great press release you wrote for me," she was saying, "I don't think any of this would have happened.

Now I don't have to take any more gigs at places like that crummy old Roxy. From now on it'll strictly be the best theatres, like the Gayety."

"That's terrific," he said.

"And it all started with you, dear Richard," she said. "Thank you, thank you, thank you." As she spoke she reached across the table and touched his hand with hers. That touch brought back those glorious weeks back in November, when her nimble fingers had helped him put on so many condoms.

"And this is for you," she said, handing him a little box. Inside was an elegant Bulova wristwatch. "A small thing, compared with what you've given me," she said.

As they ate their turtle soup, she told him about her triumphal progress across the continent, how she'd had special music written for her act, how journalists from the racier papers had interviewed her, how a Hollywood producer wanted to meet her next week.

"If you're not busy tonight," she said, "could you come to the Gayety, to see my routine?"

"Of course," he said. "I wouldn't miss it for the world."

"In my dance," she said, "you'll see me doing some of the things you suggested back in November, when I was first becoming the Girl Next Door. Like turning my back on the audience when I start taking off my bra. That really goes over good. But you know – and don't take this personally – some of that routine is starting to feel stale to me. I'm going to need new ideas. And you're such a great choreographer. So do you think, Richard, that you could help me out?"

"Absolutely," he said.

"And not just here, now," she said. "I mean when I'm on the road, too. Like I could give you a call and you could zoom out to Memphis, or Milwaukee, or wherever, and we could spend a few days working together. Even if the audience likes what I'm doing, I know I'm not doing my best if I feel stale. I need new challenges."

"That's right up my alley," Richard said, unable to believe how good all this was getting.

"I spoke to my agent," she said, "and you'll be well paid for your efforts."

"That's not important," he said. "We just want you to be the greatest, don't we?"

She responded to this with a warm smile and again reached across the table to touch his hand. He took this as a signal to start getting the ball rolling.

"By the way," he said, "do you still have that cute little portable gramophone?"

"Oh, I got rid of that long ago," she said. "I have an electrical one now. You just plug it in and off it goes. No more cranking by hand."

"Do you still have that record *The Nearness of You*?" he said. "Larry Clinton and his orchestra. Remember?" It was the music that had accompanied his historic first entry into the Garden of Eden.

She sipped her coffee in silence and then finally said, "I was afraid you were going to ask me that."

"Oh," he said. "If you don't have old Larry Clinton, some Glenn Miller would be nice."

"I can't invite you up to my room, Richard."

"Oh?"

"The Girl Next Door doesn't have men up in her room," she said. "She just doesn't do that."

"Don't tell me you don't remember November," he said.

"Of course I remember it," she said. "But Richard, I was Whirlwind Wanda then. I was wild. Now I'm Freckles, the Girl Next Door. I'm young, I'm innocent."

"But basically you're Joyce, aren't you?" he said.

"No, I'm Freckles," she said. She was looking at her watch now. "Oh dear, I'm late. I've got to get over to the theatre to rehearse with the orchestra." She signalled to the waiter to bring the bill. "After the show tonight," she said, "will you come round to my dressing room? I'm dying to know what you think of my act."

That night, with a great fanfare from the orchestra, the curtains at the Gayety opened to reveal an eighteen-year-old girl's bedroom, much enlarged and exaggerated. The bed was huge and so was the dresser. There were three large windows looking out on a garden. The draperies and bedspread were pink and frilly. On the wall, there were pictures of movie stars, all of them men – Clark Gable, Gary Cooper, Franchot Tone, Humphrey Bogart.

The fanfare subsided and the music became thin, tinkly, and tentative, to usher in a hesitant Freckles, the Girl Next Door. She was wearing a heavy winter coat, and she danced slowly and gravely as she started taking it off. Obviously she had learned how to make an innocent action vibrate with erotic promise, like Gypsy Rose Lee, who could electrify an audience by the way she slowly peeled off her elbow-length gloves.

As the coat started coming off her shoulders, she sent a small smile out toward the audience and Richard, sitting third row centre, knew it was for him. But that would be the night's only smile; like the great Lili L'Amour, and unlike strippers of the Bombshell Betty variety, she would never laugh or grin or wink as the clothes came off. No, Freckles, the Girl Next Door, was thoughtful, serious, and just a little bit frightened as she struggled to overcome her shyness.

The rest of her act, Richard felt, was magnificent, and the audience agreed, with frequent outbursts of applause. After the overcoat came off, leaving her in a girlish sweater and tartan skirt, she danced over to the room's three windows and pulled down the blinds. Sitting on the edge of the bed, she pulled up her skirt and started taking off the frilly garter that held up a long black stocking. But at this point the orchestra sounded a warning note, and she looked up in alarm to see a spotlight suddenly illuminating the picture of Clark Gable on the wall; Clark, the lecher, was watching her. Leaping up from her bed, she danced to the wall, took the picture off its hook, and somehow managed to hang it back up so that Clark Gable was facing the wall.

From then on, as this shy girl continued slipping out of her clothes to get ready for bed, there were frequent crises: window blinds kept snapping open, suggesting that there was a Peeping Tom out there; a sudden wind blew a door open, suggesting that there might be a horny ghost out in the hall; now Gary Cooper was staring at her, now Humphrey Bogart. As she became more and more naked, Freckles kept having to interrupt her disrobing to deal with these menaces – turning pictures around, pulling blinds back down, shutting the door. Eventually, in alarm, she turned the bedroom lights off, but they quickly came back on of their own accord, showing her with only the skimpiest of towels between her and the ravening bestiality of the male animal.

Finally, after much agony, and a crescendo from the orchestra, Freckles was down to the legal minimum of G-string and pasties. The audience rose in a standing ovation as she shyly took her bow. The curtain closed slowly in front of her, but the continuing applause encouraged her to make two curtain calls. Then the house lights went up, and Richard was on his way backstage to her dressing room.

He found her in a dressing gown, seemingly exhausted, slumped in an armchair.

"What do you think?" she asked. "Is the act any good?"

"I loved it," Richard said. "You're becoming a great artist, Joyce."

"Freckles," she said.

"Sorry. Freckles."

"Could we go out for a coffee?" she said.

"Yes, of course," he said.

"Then I better get dressed," she said, getting up and going behind a large screen. For a moment Richard thought of going back there, and throwing his arms around her and kissing her. But he didn't do it. Remembering their conversation at lunch, he decided that she might well have been very serious in announcing that there was to be no more hanky-panky. He would have to proceed very carefully, very intelligently.

"I forgot to tell you at lunch," she was saying, from behind the screen, "but I went to see Dr. Zilboorg in New York."

"You what?"

"I went to see Dr. Zilboorg," she said. "You remember – my psychoanalyst. You mentioned him in that wonderful press release you wrote."

"You're kidding me," he said.

"No, why should I kid you?" she said. "Dr. Zilboorg is a lovely man. He really understands me."

Richard was starting to become alarmed. If she wasn't joking, perhaps she was going round the bend; perhaps this Freckles business had caused her to lose touch with reality.

"How come you went to see Dr. Zilboorg?" he asked cautiously, humouring her.

"Well," she said, "I wanted to thank him for the treatment he gave me, showing me how taking my clothes off on the stage would cure my shyness. So when that article about me came out in *Billboard*, I sent him a copy. And he wrote back to me saying that I should come to see him when I was in New York – I was in Miami at the time, performing at the Starlight. So when I got to New York last week, I went to see him."

She came out from behind the screen, dressed like Judy Garland in *The Wizard of Oz*. "You know," she said, "since I last saw the doctor, when he was treating me – two years on the couch, remember – he has become a very big cheese. Look at this." She handed him a card that said: "Gregory M. Zilboorg, M.D., President, American Psychoanalytic Society, 1148 Fifth Avenue, New York, N.Y."

The card was real. She wasn't making all this up. And Dr. Zilboorg was real, unlike all the other ingredients in that crazy press release he had written. Richard had read an article entitled "Mental Health, What Is It?" that Zilboorg had written in *Liberty* magazine, and the name had amused him and had stuck in his mind, with its *boorg* instead of the usual *berg*. So when he wrote that press release he had used Zilboorg's name – perhaps a reckless thing to do.

"What did you and the doctor discuss?" Richard asked, as they walked down St. Catherine Street toward the coffee shop.

"Well, he wanted to know what I remembered about the treatment I had with him, and how I became an exotic dancer, and so on. He said to come and see him whenever I was in New York, and he wouldn't charge me if I needed any help. And he usually charges twenty dollars an hour, you know. Anyhow, he said I was a very interesting case. You never thought I was a 'case,' did you, Richard?"

"No, I wouldn't think that," said Richard, untruthfully.

"He said he was going to write a paper about me for a scientific journal. Of course he wouldn't use my real name. He would call me Miss F, or something like that."

It was all becoming clear to Richard. A girl Dr. Zilboorg had never seen or heard of was telling him, in detail, how she had spent two years on his couch. In his time, the good doctor had treated many different kinds of delusion, but this delusion was unique, one for the books. It would make for an important paper; it would be much discussed at meetings of the Psychoanalytic Society, especially as this beautiful but deranged patient was a striptease dancer.

"I'd really love to hear your new little gramophone," Richard said, having decided to try again and plunge right in. "I bet this one uses those steel needles I gave you. Have you still got some of those left?"

"Yes, I have," she said, as the Honey Dew waitress brought them their coffees and apple turnovers.

"Look, it's embarrassing," she said, "but can I tell you a question Dr. Zilboorg asked me?"

"Sure," he said. "Go ahead."

"It's the sort of thing psychoanalysts need to know," she said.

"Of course," said Richard.

After a long pause she finally said, "He asked me if I was still a virgin."

Richard savoured his apple turnover. "And what was your answer?" he asked, carefully.

"Come on, Richard," she said. "You know as well as I do that I'm still a virgin. That's why you and I are just friends, like brother and sister. So I said, 'Of course I'm a virgin, Dr. Zilboorg. Just as I was back then, when you were treating me for shyness. Thanks to your help I can now be an exotic dancer, but about, um, making love, I'm still absolutely shy. And I'm worried that I might still be, if I ever got married.'"

"And what did the doctor say to that?"

"He said he could help me with that problem if I came back to him for more treatment," she said.

To calm his nerves, Richard ordered another coffee and a prune Danish. He wasn't going to make love to her tonight –

and perhaps never again. But, on the other hand, he was starting to see that out of the ashes of this defeat something was arising that was perhaps even more important. Look at it this way, he told himself: in that press release, you didn't just *write about* Freckles, you *created* her. You took a randy young woman, who was highly skilled in bed, and turned her into a virgin!

To have achieved this gave Richard an exciting – and unfamiliar – feeling of power. His poetry might not be much good, and might never change the world, but he sure could write one hell of a press release.

17

It was time to start looking for a summer job. If only he could find something that wasn't too boring, something that wasn't just sorting parcels in the post office or being an office boy, carrying papers from one room to another. If only he could be hired to write press releases, or to do something like that. But where and how?

"I'd very much like something to do with show business," he said to Uncle Morty.

"Show business?" said Morty. "You want to sing and dance?"

"No," said Richard. "I thought something behind the scenes. Maybe publicity, or something like that."

"Do you think you could fit in?" said Morty. "Your mother tells me you're a writer of poetry. The guys I know in show business are pretty rough. Their English is maybe not so good."

Richard had surprised his uncle by phoning him and inviting him to lunch. This time, Richard had insisted, it would be his treat. They would eat not at Freda's, on the very Jewish St. Lawrence Boulevard, amid mountains of chopped liver, but at the very French Au 400, on the very English Drummond Street. This would surely impress Uncle Morty with his nephew's sophistication. But as soon as the waiter brought the menus, and Uncle Morty started reading his, Richard realized he had made a mistake in choosing this particular restaurant.

"What is all this?" Morty was saying, waving his menu. "Is it food?"

The menu, of course, was only in French. And Morty, despite having been born in Montreal and having grown up there, could barely speak four words of French. Richard, on the other hand, had grown up in a household that had always had a French maid, and that had helped make him quite fluent.

"What do they want me to eat?" Morty said. "Frogs' legs?"

"Well, they have them," Richard said. "Two kinds of frogs' legs. *Cuisses de grenouille à la lyonnaise* and *cuisses de grenouille à la Mornay*. You'd probably like them better with the Mornay sauce, which is how I believe they cook them at Freda's." Perhaps making a joke of this disaster would lessen the tension.

"Very funny," said Uncle Morty. "But seriously, kid, I'm starving. Is there anything here a person could eat?"

They finally settled on some harmless roast chicken with *pommes de terre duchesse*, which Morty had to admit were delicious. In fact it was these duchesse potatoes, with their subtle hint of nutmeg, that seemed to lift Morty's mood. He now looked around the restaurant approvingly, at the francophone gentry that was highly animated in discussing the wines that were being suggested by the waiters.

"So it's show business you want," said Uncle Morty.

"If possible," said Richard.

"Well, I'll give the matter some thought," said Morty, but his doubts were obvious.

When the waiter brought their coffee, Richard decided this was the time to make his major move. He would introduce Morty to Freckles, the Girl Next Door. If this didn't impress his uncle, nothing would.

Glancing at his watch, Richard said, "If you're not busy this afternoon, why don't we run down to the Gayety and catch the matinee?"

"The Gayety?" said Morty. "You go to the Gayety?"

"You took me there last summer, remember?" Richard said. "You introduced me to Lili L'Amour."

"That bitch," Morty said.

"Well, I've been to the Gayety a few times since then," Richard said. "And this Freckles they've got now is really terrific."

"So I hear," said Morty, looking at his nephew with new respect.

Richard had reserved two seats fourth row centre, and he and Morty arrived just before the curtain went up for the opening act – Alicia and Ernesto, a dance duo billed as the new, improved Rogers and Astaire. After that, they sat patiently through the other variety acts, waiting for Freckles. As they waited, Richard reflected on how much had changed in the five months since he had last seen Uncle Morty, lunching with him off boiled beef and *chrain* at Freda's. Richard then had been a pathetic innocent, so wet behind the ears that he was on the verge of becoming a Communist. He'd been a protected Westmount lad, a boy who could barely find his way down-town. As for girls, he'd still been starving in the desert. But now he was innocent no longer, as he would prove to this skeptical uncle of his, whose important connections around town would find him that great summer job.

Finally, after Marie Lévesque, the Sweet Songstress of Shawinigan, belted out "*J'attendrai*," the master of ceremonies came out to introduce Freckles, the Girl Next Door. His introduction was a long one, rehashing the poor girl's troubled past, exactly as had been invented by Richard. "Please be patient, ladies and gentlemen," the emcee said, "as you watch Freckles struggling to carry out her doctor's orders."

This time, the fourth time Richard had watched her perform, Freckles was better than ever. She could actually make you suffer with her as, tormented by shyness, she slowly and reluctantly peeled off each bit of clothing, recoiling from the lecherous gaze of those pictures on the wall – Clark Gable and Humphrey Bogart, those dirty pigs. Morty seemed transfixed as he watched her, and after she agonized her way out of her brassiere, he leaned over to Richard and whispered, "She is very, very good."

Richard watched appreciatively as the body that he had once come to know so well was slowly unveiled. She was indeed good, but nobody was as good as Lili. Watching Freckles now he could only visualize Lili, how she had electrified him the first time he had seen her, on this very stage. How, as Marie Antoinette, she had whipped off her lacy pantaloons, undeterred by the menace of her executioner. And how, later, in her dressing room, she had peeled the sequined pasty off her left breast and had given it to him as a memento. He still treasured it, in its little frame over his desk at home.

He was still thinking of this as Freckles finished her act, triumphant in nothing but G-string and pasties, with the audience rising in ovation. Dr. Zilboorg, Richard reflected, would have been proud, as she took her final bow and skipped off the stage.

As Richard and Morty worked their way from their fourth-row centre seats, toward the aisle, Richard said, "Would you like to go backstage and meet old Freckles?"

"Are you kidding?" said Morty.

"I'm serious," said Richard. "She's a friend of mine."

Morty looked dubious as they walked down the gloomy backstage corridor, as they had done back in August when they had gone to meet Lili. Richard knocked on the same dressing-room door, with the star on it, and Freckles's little-girl voice came from inside. "Who's there?" she called out.

"It's me, sweetie," Richard said. "And I've got a friend with me."

"Good," she said. "Just give me a minute to get decent."

Richard glanced at Uncle Morty; the "sweetie" had obviously made an impression on him. But there was much more to come – if Freckles did her part properly. During their last coffee at the Honey Dew, two days ago, she had reacted well to Richard's gentle reminder that she owed him a debt of gratitude. Yes, when he brought Uncle Morty round she would say exactly the right things, following the script that Richard had actually written out for her. But now, as he waited for her to open the door, he felt pangs of doubt. Could he count on her? She was so nutty these days that she could easily go off on some pointless tangent, instead of sticking to the script that was designed to gain Morty's admiration.

Finally she opened the door, demure in her little-girl dressing gown. "Pleased to meet you," she said, shaking Uncle Morty's hand. "I've heard so much about you."

"You have?" said Morty, suddenly seeming uncharacteristically unsure of himself.

"Richard tells me you have the police and the city council in your pocket," Freckles said. "I'm not sure what that means, but it sure sounds impressive."

"I've tried to explain it to her," Richard said to Morty, "but she's so innocent – aren't you, darling? – that she doesn't quite grasp it."

"Your innocence is beautiful, beautiful," said Morty, gazing at the curves of her dressing gown and the bit of cleavage that was evident above it.

"Did you like my performance?" Freckles asked.

"I loved it," said Morty. "I'll be back to see it again, and I'm going to send all my friends."

There was a pot of coffee brewing on a hotplate, and as Freckles busied herself pouring it into cups, and fussing with cream and sugar, Richard was nervously aware that this was the point where she had promised to launch into the script. But would she?

And yes, she would!

"If I have any success as an exotic dancer," she said, "I owe it all to your nephew Richard." Handing Richard his cup of coffee, she delivered a light kiss to his cheek. Exactly as scripted!

"Oh, she exaggerates," Richard said, with false modesty.

"No, I don't," Freckles said. "It was Richard who invented Freckles, the Girl Next Door."

"Invented?" said Morty.

"Shall I tell him the whole story?" Freckles asked.

"Why not?" said Richard.

He was delighted by the way her performance was going, how – in her young Judy Garland voice – she was telling Morty how she had been a failure as Whirlwind Wanda and needed a new name, a new identity, a new act. How in tears she had told Richard the whole sad story of how she had spent two long years on the couch, trying to overcome her crippling shyness, and how Dr. Zilboorg had led her to see that by becoming a stripper she could overcome that shyness. But as a stripper, as Whirlwind Wanda – the act her agent had concocted for her – she had been a failure. Until Richard came along.

"What I did," said Richard, "was to show her that being treated by a psychiatrist was nothing to be ashamed of – and she was plenty ashamed of it – and that she should tell the world that the reason she was stripping was to overcome her shyness. People would sympathize with that."

"And it was dear Richard who suggested a new name for me

– Freckles," she said. "The Girl Next Door. You understand that I can't use my real name, as my father is a prominent neurosurgeon."

"That's an incredible story," said Uncle Morty.

"And it was Richard who wrote my press release," she said, handing Morty one of the mimeographed releases that her agent had sent to *Billboard* magazine and all the burlesque and vaudeville theatres in North America.

"Your nephew is a genius," Freckles said, once again giving him a peck on the cheek, exactly as Richard had written it in the script. Yes, she was a good girl, Freckles was.

Leaving the theatre, Uncle Morty led Richard across St. Catherine Street to the Mocambo Club, where the lounge was filling up with the cocktail crowd. Morty selected a table in a quiet corner and ordered a Scotch for himself and a beer for Richard.

"Now tell me how you met Miss Freckles," Morty said.

"To start with," said Richard, "her name isn't Freckles. It's Joyce. Joyce Jaworski. And her father isn't a neurosurgeon, he's a mailman, in Minnesota. He delivers letters."

"So you made the whole thing up," said Morty.

"Exactly," said Richard. "And I also made up the shyness and the psychiatrist. It's all fiction. But the funny thing is, she now believes it herself."

"You're a smarter kid than I thought," said Morty. "This Joyce – or Freckles, or whatever – must be very grateful for what you've done for her."

"She is, she is," said Richard.

"Does that mean that you and this shy Girl Next Door, uh –" Morty paused and formed a circle with the thumb and index finger of his left hand, and with his right hand poked his index finger in and out of the circle several times.

"Well," said Richard, "let us say I knew Freckles before she became a virgin."

"Well, well, well," said Morty, summoning the waiter for another Scotch. Richard, sipping his beer, felt a pang of shame at revealing that he had slept with this girl; a gentleman just didn't name his conquests. But he had made up his mind, after inner debate, to do just this. How much loyalty did he owe Joyce? She had wounded him, hadn't she, by cutting off his bed privileges. And if he had done this great public-relations job for her, why couldn't she contribute to the public-relations job he was now doing for himself, reinventing the timid Richard Lippman as Richard Lippman, man about town and skillful cocksman?

"So how did you meet this girl?" Morty was asking.

"Lili introduced us," Richard said. "Old Lili L'Amour."

"Lili L'Amour introduced you," Morty said, dubiously.

"Yes, it was Lili," Richard said. "In fact I just got a letter from her yesterday." He took the letter from his pocket and handed it to Morty. Richard had brought it along as proof, in case Morty doubted this whole unlikely story.

Morty looked at Richard in disbelief as he took the letter from its envelope and started reading it. It was from London, England.

April 15, 1949

Dearest Richard,

You will be thrilled to hear the news! Your "Orpheus and Eurydice" has been performed! And I've danced to it! And it was a great success!

This took place four days ago, at an incredible country house called Wycombe Hall, in Warwickshire. Actually it's a huge mansion, built three hundred years ago, and it's in the middle of a vast private park. Sir Charlie was invited there by its owner, Lord Edgeworth, for a weekend party, and he took me along. There were 24 other guests.

Now Lord Edgeworth is mostly interested in fox-hunting and things like that, but Lady Edgeworth is very cultured and intellectual and at their house parties, after dinner on Saturday night, she has what she calls her "recital." Every guest is supposed to get up and provide a bit of entertainmint. Some of the men, who are only there for the fox-hunting, get away with just telling a joke (some of them not too clean) or telling some story about what they did hunting lions in Africa.

This was boring, but there were also some professionals who performed. Vera Lynn, for instance, sang "There Will Be Bluebirds Over the White Cliffs of Dover," and this made everybody sad. Evelyn Waugh (a man! did you ever hear of a man called Evelyn!) who is supposed to be a big writer read from a new story of his. This was funny mainly because he was very drunk. Then came Lili L'Amour!

I prepared for this by buying a classical Greek gown at a costume shop in Soho. And when I told Lady Edgeworth that I needed somebody to read the great poetry of Richard Lippman while I danced, she got one of the guests, the actor Lawrence Ollivier, to do the reading. And Lady Edgeworth herself sat down at the piano.

At this point, Uncle Morty looked up from his reading, held Lili's letter to his nose, and sniffed it. Like all her letters it was on her expensive mauve notepaper and was suffused with her special perfume. Morty seemed to be looking for assurance that this was not some elaborate forgery.

"What the hell is this all about?" he asked.

"It's about Lili in England," Richard said. "She writes nicely, doesn't she?"

Morty wanted more of an explanation, and Richard told him how he had come to know her, how he had written a poem for her and had sent it to her and how she had invited him to lunch at the Ritz.

"After that I saw quite a bit of her," Richard said. "And I wrote more poems for her."

Frowning, Uncle Morty resumed reading the letter.

Well, Richard, your "Orpheus and Eurydice" is sensational when you hear it in Larry's English accent. (We call Lawrence Larry.) And my dancing, if I may quote Arthur Rolfe, the critic of the *Daily Mail*, who happened to be a guest, was "breathtaking." I would have liked to slip out of my Greek gown, to cool off when I danced down into the heat of hell, as you specified in your choreography notes, but I was advised that this would not be proper at Wycombe Hall. Still, that old dog Sir Charlie had persuaded me to be nude under the robe, which was of very thin material, and I think the audience got the idea, especially when the light hit me the right way. In fact one old duffer in the audience called out, "By Jove, I think I'm seeing things!"

Well, we didn't need laughter at this point in the dance, but Larry got things back on track when he voiced that great line of yours that goes, "O wretched snake, why, why, why?" That, as you will recall, doesn't come at the exciting moment when the snake bites my ankle, but later, when I'm dead. Some of the ladies cried a bit at that "Why, why, why?"

Uncle Morty paused in his reading. "Who's this Sir Charlie?" he asked. "Her boyfriend," Richard said. "The president of the Canadian Pacific Railway." Morty looked at Richard for a long moment, before he continued his reading.

Everybody said my dance was the highlight of the weekend, but there were plenty of other great things going on. We were driven around this huge estate in jeeps, to see the sheep and the tennants. These tennants all stood at attention and took off their caps when we approached. They are sort of like slaves, I think, but I am told they get plenty to eat. Then there was the fox hunt, which I did not want to see, as I am so sorry for the poor fox.

Dinner, which we all dressed up for (some of the ladies travel with their personal maids and the men wear their medals) was something else. Can you imagine a huge dining hall with a table that seats 26 people? I sat next to the Earl of Something and I had to keep taking his hand off my knee, under the table. There is a lot of drunkenness at these weekends.

Now, back in London, we continue seeing the sights. We visited Westminster Abbey, where kings are buried, and also poets like yourself. We went to the Tower of London, and saw Tower Hill, which in the old days they used for public executions, and Tower Green, for private executions, for important people. I said I would prefer to have my head chopped off on Tower Green, as it seemed more cosy, with the hedges and all, but Sir Charlie said he would prefer a public execution, as it would give him a chance to make a speech before the axe came down. I told him that if I was in the audience while he was making that speech, I might interrupt with a few questions which he would not like at all. (I refer to a few fishy things about how he runs his railroad, which I shouldn't really know. But we won't go into that, will we?)

Last night we dined at Reggiori's and tonight we go out to Chelsea, to a district called the World's End, to dine at a place called the Ox on the Roof. But with all this glamour – weird British glamour, if you can call it glamour – I think still of those times we spent together in Montreal, dear Richard, when I shared the excitement of your poetic creativity.

Love
Lili

Uncle Morty put the letter down and called for a third Scotch. "When you and Lili 'shared the excitement,'" he said. "Does this mean you, uh –" Again he made the vulgar circle with the thumb and forefinger of his left hand and poked the index finger of his right hand in and out of the circle, several times.

Richard had been expecting this question and still hadn't decided how to answer it.

"Are you blushing?" Morty said.

"Okay, okay," said Richard. "As you may have heard, she prefers younger men."

"Jesus, you did!" said Morty.

"Look, Morty, don't tell anybody, eh," said Richard. "Will you promise not to tell anybody? I mean, we can't be dragging Lili's name through the mud, can we?"

"Okay, I promise. I won't tell a soul."

"Word of honour?" said Richard.

"Word of honour," said his uncle.

18

Uncle Morty had arranged for Richard to have an interview with Theodore Archer, the legendary public-relations man. "Teddy Archer is one of the great bullshit artists of our time," Morty had said. "You'll learn a lot from him – if he gives you a job."

Now, as the receptionist showed Richard into Archer's office, the great man rose to shake his hand. "I'm truly honoured," he said, "to meet the boy who boffed Lili L'Amour."

Richard was stunned. Uncle Morty had betrayed him, had broken his promise to tell no one about Lili.

"I bet old Lili is a real firecracker in the sack," Archer was saying, as he gestured for Richard to sit down. The reception-ist grimaced as she left the office. She didn't like to hear this kind of language, and there was all too much of it around here.

"So tell me about Lili," Archer said. "She looks like she'd appreciate a really talented muff-diver."

"Uh, I'd rather not discuss that," Richard said, by now highly uncomfortable. But he was starting to think that perhaps Lili was the reason he was being granted this interview.

"Okay, okay," said Archer, "so I'm not going to hear how you got to do it. A lot of guys would brag about it, but you're a gentleman, and I appreciate that. I too am a gentleman, although people might not immediately come to that conclusion. I mean, look at me and what do you see, at first glance? A big man, eh? A hulking brute, you might say, with rough-hewn, craggy features. That's what that magazine article about me said – 'rough-hewn, craggy features.' But underneath it all I am very sensitive. You can see that, can't you, Richard?"

"Yes, sir, I can," said Richard.

"You and I are both gentlemen," Archer said. "We don't talk about the women we screw. We have that in common, don't we?"

"That's right," said Richard.

Archer was now reading the copy of the press release Richard had written for Freckles, the Girl Next Door. As instructed by Morty, Richard had left it with Archer's receptionist the day before the interview, as a sample of his abilities. As Archer read, Richard studied the walls of his office, which were very impressive, covered as they were with framed photos of celebrities of stage and screen, of people shaking hands with each other, of people turning the first sod with a silver shovel, of mayors cutting ribbons with silver scissors, of ladies launching ships with bottles of champagne.

"And you wrote this?" Archer asked, putting down the Freckles press release.

"Yes, sir," said Richard.

"Morty Mintz tells me you're a genius. Are you a genius?"

"No, sir, I'm not," said Richard.

"Good," said Archer. "The last thing we need around here is a genius. So I'll tell you what I'm going to do: I'm going to give you a two-week tryout. If you survive that, you've got yourself a summer job. Twenty-four dollars a week. Is that all right?"

"That's just fine," said Richard.

"Now what do you know about public relations?" Archer asked.

Richard was about to say "Not much," when the door opened and the receptionist appeared. "Mr. Parrish is here," she said. "He says it's urgent."

"Show him in," said Archer. "And take Richard here and install him in the writer's dungeon."

"My name is Shirley," the receptionist said, as she led Richard down a corridor. She was a thin, tired-looking woman. "If you want to know anything around here," she said, "don't ask me. Ask somebody else."

"Mr. Archer said 'the writer's dungeon,'" Richard said. "How many writers are there?"

"There's one," she said. "You're it."

She opened a door to reveal a small, cluttered office strewn with papers. There was a man sitting behind the desk, taking papers out of a drawer and putting them into a briefcase.

"Are you still here?" Shirley said irritably.

"I'll be finished in a minute," the man said. "And who's this, the new victim?"

"This is Richard Lippman," Shirley said. "And will you please hurry up, Jimmy? Mr. Archer wants Richard to get started right away."

"Would you do me a favour, sweetheart?" Jimmy said. "Would you tell Mr. Archer to go piss up a rope? And you, young man, please have a seat. This cell will be yours in just a minute."

Richard sat down uneasily as Shirley left the office. "Just a few souvenirs of two wasted years," Jimmy said, putting more papers into his briefcase. He went over to Richard and extended his hand. "James Heffernan," he said. "Newly liberated and back on the market. I know you're going to love it here,

Richard, working for a thief who should have been put in jail long ago." As Richard shook Jimmy's hand he smelled the alcohol on the man's breath.

"Now I won't be needing this any more, will I?" Jimmy said, picking up the big, heavy Underwood typewriter. Richard watched in alarm as Jimmy took it to the open window and threw it out, down onto Peel Street, where it landed with a loud crash. Richard rushed to the window and looked down, to see white-faced pedestrians staring at the shattered typewriter and looking up at the window it came from.

"Hey, you could have killed somebody down there," Richard said.

"Well, that's the chance you take," Jimmy said. "Ours is a risky business, Richard. Farewell and good luck to you in the ordeal that lies ahead of you."

As he lurched out the door, Jimmy bumped into Theodore Archer, who was on his way in.

"Jesus, are you still here?" Archer said.

"Goodbye, asshole," Jimmy said, walking out into the corridor with head held high.

"I should have fired that son of a bitch long ago," Archer said. "But no, I was too soft-hearted. You'll find that about me, Richard. Under the rough, craggy, abrasive exterior lies a truly soft heart. You'll realize that, my boy, as soon as you start taking advantage of my good nature. Which, of course, you will inevitably do."

Archer picked up one of the press releases that were lying on the desk. "Crap," he said, glancing at it. "That bastard never could write. I'd like you to study this stuff so you'll know how not to do it. What we want here is writing that sings, writing with a punch."

Unable to think of any response to this, Richard started

gathering the papers that were strewn on the desk and putting them in an orderly pile, for future study.

"Okay," Archer said. "Now tell me what you know about the art and science of public relations."

"I'm afraid I don't know very much," Richard said.

"At least you're honest enough to admit it," said Archer. "But in future, in this business, when you're dealing with a client, never admit you don't know all the answers. If you can't wing it, just stall him, tell him you have to verify a few details, and then consult me. I'll have the answer for you right away. Okay?"

"Okay," said Richard.

"Now, what is public relations?" Archer said. "What we are put on this earth to do, Richard, is to tell our client's story in the best possible way, so he can sell his product. Okay?"

"Okay," said Richard.

"We can learn a lot about our craft if we study history," Archer said. "Do you know who the first really important public-relations man was?"

"No, I'm afraid I don't," said Richard.

"It was Moses," Archer said. "And I'm going to tell you just how he bungled the job. Picture the scene, Richard. The good Lord wakes up one morning with a great idea and he calls Moses into his office. 'Moe,' he says, 'I've got an important assignment for you,' and he hands him these two big stone tablets. 'Take these down to the multitude and proclaim them.'

"So Moses takes the tablets down the big elevator to where the multitude is assembled and he says to them, 'Okay, folks, these are the Ten Commandments, directly from upstairs, and if you know what's good for you, you'll govern yourselves accordingly. You may not like some of them, such as Number Seven, the adultery one, but believe me, it's for your own good.'

"Well, I needn't tell you, Richard, that particular product – which I call the Big Ten – never took off. If you study your history, you'll realize that damn few people over a couple of thousand years have ever governed themselves accordingly. 'Don't, don't, don't' is what the Commandments tell them and sin, sin, sin is what the multitude keeps on doing. Do you know why that is, Richard?"

"Because it's hard to be good?" Richard ventured.

"No, sir," said Archer. "It's because Moses, as the Lord's public-relations man, did a lousy job. He just read out what was on those tablets and that was that. Take it or leave it. But those tablets were just notes. What Moses needed to do was to make a presentation, proving – yes, proving – why following these ten suggestions would make each and every person in that multitude feel good. He had to give reasons why it's better not to steal, not to covet thy neighbour's wife, etcetera.

"Now I've always dreamed of having Archer Enterprises complete old Moses' work. What I see in my mind's eye is a small booklet, bound in purple leather, with a gold tassel. Inside there would be ten pages, on the best forty-pound bond paper, with the edges artistically browned to make them look like parchment. The text would be in Old English type, very black with the occasional capital letter in red. The text on each page would be not more than 150 words. But ah, what words! Each page would do what Moses neglected to do – interpret the Commandments – and tell, in dignified language, why you shouldn't steal, why you shouldn't commit adultery. It might be a little anecdote about some fictitious person who got caught, and what befell them. You see, we'd use modern situations but with old-fashioned words, like *befell*. Does that make sense?"

"Yes, it does," said Richard, marvelling at how easy it was becoming for him to lie, on any occasion.

"For instance, take Number Five – honour thy father and thy mother. Well, a lot of us love our parents, but what about the guy who hates his old man's guts and doesn't bother hiding the fact? Well, doesn't that guy realize that the old man is some day going to make a will? Does he want the estate to go to his stupid sister? There must be a way to put that idea across in a dignified, unselfish way. Do you agree?"

"Yes, I do, I do," said Richard. It was at this point that he came to a conclusion that he thought was unique to his situation but which occurs every day to people the world over: I am working for a boss who is crazy.

"Now I want you to try your talented hand at writing that little purple booklet with the gold tassel," Archer said. "I've had other writers try, like that idiot Jimmy Heffernan, but they've all failed. But something tells me Richard Lippman could bring it off. And that little booklet will be a great promotional give-away for Archer Enterprises, a great way to bring in new business. Now I've got a lot of more immediate assignments for you, Richard, so you can do the Commandments in your spare time. If you succeed you'll get a nice cash bonus. You can take a whole month to do it – unless, of course, I'm forced – reluctantly – to let you go after your two-week trial period."

"Watch their facial expressions," Eddie said, and Richard watched intently as Norma Jasper started to collapse. But Paul Paradis managed to hold her up and the two of them staggered onward. The crowd roared its approval.

"People here get their money's worth," Eddie said, and Richard had to agree. He was on his first assignment for Archer – or his second assignment, if one was to count the Ten Commandments – and he was sitting beside Eddie Harrison in the announcer's booth, watching the Speedathon Derby in the Verdun Coliseum. The derby was now in its second week and the crowds were not as big as had been hoped. The newspapers and radio stations were paying very little attention to this colourful event, and it was Richard's task to write a press release that would make reporters and radio men rush down to the Verdun to have a look.

"That Norma Jasper is a really brave kid," Eddie said. "Tomorrow night, if she survives today, we're going to freeze her in 1,200 pounds of ice."

The rules of the Speedathon Derby were simple, Richard learned. There were now eighteen speedathoners in the competition – nine boy-girl teams, people in their twenties and thirties. There had originally been twelve teams, but three had dropped out from exhaustion. Each team had to keep going around the track – walking, running, or dancing – for ten hours a day, with a fifteen-minute rest period each hour. In addition, there were songs, dances, and skits by various artists and near-swoons by speedathoners for the edification of the fans.

"But the highlight every night is the Bombshell," Eddie said to Richard. "Watch, I'm going to announce a Bombshell."

He switched on the loudspeaker system and shouted into the microphone: "Get ready, ladies and gentlemen. Here it comes, the Bombshell! One, two, three, go!"

The speedathoners, some of whom had been shuffling along listlessly, now turned on the heat and started to sprint. They would be going round and round as fast as they could for twenty minutes. The partners had to run facing each other, holding hands at arms' length, so that the men had to run backward halfway round the course and the girls backward over the next lap. They would keep going this way until one team would try to get the lead by forging out in front and starting to "jam." Horns and sirens would now start to blare, lights would flash on and off, and pandemonium would break loose.

Referees and timekeepers would dance around in the midst of the cauldron, keeping order and discouraging fouls. The couple winning the most jams in an evening would get fifteen dollars. The couple winning the most jams in the entire tournament would get five hundred dollars.

It was during these jams that a couple might collapse and be sent home. "Looks like Norma Jasper may go down!" Eddie shouted into the loudspeaker. "Oh, stay away from those pylons, Norma Jasper! Everybody help Norma!" The crowd shouted encouragement as Norma's partner, Paul, struggled manfully to keep her knees from touching the floor so that she would still be in the match tomorrow night and be able to be frozen alive in 1,200 pounds of ice.

"One minute to go," Eddie announced on the loudspeaker, as Phil Arnold and Kay Logan of New York lurched onward like the troupers they were. Louie Meredith was helping Eileen Thayer fight off that sinking feeling. Everybody wanted to collapse but managed a recovery. Miss Grace Alviso, of Georgia, was suspected of a foul and drew hisses from the audience. She responded by moving her lips fiercely, mouthing what was obviously an obscenity. The crowd, which liked spunky girls, approved of this.

Finally the referee fired his gun and the nightly Bombshell was over. The contestants now staggered offstage for their fifteen-minute rest period. Norma Jasper was helped by a shapely young woman dressed like a nurse. The speedathoners would eat and sleep backstage for the whole Speedathon Derby, which could last for up to six weeks, or until the last contestant collapsed.

"I used to be out there on the track with the rest of them," Eddie Harrison reminisced, as Richard wrote in his notebook. "You can put in your press release that I'm from St. Louis, Missouri," he said. "I used to be in the old walkathons and the eighty-six-hour dance marathons. In Wildwood, New Jersey, in 1933, I stayed on my feet for 1,786 hours, with only fifteen minutes' rest every hour.

"Eighty to a hundred couples used to compete in those days. Spectators would give the band twenty-five dollars so couples could collapse to their favourite waltz. Teams from Europe used to come to Brooklyn to compete for a five-thousand-dollar prize. Big stars like Red Skelton, Frankie Lane, and June Havoc got their start in marathons. Of course all that was back in the hungry thirties, during the Depression. Ah, those were the days."

Lili's letter arrived just as Richard was starting to write his Speedathon Derby press release. It was a long time since he had heard from her, winter months during which he had been trying to drive her out of his mind.

> 48 Grantham Grove,
> London, W. 8
> June 14, 1949.

Dear Richard,

Well, here I am, still in jolly old England and there are interesting developments. I decided to stay on here after Sir Charlie decided to go back to Canada to look after his silly old railroad. Shall we say that he and I are no longer the best of friends, but that's another story.

I have a nice little appartment, or flat, as they call it here, in the west end of London. I'm fascinated by this city, where you have history all around you. I love the fog, which can be so thick that you can't see where you're going. But everybody here is so brave that they keep going anyway.

I've been making a living by dancing at the Windmill Theatre, right off Piccadilly Circus, and a few other theatres.

The Windmill is a very famous place whose motto is "We Never Closed," which means they stayed open every night, all through the war, as the bombs fell on London.

But the exciting news is that I have met Professor Szombathely, the famous Hungarian choreographer and teacher. He heard about my "Orpheus and Eurydice" piece and he asked me to perform it for him. I did, and he asked me to become a teacher at his studio, which is called the Art of Movement. Here students learn how Modern Dance brings a new awareness of inner and outer realities – a truly beautiful concept.

But, on a more practical level, could you do me a great favor? I need a new poem and could you supply me with one? Perhaps you remember how I performed your Orpheus at Lord Edgeworth's party at his country estate. Well, I have been invited back there for another weekend, and I'd like to perform with a new poem. You once said you were going to write a poem about Diana the Huntress for me. Did you ever do that? Could you do it? The people at Lord Edgeworth's are very keen on hunting and they would love to see me dancing with Diana's bow and arrow. If you could supply me with that poem, dear Richard, I would love you forever.

Much love
Lili

P.S.: Could you send it by airmail?

Reading the letter for the second time, Richard knew that he couldn't come up with the poem she wanted. His muse had abandoned him. From now on, his typewriter could produce only prose, the unartistic prose of the press release.

That night, at home, Richard realized what he would have to do. Taking his poetry anthology from its shelf, he turned to the pages devoted to his favourite poet, Robert Herrick. Propping the book up in front of his Smith-Corona, he started typing:

Her legs were such Diana shows
When tuckt up she a-hunting goes
With buskins shortened to descry
The happy dawning of her thigh.

Good old Herrick, as good today as he was back in 1648. "The happy dawning of her thigh . . ." The poem, he realized, as he continued typing, was made to order for Lili L'Amour. For good measure, Richard threw in a few lines from another poem: "A sweet disorder in the dress / Kindles in clothes a wantonness." That was Herrick for you, always trying to get the lady out of her clothes.

Lili would take it for granted that Richard had written this. But what if somebody recognized the hand of Herrick? Well, Richard would have to take that chance. His life up to now had been far too cautious. Faint heart never won fair maid. It was time to live a bit more dangerously.

19

"This is beautifully written," Theodore Archer said.

"Thank you," said Richard.

"You certainly have a way with words," Archer said, crumpling and throwing Richard's Speedathon Derby press release into a wastepaper basket. "Beautiful, but absolutely useless," he said. "Do you know why?"

"No, I guess I don't," Richard said, wondering if his two-week trial period was coming to an end after only two days on the job.

"It doesn't grab," Archer said. "We're in the business of grabbing people, okay?"

"Okay," said Richard, almost sure that this was the right response.

"What would happen if we sent this down to the *Gazette*?" Archer said, pointing to Richard's screed in the wastepaper basket. "Randall would read it and spike it, okay? We send it down to O'Hearn at the *Star* and what happens? He reads it and he spikes it, okay?" Archer got up from his desk, went over to a cabinet, took out a bottle of Scotch, and poured some into two glasses. "Let's see if we can't figure this out," he said, handing one of the glasses to Richard.

"Excuse me, sir," Richard said, putting his glass down on the desk. "but what do you mean by 'spikes it'?"

"Randall has a big spike on his desk, okay?" Archer said. "He impales your press release on that spike, on top of a lot of other crap he figures he will reconsider when he gets a minute. But he never gets a minute, and at midnight, when the presses start rolling, he takes all the crap off his spike, throws it into the wastepaper basket, puts on his jacket, and goes home. Okay?"

"Okay," said Richard.

"But what do we want him to do?" Archer said. "We want him to read your release and be grabbed by it. To the extent that he'll yell, 'Hey, Moore,' and Brian Moore, his best feature writer, comes over to the desk and Randall hands him your release. 'Off your ass, Moore,' he says, 'and get down to this speedathon, pronto. Take Vic with you.' That's Vic Davidson, the photographer. Meanwhile, over at the *Star*, O'Hearn is grabbed by your deathless prose and he sends McCutcheon down to the coliseum. At *La Presse*, Boisvert sends Archambault down, at station CJAD Russ Hooper sends the golden-voiced Art Ainsley down, and so on. And tomorrow the whole world knows about the thrills and chills of that speedathon, and people are rushing down to Verdun to buy tickets. All because of the brilliant press release you've written, which has grabbed those editors."

"And just what is it that I've written?" asked Richard.

"That's what we've got to figure out," said Archer. "Go ahead, have a drink, let's grease the creative wheels." He pointed to Richard's glass, still where he had left it on the desk.

"Isn't it a little early in the day for, you know, a drink?" said Richard, glancing at his watch. It was three in the afternoon.

"Normally, Richard, we don't splice the main brace until the sun is over the yardarm," Archer said, taking a swig from his glass. "But in the public-relations business you've got to be flexible. If a client offers you a shot at ten in the morning, you better get it down somehow. If you don't, he'll think you're some kind of namby-pamby. But one of the consolations of our very demanding profession is that you can sometimes find yourself feeling pretty good at odd times of the day. Now let's see what we're going to put in your press release."

Archer was now pacing up and down the office, looking up at the ceiling for inspiration and sipping from his glass. Reluctantly, Richard tasted the Scotch, letting it burn its unfamiliar way down his throat. During the winter, like many other McGill freshmen, he had been learning how to drink beer at Café André, but he had always followed his father's words of advice: "Beer is all right, but lay off the hard stuff." But here he was, sampling the hard stuff – and not particularly enjoying it.

Archer had stopped his pacing and was standing rigid in the middle of the office. "I'm starting to see the light," he said. "While you were down at that speedathon, did you talk to Doctor Herscovitch?" he said.

"No," said Richard. "Who's that?"

"Doctor Herscovitch is the eminent Boston cardiologist," Archer said. "And here's our story. Take your pencil and write this down. It's our headline: 'Medical Controversy Rages Over Peril at Speedathon.'"

As Richard wrote in his notebook, Archer dictated the essence of the story. Doctor Aaron Herscovitch had visited the speedathon and had predicted disaster. The human body is not built to withstand this kind of punishment, the doctor said. There are going to be heart attacks. If they're crazy enough to freeze Norma Jasper in 1,200 pounds of ice, that girl is a goner. And there will be other fatalities. That coliseum is one big torture chamber and the police should shut it down.

"Gosh," said Richard, "that master of ceremonies guy down there never mentioned that doctor."

Archer poured himself another Scotch. "Well, he might have mentioned it if Doctor Herscovitch actually existed," he said.

"You mean this is fiction?" Richard asked.

"We don't like the word *fiction*," Archer said. "In public relations we call it *creative conceptualization*. And that's not our whole story. Write this down. The speedathon management calls in Doctor Alphonse Cornellier, one of Montreal's greatest specialists, and Cornellier says that Herscovitch's pronouncement is American hogwash. There is no danger of heart attacks. There is nothing better for the heart than exercise. And there you've got your controversy, which the press and radio will turn into a raging controversy. And people will believe Herscovitch. You know why?"

"No, why?" asked Richard.

"He's from Boston and he's Jewish," Archer said. "In this town, if you're sick, you want a Jewish doctor. Who's going to take the word of some Canadian quack over that of a towering figure like Herscovitch? So the public learns of this raging controversy and the speedathon is sold out every night. There is no bigger sporting attraction than the possibility of sudden death in the arena."

"What if the press wants to interview Doctor Herscovitch?" asked Richard.

"How can they?" said Archer. "He just sailed for England on the *Aquitania*. He's on the high seas, on his way to the World Cardiology Conference in London."

"What if they want to interview this Doctor Cornellier?" asked Richard.

"That will be arranged," said Archer. "We supply them with Corny's unlisted phone number, and my man Pierre is at the other end to take the call. Pierre is a great actor who does voice work for us. English, French, whatever. He will attack Doctor Herscovitch vigorously, following a script that you will supply. He may even make a few anti-Semitic remarks, which will add spice."

"And you arrange all that?" asked Richard, finally taking a gulp of Scotch.

"We do, we do," said Archer. "We're a full-service agency, my boy."

The press release was a great success. As Archer had predicted, it sent reporters, photographers, and radio men rushing down to the speedathon, anxious to inflame the medical controversy and to patiently await the first fatal heart attack. The papers were full of it the next day, and people were phoning the speedathon and pleading with the management not to pack poor Norma Jasper in 1,200 pounds of ice. "Let her cool down normally" was the cry, as crowds lined up to buy tickets.

"Now you know how it's done," Archer said to Richard. "I hope you appreciate that I'm grooming you for big things."

The next stage in the grooming came a few days later, when Archer came into the writer's dungeon, brandishing a newspaper. "You're famous, my boy," he said.

Richard looked up from his typewriter, where he was trying to enliven a message that the Dominion Oilcloth Company wanted to get across to the public.

"It's the third item down," Archer said, handing Richard that morning's *Montreal Herald*, open at Fitz Fitzgerald's gossip column. And there it was, in Fitzgerald's inimitable style, with three dots preceding it and three dots following it:

. . . Whiz-kid Richard Lippman, who is now pounding a typewriter for PR Supremo Teddy Archer, turns out to have been a great and good friend of the sultry Lili L'Amour. Well, Lili always did like them young, didn't she? . . .

"You're famous, kid," Archer said. "Now people will know who you are."

"Where did they get this?" Richard asked, dismayed. What if this ever got back to Lili?

"I handed it to old Fitz personally," Archer said. "What's the matter? Don't tell me you're not thrilled."

"It's embarrassing, Mr. Archer," said Richard, reading the dreadful item again.

"Look, from now on call me Teddy, eh?" said Archer. "And don't give me that shrinking-violet modesty. There's no room for that in public relations."

"But this is so personal," Richard said.

"In our business we help sell product," Archer said. "Speedathon product, Dominion Oilcloth product. By now you've probably grasped that fact. But the most important product we sell is ourselves – Teddy product, Richard product. If the client doesn't believe in us, we don't get that little old contract."

"And this . . . this mention of Lili L'Amour is going to make them believe in me?" Richard asked.

"Yes, it will," said Archer.

Richard read the item a third time. "What does he mean by 'great and good friend'?"

"It means you screwed her," Archer said. "That's the phrase Fitz always uses."

"That's terrible," Richard said.

"No, it's great," said Archer. "When you go into the El Morocco, when you go into the Chez Paree, they'll know who you are and they'll treat you with respect. Don't tell me you're not going to like that."

"I'm going into the El Morocco?" said Richard, puzzled.

"You're going to love it," said Archer. And, with enthusiasm, he outlined Richard's next assignment. Archer Enterprises was going to produce a magazine entitled *Nightlife*. It would be glossy, sophisticated, witty. It would be left for tourists in every one of the city's hotel rooms and would be sold in downtown newsstands. It would carry colourful descriptions of all the city's nightclubs, supper clubs, restaurants, and dance halls – all of which Richard would research and write. In the nightclubs, Richard would sample the food and the wine, and watch the floor shows.

At this point in Archer's spiel the door of the writer's dungeon opened and Shirley, the receptionist, appeared. "Mr. Parrish is here," she said. "He says it's urgent."

"You're going to eat and drink very well," Archer said, rushing out of the dungeon without waiting for any reaction from Richard.

Meanwhile the phone was ringing. It was Uncle Morty.

"Congratulations, kid," Morty said. "You've made it big and now the world knows who you are – and what you can do."

"Jeez, Uncle Morty, what if my parents see this?" said Richard.

"Your father has already phoned me to ask what it's all about," Morty said. "He doesn't read the *Herald*, of course, but somebody who does called him and was kidding him. Your old man said he was too embarrassed to ask you. I told him it's just ballyhoo, just public-relations hype. Flacks do it all the time to attract business. He asked me what a flack was, and I said, 'Your son's a flack now, and a damn good one. And don't worry, he's never even met this Lili L'Amour.'"

Fred Mason, the photographer, was a short, wiry man and, as Richard soon discovered, a very bitter man. "To think that I've been reduced to doing this," he said, sitting down at the table across from Richard. They were at La Bohème, the newly refurbished supper club on Guy Street. This was Richard's first research venture for *Nightlife*; he would write the article and Mason would take the photos. Mason had just taken some pictures of Ronny Matthews, who Richard would describe as "the blind keyboard wizard," whose lilting Hammond organ was entertaining the diners.

"To think that I once photographed the troops going ashore in Normandy," Mason said. "A bullet actually clipped me in the ear. Look," he said, leaning forward. "I was that close to death." After the war, Mason hoped to become a great photojournalist, roaming the world for a magazine like *Life*, covering wars in Indo-China, starvation in Africa. But that was not to be. "You just let your guard down for a minute," he said bitterly, "and suddenly you're married, with a couple of little kids. You've got to stay put and put bread on the table. You're not in Saigon with your Leica, you're in shithole Montreal taking pictures of the Kiwanis Club luncheon for Theodore Asshole Archer."

"Now wait a minute, Fred," Richard said. "This is a little more interesting than the Kiwanis Club, isn't it?" He gestured out at La Bohème's dance floor. "And this isn't just bread on the table, is it?" He pointed at what they were eating – prime rib of Alberta beef with a delicious Monte Carlo potato – all being offered to them compliments of the house, along with a bottle of choice Bordeaux. They had been seated at a ringside table by a man called Paul Babin, whom Richard would describe in his article as "your genial host." Richard would also point out that La Bohème had previously been known to Montreal's "mink-coat set" as the Orchid Room, but the flowery decor had been replaced by large reproductions of Degas ballerina scenes set against the shell-pink walls.

"I guess I better get this too, eh?" Fred Mason said, reluctantly leaving his strawberry cheesecake to pick up his camera and aim it at a tall blonde who was at the microphone now, singing "Melancholy Baby."

When the floor show was over, and Richard and Mason finished their coffees, their genial host saw them to the door. "It's been an honour for us to have you in our club, Mr. Lippman," Paul Babin said. "And if Lili L'Amour ever comes back to Montreal, don't forget to bring her here for dinner." As he said it, he winked broadly – and that wink spoiled for Richard what had been a very agreeable evening.

There was more of the same the next night, when Richard and Mason were dining amid the zebra-striped decor of the Zanzibar, in the east end. Rita, the cigarette girl, came up to their table and, with a sly smile for Richard, said, "And how's Lili these days?" The following night their reservation was at the Esquire, one of the Stanley Street nightclubs, where they were greeted by Sam Cleaver himself, who Richard – by now picking up the show-business lingo – would describe in his article as "your genial boniface."

"I see you're in the papers again," Sam Cleaver said, vigorously shaking Richard's hand. And indeed he was in the papers – in that morning's *Herald*, where the pestilential Fitz Fitzgerald's column had revealed ". . . Whiz-kid Richard Lippman making the rounds of Ourtown's niteries, but alas without his lovely Lili L'Amour. Where can she be? . . ."

As he ate his Delmonico sirloin, Richard tried to drive these words out of his mind and concentrate on writing some notes about the floor show. This show was going to be different, Sam

Cleaver had assured him. "The colourful Sam," as Richard's article would label him, had confessed a penchant for "pint-sized girls" and had imported a chorus line of six very short dancers from New York. These were called "terpsichorettes," and were very different from the tall, leggy girls who made up the standard chorus line.

"Those little ones are cute," Fred Mason said, coming back to the table after photographing them in action. For once Mason seemed not to be morose.

"It's so damn embarrassing," Richard said. "So embarrassing."

"What's embarrassing?" Mason said.

"All this Lili L'Amour stuff," Richard said. "Wherever I go."

"And you don't like that?" Mason said.

"Of course not," said Richard.

"Aw, come on," said Mason. "Don't try that act on me. I know and you know that Lili is your ticket. Why else did Archer give you this dream job, with a different nightclub every night and a different charcoal-broiled steak every night? You think you got this because you're a brilliant writer? You got it, Richard – and excuse me for being so frank – because everybody downtown wants to have a look at the high-school kid who mounted the fabulous Lili L'Amour. You're one of the seven wonders of the world."

"I'm a college kid, not a high-school kid," Richard said.

"All right, the college kid," said Mason, who seemed to be getting drunk on the cognacs he was drinking. "The college kid who parted the lovely legs of the legendary Lili," he said. "Which is exactly how Theodore Archer Enterprises has packaged you. You have glamour, you have an entree. You are the ambassador of this phony *Nightlife* magazine. People will pay attention. Advertisers will buy advertising. Money will pour into Asshole Archer's pockets."

"So Archer is using me," Richard said.

"Of course he's using you," Mason said. "He's using you, he's using me, he's using everybody he meets, the son of a bitch. He's climbing up over the bodies."

Mason signalled to the waiter for another cognac, and Richard busied himself with his notebook. The vocalist was onstage now, singing "Begin the Beguine," and Richard wondered how he would describe her. From his pocket he took out his list of possible appellations and scanned it to see which one he might use. He had been studying Vincent Geraghty's column, "Lights and Shadows of Montreal," and had been jotting down some of Geraghty's poetic terms for female nightclub singers. "Chantootsie" might be good for this one, but "vocalulu" might be better. "Songal" was a bit weak, but "a melodious eyeful" sounded right. Finally he settled on "a curvaceous thrush," and he wrote it in his notebook.

Was it plagiarism if you used another writer's metaphor? Richard would think about that later. But in this type of work, you didn't have to adhere to the highest standards of literary morality, did you? And wasn't there an eminent literary figure who once said that mediocre writers borrow, while great writers steal?

Night after night, Richard and Fred Mason worked their way through Montreal's nightclubs – Ciro's, the Tic Toc, the Copacabana, the Blue Angel, the Samovar, Rockhead's Paradise, and others. They saved the best for the last, the elegant Normandie Roof, dubbed "Ourtown's swankiest watering hole" by the perspicacious Vincent Geraghty. It was indeed the resort of the carriage trade and, it being Saturday night, many of the customers were wearing dinner jackets and evening gowns. Noting this as he and Mason came into the huge, lavishly appointed room, Richard wished he had thought to wear his Royal Northumberland Fusiliers necktie; these people would recognize its significance.

Norbert, the maître d', showed them to their ringside table, and they settled in to order dinner and watch the carriage trade dancing to the music of Neil Golden's orchestra. Before long the *consommé houblonnière* arrived, and a moment later the substantial bulk of Theodore Archer himself was looming above the table.

"May I?" he said, gesturing at a vacant chair.

"Why not?" said Mason, and the boss sat down.

"I was working late, so I thought I'd come up and take a breather," Archer said. The Normandie Roof was on the ninth floor of the Mount Royal Hotel, and the offices of Archer Enterprises were on the mezzanine floor.

"So how's it going, young man?" Archer said. "Are we making progress?"

"We're doing great, sir," Richard said. He had not yet mustered the courage to call Archer Teddy, as Archer had requested.

"It's going to be a great magazine," Archer said. "I really like what you've written so far, Richard, even though some of it does sound a bit like my friend Vince Geraghty. But tell me, I hope all this high living hasn't kept you from working on the Ten Commandments."

"Oh no, I'm working on them all the time," said Richard, who hadn't yet given a thought to this idiotic assignment.

"Which one are you on?" Archer said. "Have you done the adultery one yet?"

"Not yet, sir," said Richard. "I'm on Number Nine. I'm not doing them in order, I'm sort of jumping around." Archer had wanted to see each commandment as soon as Richard had rewritten it, but Richard had persuaded him to wait until he had done the whole shebang – and "polished" it.

"Number Nine," said Archer. "Refresh my memory, which one is Number Nine?"

"'Thou shalt not bear false witness against thy neighbour,'" Richard said.

"Ah, false witness," said Archer. "That's always been one of my favourites." And he held a finger to his lips, to call for silence. Tommy Dix, "the Baby-Faced Song Man," was at the microphone now and was starting to sing "Best Foot Forward."

False witness . . . Lately Richard had been giving some thought to this matter, to whether it was always wrong to tell lies. After all, the whole public-relations business seemed to be based on stretching the truth, or inventing things that would pass for truth, like Dr. Herscovitch and Dr. Zilboorg. Richard realized how very good he was at this sort of thing, and if lying made good things happen – like the career of Freckles, the Girl Next Door – could it always be wrong? After all, Commandment Number Nine tells you not to bear false witness against your neighbour, but it doesn't forbid you to bear false witness against somebody else's neighbour, does it?

"Okay, everybody smile." Richard turned to see a girl photographer pointing her camera at their table.

"Aw, cut it out, Angie," Archer said.

"Come on, Teddy," the girl said. "This is a historic picture." And her flashbulb popped. "Can I join you gentlemen for a moment?" she said.

"No, you can't," Archer said.

"Thank you," said the girl. And putting her camera on the table, she sat down in the chair next to Richard's, which was vacant. "I'm Angela," she said. "You must be Richard, *the* Richard." Looking into his eyes, she extended her hand to shake his.

"How do you do?" Richard said uneasily. Angela was a tall, svelte ash blonde with big blue eyes and a smile that struck Richard as being quite cynical.

"I've been wanting to meet you, Richard," Angela said, "but this monster has been keeping us apart." She nodded at Archer.

"Will you please cut it out, Angie?" Archer said.

"You see what I mean?" Angela said. "Wait till I tell the girls I've actually met you, Richard. We do talk about you, you know. About you and Lili."

"Is she boring you, Richard?" Archer said.

"No, not at all," Richard said truthfully.

At this point Norbert, the maître d', came up to the table and whispered in Angela's ear. With a grimace, Angela stood up. "Gotta go," she said, picking up her camera. "See you later, Richard," she said, with a large wink.

Richard watched as she followed Norbert around the edge of the dance floor to a distant ringside table, where a middle-aged couple was waiting for her. She arranged them in a good pose and her flashbulb popped. Then she followed Norbert to another table, where she took another picture. As the Normandie Roof's official photographer, Angela offered you a photo of you and your lady for five dollars – developed and printed within an hour. For ten dollars you could get a special deal whereby you received not only the print but also the negative. The special deal, which offered you the luxury of destroying the negative personally, was, of course, for the man whose lady was not his wife.

"Well, it's back downstairs for old Teddy," Archer said, rising. "Enjoy your dessert, gentlemen. And let me know if Angela bothers you any more." They watched as he walked off, stopping at tables to greet various of Montreal's movers and shakers.

"Does Angela work for him?" Richard said. "I mean, the way he talks to her –"

"Yes, she does," Mason said. "Archer has the photo franchise up here, so Angela is one of us, one of our brave little band of slaves."

"You say 'little band,'" said Richard. "How little is it?"

"He tries to keep the number secret," Mason said. "He pretends that Archer Enterprises is a big empire, but actually the bastard has only four and a half employees. I hope you don't mind me calling you half an employee, but you're just here for the summer, eh? The full-timers are me, Angela, sourpuss Shirley on the reception desk, and pathetic Molly on the mimeograph machine. Actually, I officially work for XYZ News Pictures, which is a subsidiary of Archer Enterprises. I am the only employee, but he likes to have a second letterhead for various kinds of swindles."

"But that Angela," said Richard. "She's quite a number, isn't she?"

"If you think she's available, forget it," Mason said. "She's Archer's mistress."

"Aha," said Richard. "But that's quite an act she puts on."

"She tries to make him jealous," Mason said. "She'd like him to get rid of his wife."

"He's got a wife?" said Richard.

"Of course," said Archer. "A wife and three kiddies in a house up in Outremont. And another little house right here in the hotel, room number 735, known as the Archer Enterprises Hospitality Suite. That's where he offers hospitality to little Angela. Because she works nights, up here on the Roof, it's usually a nooner with Angela. But at nights he's free to offer hospitality to other women he meets."

"So Teddy is a real cocksman," Richard said. It was a word that increasingly intrigued him.

"He's more than a cocksman," Mason said. "He's a whore-master. But that's not his greatest sin."

"What's his greatest sin?" Richard said.

"You'll find out, eventually," Mason said.

Richard let his mind run down the tablets of the Ten Commandments. "He doesn't make graven images, does he?" he said.

"No, that's what I do," said Mason, pointing at his camera.

Eating his baked Alaska and watching the chorus girls do their number – in his article he would call them "chorines" – Richard felt sad that tonight would be the end of his voyage through nightclub-land. This would be his last article for the magazine. These freebie dinners had been wonderful, and it would be a long time before he would be able to pay for evenings like this one himself. It had all been immensely enjoyable, moving in this glamorous world, meeting glamorous people. And he had to admit that he no longer objected to being stared at as Lili L'Amour's lover. In fact, he had come to like it. It was nice to be important.

In the mornings, coming to work through the lobby of the Mount Royal Hotel – the city's biggest and most worldly hotel – he had got into the habit of stopping at the newsstand to buy a copy of the *Herald*. At his desk, in the writer's dungeon, he would quickly turn to Fitz Fitzgerald's column, hoping to see his name there. But Fitz seemed to have lost interest in him. Then, one day early in August, his name leapt out at him from the column, in an item that sent his spirits sinking through the floor:

. . . When will Montreal see the luscious Lili L'Amour again? striptease aficionados are asking. Well, the sad answer is almost surely never. My informants down at Station 10, the downtown cop shop, assure me there's still a warrant out for her arrest on charges indecent dancing. And we know that

Lili is not cut out for life behind bars. Besides, Lili is making heads turn all over England, and that is where she plans to make her nest. All of which brings a tear to the eye of PR whiz-kid Richard Lippman . . .

It was like an official confirmation of something that Richard had suspected for months, but had never really admitted to himself. He would never again see his Lili.

20

But yes, he would see her again. Definitely. It was simply a matter of getting over to England as soon as possible. The plan became clear in his mind by the time he finished reading Lili's letter for the fourth time. It was a wild plan, but he knew he was thinking clearly, even though he was intoxicated by the perfume arising from her fancy mauve notepaper.

Burghley Manor,
Hampshire, England.
July 20, 1949.

Dear Richard,

I write this in the morning, in my very beautiful bed-room. The maid (one of the maids) has just brought me breakfast. This includes sausages and a fried tomato. Is not England wierd? As I write I look out at a fountain decorated by nimphs. I think those sculptures are nimphs. Beyond the fountain is the park. It goes on forever. Lord Burghley's layout makes Lord Edgeworth's estate (huge) look like a small backyard.

Last night I danced for the weekend guests (40 people). I danced to your Diana poem and they loved it. But I must confess – can I be very frank? – that I too loved it but I didn't love it quite as much as your Orpheus and earlier works. It seemed to lack the zing. Also, the reading was not too great. It was read by Sir Anthony Eden, the former foreign minister before this terrible Labour government got in. (We all hate this government). Even though Sir Anthony is even more handsome than Larry Ollivier, he just doesn't have the voice. As Lady Elphinstone whispered to me, Sir Anthony made your poetry sound like a speech in the House of Commons.

Still, they loved it. And thank you, thank you, thank you. But if only I could have some new poems. Still, I know how busy you must be with your interesting summer job.

I am in demand. I am invited, three weeks from now, to the Duke of Somerset's annual summer bash. He is not a Royal Duke (there are only 5 of those and you have to call them Your Royal Highness in your thank you note after the party) but Mr. Somereset is still a Duke (you call him Your Grace) and that's right up at the top, ahead of the Marquesses, the Vycounts, the Earls, etc. (Did you know that the wife of a Marquess is a Marchioness?) It's all very complicated, and you can't ask the other guests because you're supposed to be born knowing all the details. But when I need information I get it from the servants. The servants here like me, especially after I went below stairs and did a little dance for them in the huge kitchen. Lady Burghley didn't like me doing that, but to hell with her, the old bat.

One servant I really like is Biddulph, who is in charge of the stables. Biddulph is teaching horsemanship to three small children who are among the guests here and I asked him if I could join the class. He said sure. I was never on a horse before and I started on a lovely, quiet mare (female horse) called Sally. The children found this very funny as they never heard of an adult who didn't know how to ride. But I love it and some day I will have a horse of my own (a stalion) and I will teach him how to dance.

Richard, I am again hearing the name of Isadora Duncan. After my recital last night three of the ladies came up to me to tell me that they saw Isadora dancing in Paris and Viena and other places 30 years ago. She was the toast of Europe and they tell me I'm every bit as good. It's all very well to dance in the ballroom of stately houses, for 40 people sitting on folding chairs, but what I really hanker for is a real theatre, with a thousand people out there and the crowned heads of Europe up in the boxes, watching my Eurydice and listening to the words of Richard Lippman. And I'd like to make big money like Isadora did, but I wouldn't use it to get drunk half the time the way she did and give it away to a crazy Russian poet the way she did. But I would certainly pass some of that money on to a certain very deserving Canadian poet.

Too bad you're not here, Richard. At these weekends people ask me where I get my poetry, and when I tell them it comes from a young man who is still at university they are very intrigued. One man – Vycount Somebody – told me your Diana poem was so good it reminded him of Robert Herrick, whoever that is or was. But I am sure you are better than this Herrick.

Could you possibly ever make a trip to England? Perhaps after you graduate. You would enjoy meeting the aristocracy and perhaps you could try your hand at fox-hunting. And you would enjoy meeting Professor Szombathely, who has that studio in London where I teach clumsy children how to dance. Szomby, who is crazy, and his crazy wife Jacinthe, who used to be a great dancer before she broke her leg, think I could make a tour of Europe, performing in big theaters, and they say they are working on it. Isn't that exciting?

By the way, in London last week, I went to Harrod's, the fancy department store, and bought three neckties for you. They have the regimental stripes that you like and are authentic, not like the American copies. I also got you two sweaters, one Cashmere and one Shetland. They are in the mail and should arrive soon, a small token of my esteem. And oh yes, at Harrod's I also got you a pot of home-made, thick-cut Seville orange marmalade. It's delicious. You can think of me when you have it on your toast at breakfast.

With love
Lili

Yes, he would think of her at breakfast, at lunch, and at dinner – and during all the hours in between. And if she wanted new poems, she would have new poems – scads of poems, trunks full of poems. He was at home, late at night, when he read her letter for the fourth time, and when he finished it he leapt up and ran down the stairs to the basement to get the maid's feather duster out of her closet. In his bedroom again, he flicked the dust off the keys of his typewriter, which had stood idle all spring and summer. Yes, his muse was definitely back; he had heard her whooshing in through the window while he was reading Lili's letter and now, sparkling and transparent, she was floating around up near the ceiling and pointing down at his trusty Smith-Corona typewriter with her magic wand.

He immediately attacked the keys. He had always wanted to write a poem about the execution of Anne Boleyn, Queen of England, in 1536, and this would be it. At the Duke of

Somerset's summer party they would know what he was talking about, and Lili would adore it. She loved to dance in the role of a woman who was about to die or who had recently died, preferably violently. Hadn't she been inspired by Richard's sequel to *The Divine Comedy*? In that one, his suicidal Beatrice had danced her way into a bathtub, to cut her wrists. Once dead, she arose from the encrimsoned, soapy water to become a lovely, naked, dancing ghost – lovely but vindictive, as Richard's poem had her cursing out that miserable, two-timing Dante Alighieri. Richard's Orpheus and Eurydice was, of course, another nifty dance of death, with Eurydice – a gorgeous girl but dead as a doornail – dancing lightly up the stony path from the underworld to the upperworld, despite her sore ankle, where that dastardly snake had bitten her, causing her death. Richard's poem had some harsh words for that snake, as well as for that blockhead Orpheus, for handling the whole thing so badly.

It was always good to have a villain to work with, and in this new epic poem, Richard would not spare King Henry VIII, the rotter who sent his loving wife Anne Boleyn to the chopping block. Mind you, Henry did have the occasional ounce of decency, as when he imported a very high-priced executioner from France because that fellow did it with a big sword, very neat and fast, as opposed to the Tower of London's staff executioner, who used an axe and, often suffering from a hangover in the morning, could sometimes do a very messy job, taking several chops to get the head off. Richard's poem would have some thought-provoking things to say about the executioner's craft in general, and he would not be kind to Anne's lady-in-waiting who, when Anne knelt down at the block, came forward to pin up her long black hair so the back of her neck would be exposed to the sword.

Richard would have some sarcastic lines about that horny swine Henry VIII, over at Hampton Court, waiting for the messenger who would tell him that the dirty deed had been done and that he was finally a free man, wifeless and queenless once again, and thus able to marry that vamp Jane Seymour right away. But then, rising from the chopping block, hooded to suggest headlessness, Lili would be Anne Boleyn's ghost, dancing defiantly to the reading of Richard's withering lines about King Henry, Jane Seymour, and the British judicial system of the time.

It took Richard four days to write the Anne Boleyn epic, working half the night at home and much of the day at the office, when he should have been working for Archer Enterprises. When he finished the poem, Richard wondered whether his future biographers might not consider it his masterpiece. Typing it on his best heavy paper made sending it by airmail to Lili rather expensive, but it didn't seem right – what with the poem's royal theme – to type it on the lightweight onion-skin paper that you were supposed to use for airmail.

With the poem dispatched, Richard had to figure out how to get over to England as soon as possible. After some research into steamship fares and timetables, he realized that as soon as possible might not be possible. This venture wasn't going to be cheap, and at this point he simply didn't have the money. He spent many hours calculating just how much he would need for fares, hotels, meals, etcetera. It was a substantial sum, but with any luck he might be able to accumulate it by Christmas; he would save all his pay for the remaining weeks of his summer job, and Archer had hinted that there might be spare-time work for him in the fall, after he went back to McGill. Yes, by Christmas he could do it. And from a travel agent he learned that the *Île de France*, the ship that had taken Lili across the

Atlantic, would be sailing from New York on December 21, the day after the beginning of McGill's Christmas break. Yes, he would sail on the *Île de France*. Of course he would not be dining at the captain's table, as Lili did, but way down in third class, where you probably had to bring your own sandwiches.

When would he come back? The McGill calendar told him that lectures would resume on January 11. He would have to be back for that. But what if he wasn't? What if he came back much, much later? What if by then Professor Szombathely had organized Lili's European tour, and Richard would have to go along as staff poet and public-relations officer? He visualized himself sitting across from Lili at their table in the dining car of the train, the romantic Orient Express, steaming through the Alps from Paris to Vienna. They were sipping their after-dinner Chartreuse, speculating about the other passengers. Which of the beautiful ladies were famous courtesans? Which of the elegant gentlemen were ruthless international financiers? Which were high-society jewel thieves? Which were dangerous Russian spies? Ah Europe, so fascinating . . . Why come back to Canada at all?

21

Archer was in one of his sky-high moods, in a state of dangerous enthusiasm. Richard had seen this before, the last time being when Archer had instructed him to think up two new commandments, to make it an even dozen. Today the PR supremo was in full flight, pacing up and down in his office while brandishing a small machine.

"Do you know what this is?" Archer asked, as Richard came into the office.

"Uh, no, I guess I don't," Richard said, as Archer put the machine down on his desk. "It's an electric can opener," Archer said. "Have you ever heard of an electric can opener?"

"No, I haven't," said Richard.

"Of course not," Archer said. "This is a prototype. Very few people have seen it. But when it goes into production and is unleashed on the market, Archer Enterprises will make every housewife in Canada miserable until she buys one. Richard Lippman's magic prose will be a key element in that campaign. Can you start thinking about that right away?"

"I'll do that," said Richard. But actually his mind was far away, in England. Five minutes ago, when he was summoned from the writer's dungeon into Archer's office, he had been studying a tourist guidebook to London and had almost decided that his first celebratory dinner with Lili would have to be at a restaurant called Boulestin's.

"Okay," Archer was saying. "Now if I say 149 days, what does that say to you?" He was pointing at a calendar on the wall. "One hundred and forty-nine days," he repeated.

"Give me a minute to think," Richard said. But his mind was still in London. Boulestin's was horribly expensive, but . . .

"Oh, for Christ's sake," Archer said. "This whole town is asleep. It's going to be up to Archer Enterprises to wake them up. To make it dawn on them that in 149 days, or however many days" – he took the calendar off the wall and was waving it – "it will be January 1, 1950. Nineteen fifty." He seemed out of breath now as he slumped down into his chair behind his desk.

"Oh, 1950," Richard said. "Of course."

"We will be exactly halfway through the twentieth century," Archer said. "We'll be halfway on toward the year 2000. It's going to be a turning point. Everything is going to be different."

"Like the electric can opener," Richard said.

"At last you're catching on," Archer said. "Like the Whizza-Can, like the coloured telephone – pink telephones, green telephones, not just the gloomy old black telephone. And above all, television. The fifties will take us into a great new age."

"When are we going to have television?" Richard asked.

"In two years' time," Archer said. "They already have it in the States and we're going to have it here, too. And we have to be ready for it." He was getting up from his desk now and was going over to the window. "Come here," he said. "Have a look at this."

Richard looked down at Peel Street, where people were hurrying through the rain.

"It's a grey city, isn't it?" Archer said.

"Yes, I guess it is," said Richard, wondering whether London would also be grey or, with its fog, more brownish. Either way, it would be beautiful.

"But Archer Enterprises," Archer said, "is going to take this grey city – in fact this grey country – and bathe it in bright colours. Which is what we're going to do in the 1950s. How do you feel about that, Richard?"

"I feel good about that."

"Great," said Archer, glancing at this watch. "Now let's hurry. I'm taking you to lunch. Or should I say Mr. Parrish is taking us both to lunch. This lunch, my boy, may be a turning point in your career. And mine, too, for that matter."

Lunch was to be at Chez Ernest, on Drummond Street, around the corner from the Ritz. It was another resort of the upper crust, with crystal glasses and gleaming silverware. As soon as they sat down, Archer ordered two martinis.

"You're going to meet a financial genius," Archer said. "He's a visionary, probably as crazy as I am, but he's quiet. If he needs any noise to be made – and he will need it – we'll be the ones to make it. Which, of course, is public relations."

Parrish turned out to be a tall, aristocratic-looking man with a pencil-thin moustache and distinguished grey hair swept back on the sides. He wore a beautifully cut British suit and Richard noticed a diamond ring on his finger.

"So you're the writer," Parrish said, shaking Richard's hand.

"I guess so," said Richard, eliciting a frown from Archer, who had warned him never to be modest.

"He's a brilliant writer," Archer said.

"That's what we're going to need," Parrish said, as the waiter approached to suggest the rosette of baby lamb vert-pré and the glazed julienne of beetroot. This did not appeal to Parrish and there followed considerable palaver about the menu and the wine list. Finally the three of them made their decisions and ordered. Now it was time to get down to business.

"Tell me, Richard," Parrish said, "have you ever heard of Levittown?"

"No, can't say that I have," said Richard.

"Levittown is the eighth wonder of the world," Parrish said. "It's a planned community that has gone up overnight. Thousands of houses, all alike, built on a kind of assembly line, only twenty-five miles outside of New York City. People are lining up to buy those houses. It's the greatest real-estate venture of all times."

"It's the suburbs," Archer said. "The future is in the suburbs. Get out of the dull, grey city and move into the bright colours of the new suburbs. That's going to be the 1950s."

"Our development," Parrish said, "is going to be out on the lakeshore, half an hour from downtown Montreal. It's going to be called Futureville."

"And Archer Enterprises will make Futureville known to the world," Archer said.

"What we're going to need, as soon as possible," Parrish said, "is a handsome, full-colour brochure, to show to investors and to future home buyers. Would you be willing to write that brochure, Richard?"

"If you can do it fast," Archer said, "there will be a handsome bonus in it for you."

"I'm ready to start," Richard said. The word *bonus* did the trick. How big would it be? Could it possibly be enough to get him over to London very soon, without having to wait for Christmas? As Parrish and Archer raised their glasses in a toast to the Futureville brochure, Richard silently toasted Lili.

"We want you to go down to Levittown, to get ideas," Parrish said. "Is that all right?"

"Just fine," said Richard.

"You're going to see a miracle," Parrish said, reaching into his pocket. "Here's your ticket, young man. The plane leaves at seven-thirty tomorrow morning. Is that all right?"

"Just fine," said Richard.

The big DC4 Skymaster of Colonial Airlines took only an hour and forty-five minutes to get from Montreal to New York. For Richard they were very nervous minutes; this was his first time up in an airplane and he thought he was hearing subtle changes in the roar of the engines that suggested trouble. And just as worrisome was the fact that he was flying under false colours – as an imposter, a spy. At Archer's suggestion, he had phoned ahead to the Levittown office to introduce himself as a reporter for the Montreal *Gazette*, coming down to do a feature story on their great housing development. The builders of Levittown, New York, were about to start another such development in Pennsylvania, and there were rumours that they were considering one for somewhere in Canada. It wouldn't do for them to think that Richard was looking for trade secrets on behalf of a potential competitor, so he was coming in the guise of a newspaper reporter looking for a feature story.

The DC4 put down at LaGuardia Field at 9:15 in the morning. Jack Gilroy, the Levittown public-relations man, was waiting for him. "What you're going to see, Richard, is the American dream come true," Gilroy said, as they got into his car and headed out toward Long Island.

"It all started in the mighty brain-box of a man called William Levitt," Gilroy said. To Richard, this Gilroy, wearing a white summer suit and white Panama hat, sounded very much like a radio announcer. "What Bill Levitt had," Gilroy was saying, "was vision, with a capital *V*. You and I, Richard, would have looked out of our car two years ago and would have seen just a big farm, just a typical Long Island potato field. Fourteen hundred acres of it. But Bill Levitt saw more than just potatoes. He saw a town, a town that has become . . . Levittown!"

As they drove, Gilroy handed Richard a brown envelope. "There's some facts and figures in there," he said, "plus a picture of Bill Levitt. There was a fellow from the *Toronto Star* down here a few weeks ago and he did a terrific story. We have it framed and on the wall in the sales office. I trust you'll send us a clipping of your story, Richard, from the Montreal *Gazette*."

"Oh, definitely," said Richard. "I'll send you several clippings. I may be writing a series." As he said it, he wondered if he could possibly carry out this monstrous – and perhaps dangerous – deception if it were not for his desperate need for money, that bonus that would get him across to England.

"Bill Levitt saw a need," Gilroy was saying. "He saw young men coming home from the war, veterans who wanted two things – a wife, and a house where they could raise a family. The wife part was easy, but there were no houses. Nothing was built during the war and damn little was built during the Depression years before the war. So Bill Levitt decided to give them houses – and here they are."

Gilroy brought his car to a stop at the entrance to Levittown and Richard was confronted by an astonishing sight – row after row of small houses, identical small houses, each sitting on its front lawn. There was street after street of them, streets that seemed to stretch to the horizon. "You're looking at the first four thousand houses," Gilroy said. "They're all sold and occupied, and there's a waiting list for the new ones we're building right now. There's eventually going to be seventeen thousand houses by the time we've covered all our land."

The press release that Gilroy had given him told Richard

that these were Cape Cod houses, built on lots that measured sixty by one hundred feet. Each house, with four and a half rooms, occupied only 12 per cent of its lot; the rest was front lawn and backyard. A house would cost $7,995. Construction crews, working with Levitt's radical assembly-line methods, were building them at the rate of thirty-six houses a day.

"Now let's have a look inside," Gilroy said, driving down President Garfield Street and stopping in front of a house that looked exactly like all the others.

Gilroy rang the doorbell and a young woman in a frilly apron opened the door. "Howdy," she said. "Come on in, coffee's perking."

"This is Richard Lippman," Gilroy said. "He's a big-time writer from Canada. And this is Madge, a typical Levittown housewife."

"Pleased to meet you," said Madge. "This is the living room. Twelve by sixteen feet."

"That's the latest twelve-inch Philco television set," Gilroy said. "Comes with the house."

Madge led them into the kitchen, where Iris, the next-door neighbour, was setting out some apple pie to go with the coffee. Presumably Iris was also a typical Levittown house-wife, and Richard guessed he was witnessing a well-rehearsed routine, designed for journalists and other important visitors.

"General Electric stove, Bendix washer, Kelvinator refriger-ator," Gilroy said. "Comes with the house."

"Before we got this place," Madge said, "my husband and I were squeezed into a small room in my parents' apartment. Which was not good, at least not from Arthur's point of view."

"Terrible housing shortage," Gilroy said. "Terrible. People living on top of each other."

As he ate his pie and sipped his coffee, Richard listened to the two women and the public-relations man expounding on the wonders of Levittown – the schools, the churches, the swimming pools supplied by Bill Levitt, one swimming pool for every one thousand houses. But after a while Richard, who was taking notes, sensed a note of discord creeping into the conversation.

"Now that you're here, Jack," Iris was saying to Gilroy, "what about my fence? When do I get an answer?"

"I really don't know," Gilroy said. "Have you spoken to Sam?"

"Sam is useless," Iris said. She turned to Richard. "I've always dreamed of a white picket fence in front of my house. But we can't put one up. Mr. Levitt says no fences."

"It's in the purchase agreement," Madge said. "And in your backyard you can't dry your laundry unless it's on a special rack you get from Levitt. You can't put up a clothesline."

"Now, Madge, you wouldn't want your house to stand out like a sore thumb, would you?" Gilroy said. "I mean, what would the neighbours say?"

"Yeah, I guess you're right," Madge said, pouring more coffee from the percolator.

"One thing you can put in your story," Gilroy said to Richard, "is a quote from Bill Levitt. He said, God bless him, that a man who owns his own home will never become a Communist. He's got too much to keep him busy."

"I've been there," the man said. "It's a nightmare."

"Exactly," said Richard.

The man, a New Yorker, was sitting beside Richard in the five o'clock plane going back to Montreal. Richard, still pretending to be a journalist, had told the man about his visit to Levittown.

"A guy in my office bought one of those houses," the man said. "He invited me out for dinner. We drove out from the city in his car and when we got there and went into the house a woman came out from the kitchen and started to scream. People don't lock their doors in Levittown. We were in the wrong house. They all look the same, white houses with grey roofs, and they won't let you paint them another colour. All the streets look the same. It happens all the time, husbands who can't find their house, especially if they've stopped on the way home for a drink."

As the New Yorker reeled off more of the horrors of life in Levittown, Richard took notes industriously. All the new suburbs of the 1950s would be just as bad, the man said. The main food at their parties would consist of tiny cubes of orange-coloured cheese, with a toothpick stuck in each cube.

"Frozen TV dinners," Richard wrote in his notebook. "Tuna casseroles." Richard felt he had to keep writing as his talkative companion became more and more worked up. Of course Richard had no intention of using any of this material in the brochure he would write for Montreal's Futureville. But it was interesting and you never knew when it might be useful.

There was not the tiniest hint of negativism in the text he delivered to Archer a few days later. Instead, there were only quiet superlatives, often verging on the poetic. This brand-new town would be a sylvan paradise, with many a shady glade. The twitter of birds would mingle with the gleeful cries of children in the swimming pools. In the evening, Dad would relax in his lawn chair, puffing his pipe, content in the knowledge that at last he owned his own home, far from the dust and danger of the big city. Mother would be on her way to a meeting of the Home and School Association and young Johnny, in his Boy Scout uniform, would be saying, "Dad, we just learned how to tie three new knots."

Some of this was original with Richard, but much more was lifted wholesale from the Levittown brochure the PR man had given him. It was disgusting to have to produce this kind of stuff, but this was what they wanted, this was professionalism, this was what would get him his bonus.

In Archer's office, Archer, Parrish, and Richard were celebrating the birth of the Futureville brochure, which had just been delivered by the printer.

"To Futureville," Parrish said, lifting his glass in a toast. He had brought a bottle of Scotch – Johnny Walker Black Label, the expensive version, as opposed to the standard Red Label that Archer usually drank.

"This is beautiful," Archer said, riffling through the full-colour brochure, which featured not only Richard's prose but also drawings of the ranch-style houses that would be available, photos of refrigerators and washing machines, and maps of the landscaping, inspired by the gardens at Versailles.

"And here's your bonus, Richard, for doing it so fast," Archer said, handing him a fifty-dollar bill. Richard had never seen one of these powerful banknotes before.

"Now here's the next step," Parrish said, opening his briefcase and taking out some stock certificates. "They did a nice job, didn't they?" he said. He handed one of the newly printed certificates to Archer and one to Richard, to examine.

They were engraved with the same sort of intricate, old-fashioned artistry as the fifty-dollar bill. Across the top of the certificates, in ornate lettering, were the words FUTUREVILLE INC. Under this, there was an engraving of a ranch-style house, with children playing on the front lawn. Under this was the statement "Authorized Capital Stock $1,000,000. Shares $100 each."

"The faster the investors start coming in, the faster we can start construction," Parrish said. "So we're going to be giving our salesmen a 20 per cent commission."

"I think I could place some of those," Archer said.

"By all means," Parrish said. "And how about you, Richard? All those nightclub owners you met. All potential investors, aren't they?"

"I don't know," Richard said. "I'd have to think about it." It was all too weird. He had never in his life sold anything.

"Just show them the brochure and the financial prospectus, and they'll see that there's a big profit to be made," Parrish said. "And remember, Richard, for every hundred-dollar share you sell you get twenty dollars cash."

As Parrish refilled their glasses with his Johnny Walker Black Label, Richard imagined the "lush, orgiastic richness" of Les Ambassadeurs, which the guidebook said was London's fanciest nightclub. It cost you five guineas just to get in. He would dance there with Lili, holding her tight, with the music slow.

"Why not?" Richard said, sipping his Scotch and picking up one of the stock certificates. "Why don't I give it a try?"

He would give it a try with Aunt Harriet, who was a wealthy widow. He could never remember whether it was Aunt Harriet who considered him handsome or whether it was Aunt Evelyn. On the infrequent occasions when he saw them, usually at one of his mother's Sunday luncheons, they would debate the matter at length, to his great embarrassment. One of the aunts would exclaim that Richard was becoming so handsome, while the other would maintain that he was extremely good-looking, but not handsome. Why? Because handsome men were not to be trusted.

Harriet was delighted when he phoned and insisted that he come to tea at her apartment. And while he sipped his tea and ate two of her homemade scones, with blueberry jam, she pored over the Futureville brochure, seeming to read every word.

"And you wrote this?" she asked.

"Yes," he said.

"It's very eloquent," she said. "I want to get in on the ground floor. What do I get for a thousand dollars?"

"Ten shares," Richard said, taking a stock certificate from his briefcase, inscribing the word *ten* on it, and handing it to her.

"I'll go get my chequebook," Aunt Harriet said. "Have another scone. And try the raspberry-rhubarb, it's better than the blueberry."

Three days later Uncle Morty phoned him. "I hear you sold your Aunt Harriet some interesting shares."

"That's right," said Richard.

"Maybe you can sell me some," Morty said.

"I'd love to," Richard said.

"Then why don't you come round and see me tonight," Morty said. "At the casino."

"Uh, just where is the casino?" Richard said.

"Just tell the taxi driver you want to go to the White House in Côte Saint Luke," Morty said. "He'll know where it is. My doorman will pay the taxi."

If Aunt Harriet could buy ten shares, Uncle Morty should be able to buy one hundred. Then Richard wouldn't have to wait until Christmas to have enough money to go to London; he'd have enough to go next week. He wouldn't wait for the *Île de France* from New York; there were ships leaving from Montreal all the time – the *Empress of Britain*, the *Ascania*, and others. He saw himself now with Lili in one of those big black London taxis. They had been dancing cheek-to-cheek at Les Ambassadeurs and now they were on their way to Lili's apartment – or flat, as they called it in England – for a nightcap.

Yes, the *Ascania* or the *Empress of Britain*. He would take his portable typewriter with him and write poems for her all the way across the Atlantic.

"Roulette, baccarat, blackjack, barbotte – you name it, we've got it," Uncle Morty said. He was showing Richard around his casino. "And if you're hungry, we've got a filet mignon for you in the dining room, free of charge. Also a Scotch and soda. I know your mother never wanted you to see this place, but I figure you're old enough now to know what goes on in the world."

The activity in the big rooms was brisk, with croupiers in tuxedos scooping up chips at the roulette tables and dealers dealing cards swiftly at the blackjack tables. The patrons of this highly illegal establishment were, as Uncle Morty put it, "the *crème de la crème*." "You see that old guy over there," Uncle Morty said, "that's Judge Montpetit. And that's Senator Verrall."

"Cute kids, aren't they?" Morty said, nodding to a waitress and a cigarette girl, both dressed as French maids, who were bringing free drinks and free smokes to the patrons. Morty introduced Richard to several of these gamblers, including Henry Holland, president of National Linoleum, and Madame Menard, an elegant woman smoking through a long ivory cigarette holder. As she moved away, toward a roulette table, Morty whispered to Richard, "She's Premier Duplessis' mistress."

"And the police never raid the place?" Richard asked.

"Never," said Morty. "There's only one policeman for the whole village of Côte Saint Luke, and we look after him very nicely. He's more interested in kids stealing melons from the farms." The White House was surrounded by farms and it too was once a farmhouse, an old building in the classic Quebec style that had been completely refurbished, with a large addition at the back.

"Now let's go and talk business," Uncle Morty said, leading Richard into his upstairs office, where the walls were decorated with framed photos of boxers, wrestlers, hockey players, jockeys, and racehorses. All the photos were signed and dedicated to Morty.

"Futureville, eh?" said Morty. "Your Aunt Harriet bought ten shares?"

"That's right," said Richard. "There's more available if you're interested."

"I'm very interested," said Morty. From his desk he picked up the familiar green stock certificate. "This is Harriet's," Morty said. "I want you to take it back to those guys downtown and get her money back."

"Huh?"

"This is a fraud," Morty said. "Those guys are crooks, or at least Parrish is."

"I can't believe that," Richard said, his spirits sinking. "They're very serious. Look at this." He took the brochure from his jacket pocket and handed it to Morty, who threw it into his wastepaper basket.

"I've seen it," said Morty. "It's a work of art."

"Mr. Parrish has an option on a thousand acres of farmland out in Baie d'Urfé," Richard protested. "That's where Futureville will arise."

"Mr. Parrish has an option on a train ticket to Chicago, or somewhere like that," Morty said. "As soon as he collects his bundle, which guys like you will supply." He picked up the phone on his desk and said, "Alice, will you ask Mr. Galipeau to step in for a minute?"

While they were waiting for this man, whoever he was, Richard got up nervously and pretended to study a large photo on the wall, a group photo of a hockey team.

"The Montreal Maroons," Morty said. "They cost me a lot of money, but they were a beautiful team."

When Galipeau came in – a wiry little man in a salt-and-pepper suit – Morty introduced him to Richard and said, "What can you tell us, Pierre, about Albert Parrish?"

"Albert Parrish," Galipeau said, "was known as Alan Palmer

when he did two years in jail in Toronto, for fraud. At this very moment they are looking for him in Halifax, where they think his name is Arthur Patterson."

"Mr. Galipeau is a private investigator," Morty said. "He does various things for us. He knows everything, Richard. For instance, Pierre, can you tell us what was the last time Richard here visited Lili L'Amour in her room in the LaSalle Hotel?"

Galipeau consulted his small black notebook. "Five p.m.," he said. "September 11, 1948. That was the day Miss L'Amour left for New York in Sir Charles Hammond's private railway car."

"Thank you, Pierre," Uncle Morty said. "And you're watching the fat guy, eh?"

"Yes, I am watching," the detective said, and he left the room.

"The fat guy is a new client," Morty said. "He's winning too much at blackjack. We think he might be a card counter." Morty picked up the Futureville stock certificate and held it up by its edge, with two fingers, as though it were dirty, or infected. He sniffed at it and grimaced, as though it were emitting a bad odour. "Now you'll take this back to those crooks first thing tomorrow morning, eh?" He handed the certificate to Richard. "I told Harriet she'd have her money by lunchtime."

This was too painful. Richard had to hit back, even if only with a joke. "What if this is slightly illegal?" he said, waving the stock certificate. "All this is illegal too, isn't it?" He gestured out at the casino, at all the patrons being separated from their money. But Uncle Morty wasn't amused.

"Look, Sonny-boy," he said, "the difference between you and me is that I'm an adult and I know what I'm doing. And you're still a boy, a boy with lots to learn."

"Well, I guess I'll be running along," said Richard, badly wounded.

"Yeah, we'll get you a taxi," said Morty.

"By the way," Richard said, at the door, "is Archer a crook too, or just Parrish?"

"I think it's just Parrish," Morty said. "When I got that job for you I told you Archer was one of the great bullshit artists, and you could learn a lot from him. But I never said he had any brains, did I?"

"I guess this will finish me in the public-relations business, eh?" Richard said.

"Of course," said Uncle Morty. "But look at it this way: you've had the experience and now you can move on to other things."

Yes, but he would not be moving on to London as soon as he had hoped.

"Sonny-boy." The ugly phrase rang in his ears and kept him awake half the night. Uncle Morty had called him "Sonny-boy." When it came to what was really important in life – business, money, etcetera – Richard was still a boy, not yet a man. He was now fully eighteen years old, and had been since February, but he was still a boy.

During this landmark summer he had been involved with people more than twice his age and had never felt out of place. But in the eyes of those people, he now realized, he had obviously been just a boy, a precocious boy but still just a boy. That's the way they had sized him up in places like Levittown, in the nightclubs, at the speedathon. And, worst of all, that's the way Lili saw him – just a boy. This thought, in his restless bed at three in the morning, was the most agonizing thought of all – that for Lili he was just a boy.

22

Awake at dawn, after a few hours of troubled sleep, Richard finally started grappling with the problem. Just how would he confront Archer and Parrish and get Aunt Harriet's money back?

Several scenes formed themselves in his mind. Perhaps he would invite them out to a lavish lunch and would bring the matter up casually, a throwaway line, *en passant*. During the lamb chops, after a conversation during which he would extol the future greatness of Futureville, Richard would casually say, "By the way, seeing you two gents are thieves, would you mind forking over my auntie's thousand dollars? If you do, I'll give you this worthless piece of paper, which you can use to screw somebody else." And he would take the stock certificate from his pocket.

Idiot.

No, he would have to creep apologetically into Archer's office and tell him that poor Aunt Harriet, in her dotage, had been listening to some fraudulent financial expert who had told her that Futureville was too speculative a venture for her to risk her life's savings on. "I tried to reassure her," Richard would say, "but she wouldn't listen."

Rehearsing his lines in the streetcar going downtown, a brilliant idea came to him in a flash. Rather than just standing there, waiting to be fired by Archer Enterprises, he would say that he personally believed deeply in Futureville and was anxious to get going again, selling shares far and wide. The nightclub owners he had met would surely be anxious to invest.

But if he started selling these smelly stock certificates, would he be as much of a criminal as Archer and Parrish? Maybe not. It was Uncle Morty's word against that of Theodore Archer's. What if Uncle Morty was having a feud with Archer and this was his way of taking a whack at him? That could be. Futureville might be a good, legitimate investment. But if it wasn't, Richard wouldn't be all that much of a thief, would he? All he would have to do was sell thirty shares to get six hundred dollars as his commission. That would be more than enough to buy a third-class return ticket on the SS *Ascania*, which was sailing from Montreal on Saturday. And there would be plenty left over to buy a lot of wining, dining, and dancing – cheek-to-cheek – in London.

"He's very busy," Shirley said when Richard asked to be shown into Archer's office. "He doesn't want to be interrupted."

"I know he'll want to see me," Richard said. "What's making him so busy?"

"He's with Mr. Parrish," Shirley said. "They're getting ready for the lunch."

"What lunch?" Richard said.

"Didn't you know?" Shirley said. "Lunch in the Champlain Room. *Paté de foie gras* for twenty important investors."

"Please," said Richard. "He really wants to see me."

Reluctantly Shirley opened the door to Archer's office and waved him in. "The boy genius," she announced, closing the door behind him.

Archer and Parrish were standing at Archer's desk, examining a scale model of a split-level suburban house. "We've got to draw attention to this carport," Parrish was saying, pointing at the side of the model.

"That's called a carport?" Archer asked.

"Yes," said Parrish, "it's called a carport. And this here is a breezeway. Remember, Teddy, we're going into the 1950s. We don't talk about siding, we talk about cladding. We don't talk about windows, we talk about fenestration treatment."

Archer and Parrish had looked up to see Richard come in, but they were paying no attention to him.

"Don't forget to tell them that there'll be a helicopter landing pad right next to the clubhouse," Parrish was saying. "You'll be able to get to the hospital in a jiffy."

This, Richard thought, was the moment for him to begin his speech. "That's a really beautiful model," he said, pointing to the little house on Archer's desk.

Archer looked up at Richard, picked up an envelope from his desk, and handed it to him. "Here's your aunt's money," he said. "Ten one-hundred-dollar bills. Exactly as your stupid Uncle Morty requested."

"You – you spoke to my uncle?" Richard said, almost stammering in his nervousness.

"Of course," said Archer. "He phoned me. He didn't think you'd have the guts to tell Mr. Parrish and me that we're just a couple of crooks."

"Never send a boy on a man's errand," Parrish said.

Archer flipped the switch on the intercom on his desk, to speak to the receptionist. "Shirley," he said, "Mr. Lippman will be leaving our employ immediately. Will you escort him to the writer's dungeon and watch while he collects any personal items from the desk? And don't let him throw the typewriter out the window or make any other childish gesture."

"Will do," came Shirley's voice.

"And so goodbye and good luck, young fellow," Archer said.

Richard thought he should say something at this point, but he could think of nothing. Like a condemned man, contemptuous of the hangman, he would make no final statement.

"Whenever I hire a new employee," Archer said to Parrish, "I always tell them that they will eventually take advantage of my good nature. I always hope I'll be proven wrong, but so far I never have been."

"You're too soft, Teddy," Parrish said.

"We're both of us too soft, Albert," Archer said.

The door opened to reveal Shirley standing there with an empty cardboard box for Richard's belongings. "Okay," she said to Richard. "Let's go."

The situation was hopeless, but not entirely without hope. It called for desperate measures. Now more than ever he absolutely had to get across that ocean to see Lili. And there still might be a way.

Back home now, sitting in his room, on the edge of the bed, he opened the envelope that contained Aunt Harriet's money, ten one-hundred-dollar bills. He counted them slowly. Five of these beauties was all he needed.

Seeing that Aunt Harriet was the aunt who considered him very good-looking, as opposed to being handsome – and you could never trust a handsome man – she would listen to his problem and would trust him. He would give her five hundred dollars and ask her if he could please borrow the other five hundred. It wasn't for himself, it was for his friend Stanley, who was in terrible trouble. Foolish Stanley had been betting on the horses and had lost five hundred, which he didn't have. If he didn't pay up by Saturday, the bookie's enforcers might break his kneecaps. Stanley would be able to pay back Richard, and thus Aunt Harriet, in six weeks' time, with money from a source that Richard had not yet invented. But he knew he could figure that out by the time he visited Aunt Harriet at noon. He was now fully confident in his ability to tell lies smoothly. Lies were coming more easily all the time. It was nothing to be proud of, but it was extremely useful.

He put the money away quickly when his mother knocked on the door, as he was training her to do, and came in with his mail. "It's got a funny stamp on it," she said, sniffing the envelope, "but it's the same perfume. What kind of a female uses perfume like this?"

"I told you, she's a striptease queen," Richard said.

"Can't you ever be serious," his mother said. "Is she at least a nice girl?"

"She's very nice," said Richard, snatching the envelope from her.

The stamp was indeed a funny one: instead of the reassuring picture of King George VI it bore a portrait of a strange man in a black hat, with a moustache. The writing on the stamp was in Arabic.

The news in the letter was devastating.

Shepheard's Hotel
Cairo, Egypt
August 10, 1949.

Dear Richard,

What am I doing in Egypt? Well, first let me tell you my big news. I am married! Yes, married! My husband is Sir Geoffrey Maynard.

Geoff and I met at one of those great weekend parties, this one at the estate of the Marquess of Milford Haven. I was invited to give one my recitals and this time I was going to interprit your wonderful poem about the execution of Anne Boleyn. (Oh thank you so much for that, Richard!) The Marquess asked Geoff to read the poem, while I danced.

Geoff has a beautiful voice, as he was involved in amateur theatricals when he was at Oxford. The lords and ladies in the audience, and the distinguished commoners, were deeply moved. Especially by that great bit when Anne's ghost defiantly says, "My head? I need it not. From the basket, where it rests, it still can curse the King."

A few days later, in London, Sir Geoffrey Maynard came to see me at Professor Szombathely's studio, where, as you will remember, I teach Modern Dance. Geoff is a widower and he brought with him his twin daughters, Miranda and Elspeth, 13 years old. He thinks, correctly, that they are becoming tomboys, interested only in playing field hockey. He wanted me to teach them how to move in a feminine way. I agreed to do this, even though the girls were not too enthusiastic. But being British they do as they are told.

During the next few weeks, Geoff came around to the studio quite often, to see what progress we were making. Then I went out to dinner with him, etcetera, etcetera. It didn't take us too long to realize that we were desperitely in love. We were married two weeks ago in a little country church.

Now why are we in Egypt? Well, Sir Geoff is a high official in the Colonial Office, in London, from where they run the British Empire. And now he has been appointed Governor of Hong Kong. And so we are on our way to Hong Kong, us newlyweds plus Miranda and Elspeth, plus Robert Rowley, Sir Geoff's secretary. Robert refers to me as Lady Lili, so I guess I am officially Lady Lili. But please continue to call me just Lili.

We are flying to Hong Kong in one of those big BOAC flying boats. We fly by day and in the evening we land (is that the right word?) on a lake or a river or in a bay. The passengers disembark on a local boat and spend the night in a hotel, always a luxurious hotel, and in the morning we take off on the next lap. That way it takes only eight days to get from England to Hong Kong, which is a lot better than five weeks on a ship. Since London we have stopped in Marseilles and in Sicily. Now Cairo. Then Basra, then Karachi, then Calcutta, then Rangoon and then Hong Kong, which will be home for at least four years.

Actually we will spend three days here in Cairo and catch the next ongoing plane on Friday. Geoff has some business to do with the British ambasador here, and we want to visit the piramids. At every stop, we usually have dinner with some high local officials, which can be quite stuffy. But I am very anxious to meet this ambassador tonight. Can I tell you a secret? Promise not to tell anybody? Geoff tells me that the ambassador gets his jollies by dressing up like an Eton schoolboy and being whipped on his bare bottom by a girl dressed (or partly dressed) like a schoolmistress. Isn't the British Empire wonderful?

I am in charge of the girls, Miranda and Elspeth, and believe me they are quite a handful. They disappeared yesterday afternoon and I finally found them behind the hotel where some boys from the kitchen were teaching them how to speak Arabic – and God knows what else. Can you picture me as the cruel stepmother?

When we get to Hong Kong I will have to learn how to run the Governor's mansion, which is huge. I will arrange receptions and will supervise the servants, of which there are a great many.

Oh, Richard, this is all so wonderful, especially as I am in love. Are you by chance in love too? You should be by now, with one of those cute college girls wearing their cute tam-o'-shanters.

And to think that none of these wonderful things would have happened to me if you hadn't written that Anne Boleyn poem and Sir Geoffrey Maynard hadn't read it at my recital. How can I ever repay you? Perhaps some day you'll come out to Hong Kong on a visit and we will put you up in the best guest room in the Governor's mansion. You will have a wonderful time. You'll like Geoff, who is a fine man with a great sense of humour. And Miranda and Elspeth can be a lot of fun too.

So do think about it.

Love
Lili

This horrific letter arrived the day before the beginning of lectures at McGill. After the Futureville debacle, Richard had promised himself that he would try to do something during his second year at university that he had neglected to do during his first year: he would try to learn something. And now, this bombshell . . . Could he now possibly concentrate on the Theory of Something in Economics 1? Would there ever be room in his head for anything beside the cruelty and treachery of Lady Lili, who would soon disappear into a mansion in China?

23

Richard found a quiet table, sat down, and ordered a pint of beer. He was ten minutes early, so he would have to wait for Stanley and Martin. The three friends had seen almost nothing of each other all summer and now, with lectures starting at McGill, they had arranged to meet and catch up on what they had been doing during the past few months.

Arranging this meeting on the phone, Martin had suggested that they go to their old high-school haunt, Gagnon's Ice Cream Parlour, but the others said that would be far too juvenile. No, they would meet here, at Café André, McGill's beer dispensary, just across the street from the campus. In Gagnon's you would listen to things like Benny Goodman's "Flat Foot Floogie," but here your dime in the highbrow jukebox could elicit "Cavaliera Rusticana."

As he took his first sip of beer, Richard tried to get his mind off Lady Lili, probably settled in at the governor's mansion by now. Unfolding his copy of the *McGill Daily*, he tried to interest himself in the schedule of upcoming events. But in his low mood they all seemed so boring, things like the torchlight parade from Dominion Square up to Molson Stadium, where the moronic marchers would hold a football rally, complete with clowns and cheerleaders, for God's sake.

Turning the page in the *Daily*, he came on a story about the McGill Beautiful Baby Contest. Across the top of the page were photos of eight beautiful babies, all the offspring of fourth-year students living with their wives up in the Peterson Residence. These senior students were all army, navy, or air-force veterans, back from the war in 1945 and now getting their education late in life. With their young wives they were creating such a popping-out of babies that the Peterson Residence was becoming known as Fertility Hall, or the Rabbit Warren. Students were invited to come over to the residence and vote for the most beautiful baby. Would it be cute little Caroline? Or adorable Andy? Or cuddly little Cathy?

Would Richard ever be a father, he wondered, with beautiful babies like these crawling around at his feet? It was a thought that had never before entered his mind. He'd never had much experience with children, and on the few occasions when he encountered them they seemed to be more of a nuisance than anything else. But surely procreation – one's personal contribution to the survival of the human race – was the essence of maturity and responsibility. And shouldn't maturity be the goal at this point in Sonny-boy's life? Yes, maturity – no matter how boring it was, how unpoetic.

So if he could ever break free from his commitment to Lili, if he could ever find himself a nice, ordinary wife, he could start procreating with her. In that event, of course, he would have to throw away his supply of condoms. And actually that might be quite nice: he'd heard it said that once you experienced the joy of doing it bareback, you never again wanted to be rubberized. And that, surely, was the reason for the existence of large families.

He was pondering this new insight when Stanley and Martin came in. The three of them shook hands and sat down.

"Too bad Harold can't be here," Richard said.

"Anybody heard from Harold?" Stanley asked, but nobody had.

"When they go to Toronto it's like they drop off the face of the earth," Martin said.

They all ordered some beer and settled in to review the summer's activities.

"Well, if you want me to start, it was a great summer for me," Stanley said. "Sophia and I went over to Yugoslavia to help build the Youth Railroad. It was a wonderful experience. Brigades of socialist youth from all over – England, Italy, Austria, Romania, Sweden, everywhere. We Canadians called ourselves the Beaver Brigade." Richard avoided catching Martin's eye. Stanley was being very serious.

Yugoslavia had been devastated by the war. The railroad, which would run 150 miles from Sarajevo to Samac, would help a very poor part of the country export coal and minerals. The young workers didn't have any fancy equipment so they worked with picks and shovels and wheelbarrows.

"When we built an embankment on the approach to a bridge, we tamped down the earth with our bare hands," Stanley said. "We sang Serbian partisan songs while we worked and at night, in the camp, we danced the *kola*. We slept in rough bunkhouses, which we helped build. We painted murals of Marshal Tito on the outside of the bunkhouses, and slogans from the Five-Year Plan."

Stanley showed them photos he had taken, with Sophia prominent in most of them – Sophia with a shovel, Sophia with a wheelbarrow, Sophia at a stove, frying something. And at a lake, Sophia sensational in a bathing suit. It was clear to

Richard that the problem the boys used to discuss in the ice-cream parlour a year ago – sexual starvation – no longer tormented Stanley, who today looked skinnier and scrawnier than ever.

"So what are your plans now?" Martin asked.

"I've signed up for a lot of economics and political science," Stanley said. "But I don't know if I'll be able to last three more years at McGill. Basically it's all irrelevant. The best Marxist study groups are off-campus. And my ultimate goal is to get involved in the labour movement. As an organizer, probably. So I don't know. We'll see."

"Well, I'm going to be here for a lot more years," Martin said. "It's going to be medicine for me, specializing in psychiatry."

"I thought you were going to be a lawyer," Richard said.

"That's all changed," Martin said. "Marjorie and I have been spending a lot of time reading the works of Sigmund Freud. And that has really opened my eyes. Also, Marjorie's father is a psychoanalyst in New York, and he has a summer house in East Hampton. So we spent the month of July on the beach out there. And it was incredible. Every weekend, analysts would come out from New York and there were terrific dinner parties and gabfests. Jungians fighting with Freudians, one crazy Romanian spouting Wilhelm Reich and orgone energy, Otto Rank's theories, Melanie Klein, everything. Marjorie and I took it all in, and Marjorie even butted in on some of the discussions."

"Did you ever run into a psychiatrist called Dr. Gregory Zilboorg?" Richard said.

"Did I ever!" said Martin. "A fantastic man. He's become famous for treating a certain striptease dancer, helping her overcome her pathological shyness. Yes, my friends, I learned a lot out there in East Hampton."

"Like what?" Stanley asked.

"Well, let me give you an example you might be able to understand," Martin said. "You remember last year, we were talking in Gagnon's. I told you how I was parked in my father's car, up at the Summit, with that girl. I told you how I achieved bare tit, but she wouldn't let me into her Garden of Eden. You remember that?"

"Vividly," said Richard.

"Of course those were our childish terms for the breast and the vagina," Martin said. "But do you know what my motive really was, for what I was doing up in that car?"

"You were trying to get laid," Stanley said.

"There you go," Martin said. "For you, the surface is everything. The workings of the unconscious mind are beyond your understanding. If I told you I was trying to work out some Oedipal problems, would you know what I was talking about? To start with, let me tell you what Otto Rank says about precopulatory fantasies."

"Please don't," said Stanley, glancing at his watch. "How about you, Richard?" he said. "What did you do all summer?"

"Well, I made a few dollars," Richard said. "But it wasn't anything interesting. Just a joe job in an office."

While the others had been speaking about their summer's achievements, Richard had decided not to tell them that during the past few months he had been acknowledged as the creator of Freckles, the Girl Next Door; that he had starred in the gossip columns as the lover of a legendary striptease dancer; that he had brought success to the speedathon; that he had been instrumental in keeping Norma, the speedathon girl, from being frozen in 1,200 pounds of ice; that he had wined and dined lavishly at every nightclub in Montreal; that he had written most of the contents of a cheesy magazine called *Nightlife*; that he had flown down to Levittown and back; that he had written a brochure that was the basis for a massive stock fraud; that he had almost become a con man himself; that he had considered robbing his old aunt. He had done all this without his parents being aware of any of it. As far as they were concerned, he'd had a simple office job that sometimes kept him working at night.

Yes, while Martin and Stanley had been preparing for careers that would benefit the human race, Richard Lippman had been capitalizing on his talent for lies and deception.

"Sorry that I don't have anything very interesting to report," he now said to his two friends. "But maybe one thing. I got started a while back on a big rewrite of the Ten Commandments. Not just to tell people what they have to do and what they must not do, but to explain – clearly – just why it's in their interest to act that way. Also, I'm introducing two new commandments, to round it out to an even dozen."

After Richard finished this little speech, Stanley and Martin simply sat looking at him without expression. If these two ever had a sense of humour, Karl Marx and Sigmund Freud had taken it away from them.

"Well, I guess I'll be running along," Stanley said. "I'm already late for a meeting. Sophia and I would like you to come to one of our meetings, Richard, or a study group. Give it another try. It might do you a lot of good."

"I'll think about it," Richard said, but of course he wouldn't. What he would surely think about – brood about – was that each of his friends now seemed to have a stable relationship with a woman and each of them knew where he was going in life. But for Richard, there was no woman and no career in sight.

"You're not your old self, Richard," Martin said, when Stanley departed. "You don't look happy."

"I'm fine," Richard said. "Just fine."

"I'll be frank with you," Martin said. "That Ten Commandments thing is worrisome. Taking refuge in religion may not be the answer. And there's the fact that you didn't really do anything all summer. What I'm driving at, Richard, is that you may need help. I can put you in touch with a very good analyst."

"Thanks," Richard said. "I'll think about it." And he would. Perhaps some Freudian probing could free his mind from the clutches of Lady Lili.

WOE

Associate Professor Jock Ramsay wrote the word on the blackboard in large capital letters. Then he turned to peer out at the class in one of his most effective theatrical poses, gazing at the second-year students with a blank, distracted expression on his handsome face, as though poetry were transporting him elsewhere, to empyrean heights. The students waited patiently, studying the chalk stains on his flowing black gown. Professor Jock's Woe lecture was as famous as his first-year Byron lecture; it was perhaps not quite as popular with the boys, because it didn't deal with sex, but it was still a favourite with the girls, because it dealt with tragic love.

Finally Jock snapped out of his trance and uttered the pivotal line: "'I sought fit words to paint the blackest face of woe.'" He was, of course, quoting Sir Philip Sidney, the greatest sufferer among all the poets who wrote about their suffering. And this lecture was about the joy of poetry that expressed misery.

Richard listened attentively. The man was right. Richard's "Ode to Zero," written in the gloom that followed Lili's departure to New York in Sir Charles Hammond's private railway car, was surely his most effective poem. It was the one that had moved Sophia Bruce to tears and might have led into her bed, if it hadn't been for those damn Communists.

Professor Jock was continuing to quote: "'And yet she hears, yet I no pity find / But more I cry, less grace she doth impart.'"

259

Sir Philip Sidney, the professor explained, was hopelessly in love with Lady Penelope Devereux, who was married to another and had no time for Sir Philip, who could only deal with the situation by writing poetry about the lady's beauty, her perfection in all things, and her cruelty – and the agony of his love. He wrote a cycle of 108 sonnets on these subjects and eleven songs, a work entitled *Astrophel and Stella*, one of the great classics of English literature, by a poet who, in his time, was considered to be greater than Shakespeare.

"Of course Astrophel was Philip Sidney," Jock said, "and Stella was Penelope Devereux. Everybody knew that and felt sorry for him, especially after he died on the battlefield in 1586. And especially when they learned that as he lay dying, Sir Philip, a knight, passed his cup to a humble, wounded soldier, saying, 'Thy necessity is yet greater than mine.'"

As he listened to this, an idea started forming in Richard's mind. There was no doubt that Astrophel was Richard Lippman and Stella was Lili L'Amour.

That night, at his desk at home, Richard stared at his holy relic, the pasty that once adorned Lili's left breast. It seemed so long ago that she had given it to him in her dressing room, after he had seen her undress for the first time, as Marie Antoinette, on the stage of the blessed Gayety Theatre.

Richard had enshrined the pasty in a little silver frame that stood on his desk. When his mother had first seen it, she wanted to know what it was.

"I wish I could tell you, Ma," he had said. "But I can't."

"What do you mean, you can't?" Mrs. Lippman said.

"It's a secret society at McGill," he said. "We're not allowed to talk about it. All I can say is that it's a talisman and it exudes a powerful magic."

"Richard, you're becoming more of a mystery to me every

day," his mother had said, picking up the framed pasty to have another look at it.

Now, turning to Sir Philip Sidney in his poetry anthology, Richard realized that what he felt about Lili had been perfectly expressed to Stella by Astrophel: "Fair eyes, sweet lips, dear heart, that foolish I / Could hope by Cupid's help on you to prey."

Why had Philip Sidney written all those sonnets? He made his motive quite clear in the very first lines of his first sonnet:

Loving in truth, and fain in verse my love to show,
That she (dear She) might take some pleasure of my pain:
Pleasure might cause her read, reading might make her know,
Knowledge might pity win, and pity grace obtain.

Yes, that was it. Grabbing his legal-size yellow pad and two pencils, he ran down the stairs to the kitchen, to brew himself a cup of Ovaltine, the nectar his muse demanded. If Sidney wrote 108 sonnets to Penelope, Lippman would write 112 to Lili; if Sidney wrote eleven songs for Penelope, Lippman would write fifteen songs for Lili.

How long would this take? A year? Two years? And how many lectures would he find himself missing at McGill? What if he became so enveloped in this task that he failed his second year? Did that matter? Probably not, especially as he still had no idea of what kind of career he might try to follow, what – besides public relations – might be open to a fellow whose main talent was for falsehood and deception. Of course it could be politics, or business, but Richard shuddered at the thought of those grubby occupations.

Yes, he would write those 112 sonnets. It was obvious that Sir Philip's muse was still going strong four centuries later, and that she had now become Richard's muse. Her instructions to the noble knight of old were clear in that first sonnet, and they were obviously also aimed at this hesitant, bumbling student, across the ocean in Montreal in 1949. As Sir Philip had put it: "Thus . . . helpless in my throes, / Biting my truant pen, beating myself for spite – / 'Fool,' said my Muse to me, 'look in thy heart and write.'"

Would Lady Lili read those sonnets and songs Richard was going to write? Perhaps. Would they be enough to make her leave her husband and rush into Richard's arms? Probably not. But he would have expressed his misery and perhaps he would have purged it. Like Sir Philip Sidney he would have failed to win fair lady and would have had to settle for something less – immortality as a poet. Yes, Richard would write it. And only after he had written it would he be set free, able to turn his attention to that irritating question his father used to ask him: "What, if anything, do you plan to do with your life?"

His Ovaltine was bubbling on the stove. He poured it into a cup, brought the cup to the table, and sat down. He picked up one of his pencils and held it over his yellow legal-size pad, waiting for the idea that would give him his first word.

But before the word came to him, the telephone rang in the hall. His mother answered it and came into the kitchen. "It's for you," she said. "It's a female. A new one, I think."

ACKNOWLEDGEMENTS

Thanks to Joseph Blumer and Gerald Feil for help with research – W.W.

The lyrics on pages 82 and 83 are from "Moonlight Cocktail" from *A Night In Casablanca*. Lyrics by Kim Gannon; Music by Lucky Roberts. ©1941, 1942 (Renewed) by Jewel Music Publishing Co., Inc. (ASCAP) and Rytvoc, Inc. International Copyright Secured. All Rights Reserved. Used by permission.

The lyrics on page 133 are from "That Old Black Magic" from the Paramount Picture *Star Spangled Rhythm*. Words by Johnny Mercer; Music by Harold Arlen. © 1942 (Renewed 1969) by Famous Music Corporation. International Copyright Secured. All Rights Reserved.

The lyrics on page 133 are from "Taking A Chance On Love" by Vernon Duke, Jon Latouche, and Ted Fetter. ©1940 (Renewed 1968) EMI Miller Catalog Inc. All Rights Controlled by EMI Miller Catalog Inc. (Publishing) and Warner Bros. Publications U.S. Inc. (Print). All Rights Reserved. Used by permission Warner Bros. Publications U.S. Inc., Miami, Fl. 33014.

The lyrics on pages 135 and 136 are from "The Nearness Of You" from the Paramount Picture *Romance In The Dark*. Words by Ned Washington; Music by Hoagy Carmichael. © 1937, 1940 (Renewed 1964, 1967) by Famous Music Corporation. International Copyright Secured. All Rights Reserved.

THE QUOTABLE ROBERTSON DAVIES: The Wit and Wisdom of the Master *selected by* James Channing Shaw
More than eight hundred quotable aphorisms, opinions, and general advice for living selected from all of Davies' works. A hypnotic little book.
Non-fiction, 5¼ × 7, 176 pages, hardcover

ALICE MUNRO: Writing Her Lives. A Biography *by* Robert Thacker
The literary biography about one of the world's great authors, which shows how her life and her stories intertwine.
Non-fiction, 6½ × 9⅜, 456 pages plus photographs, hardcover

MITCHELL: The Life of W.O. Mitchell, The Years of Fame 1948–1998 *by* Barbara and Ormond Mitchell
From *Who Has Seen the Wind* on through *Jake and the Kid* and beyond, this is a fine biography of Canada's wildest – and best-loved – literary figure. *Non-fiction, 6½ × 9⅜, 420 pages plus photographs, hardcover*

TO EVERY THING THERE IS A SEASON: A Cape Breton Christmas Story *by* Alistair MacLeod, with illustrations *by* Peter Rankin
A "winsome tale of Yuletide past," almost every page of this beautiful little book is enriched by a perfect illustration, making this touching story of a farm family waiting for Christmas into a classic for every home.
Toronto Star   *Fiction, illustrations, 4⅝ × 7¼, 48 pages, hardcover*

RUNAWAY *by* Alice Munro
The 2004 Giller Prize-winning collection of short stories by "the best fiction writer now working in North America.... Runaway is a marvel."
The New York Times Book Review   *Fiction, 6 × 9, 352 pages, hardcover*

HERE BE DRAGONS: Telling Tales of People, Passion and Power *by* Peter C. Newman
The number one bestseller by the man whose books on politics, business, and history have sold two million copies, *Here Be Dragons* tells the story of his own life, from child fleeing the Nazis to editor of *Maclean's*. The *Globe and Mail* calls this autobiography "a work of genius wit and insight."
Non-fiction, 6 × 9, 736 pages plus photographs, trade paperback

ON SIX CONTINENTS: A Life in Canada's Foreign Service 1966-2002 *by* James K. Bartleman
A hilarious, revealing look at what our diplomats actually do, by a master story-teller who is a legend in the service. "Delightful and valuable." *Globe and Mail*   *Autobiography, 6 × 9, 256 pages, trade paperback*

ROLLERCOASTER: My Hectic Years as Jean Chrétien's Diplomatic Adviser 1994–1998 *by* James Bartleman
"Frank and uncensored insider tales of the daily grind at the highest reaches of the Canadian government. . . . It gives the reader a front row seat of the performance of Jean Chrétien and his top officials while representing Canada abroad." – Ottawa *Hill Times*
Autobiography, 6 × 9, 358 pages, hardcover

WORTH FIGHTING FOR *by* Sheila Copps
The former Deputy Prime Minister and life-long Liberal tells all in this revealing look at what really goes on behind the scenes in Ottawa. "Copps gives readers a blunt, no-holds-barred glimpse into the seamy backrooms of Canadian politics." Montreal *Gazette*
Non-fiction, 6 × 9, 224 pages, hardcover

DAMAGE DONE BY THE STORM *by* Jack Hodgins
The author's passion for narrative glows through this wonderful collection of ten new stories that are both "powerful and challenging." *Quill & Quire.*
Fiction, 5⅜ × 8⅜, 224 pages, hardcover

DISTANCE *by* Jack Hodgins
"Without equivocation, *Distance* is the best novel of the year, an intimate tale of fathers and sons with epic scope and mythic resonances. . . . A masterwork from one of Canada's too-little-appreciated literary giants." *Vancouver Sun*   *Fiction, 5⅜ × 8⅜, 392 pages, trade paperback*

BROKEN GROUND: A novel *by* Jack Hodgins
It's 1922 and the shadow of the First World War hangs over a struggling Soldier's Settlement on Vancouver Island. This powerful novel with its flashbacks to the trenches is "a richly, deeply human book – a joy to read." W.J. Keith   *Fiction, 5⅜ × 8⅜, 368 page*

THE MACKEN CHARM: A novel *by* Jack Hodgins
When the rowdy Mackens gather for a family funeral on Vancouver Island in the 1950s, the result is "fine, funny, sad and readable, a great yarn, the kind only an expert storyteller can produce." *Ottawa Citizen*
Fiction, 5⅜ × 8⅜, 320 pages, trade paperback

RAVEN'S END: A novel of the Canadian Rockies *by* Ben Gadd
This astonishing book, snapped up by publishers around the world, is like a *Watership Down* set among a flock of ravens managing to survive in the Rockies. "A real classic." Andy Russell

Fiction, 6 × 9, map, 5 drawings, 336 pages, trade paperback

THE SELECTED STORIES OF MAVIS GALLANT *by* Mavis Gallant
"A volume to hold and to treasure" said the *Globe and Mail* of the 52 marvellous stories selected from Mavis Gallant's life's work. "It should be in every reader's library." *Fiction, 6⅛ × 9¼ , 900 pages, trade paperback*

AT THE COTTAGE: A Fearless Look at Canada's Summer Obsession *by* Charles Gordon *illustrated by* Graham Pilsworth
This perennial best-selling book of gentle humour is "a delightful reminder of why none of us addicted to cottage life will ever give it up." *Hamilton Spectator*

Humour, 6 × 9, 224 pages, illustrations, trade paperback

A PASSION FOR NARRATIVE: A Guide for Writing Fiction *by* Jack Hodgins
"One excellent path from original to marketable manuscript. . . . It would take a beginning writer years to work her way through all the goodies Hodgins offers." *Globe and Mail* The Canadian classic guide to writing fiction. *Non-fiction / Writing guide, 5¼ × 8½, 216 pages,*
updated with a new Afterword, trade paperback

TEN LOST YEARS: Memories of Canadians Who Survived the Depression *by* Barry Broadfoot
Filled with unforgettable true stories, this uplifting classic of oral history, first published in 1973, is "a moving chronicle of human tragedy and moral triumph during the hardest of times." *Time*

Non-fiction, 5⅞ × 9, 442 pages, 24 pages of photographs, trade paperback

HOW I SPENT MY SUMMER HOLIDAYS *by* W.O.Mitchell
A novel that rivals *Who Has Seen the Wind.* "Astonishing . . . Mitchell turns the pastoral myth of prairie boyhood inside out." *Toronto Star*
Fiction, 5½ × 8½, 276 pages, trade paperback

JAKE AND THE KID *by* W.O. Mitchell
W.O.'s most popular characters spring from the pages of this classic, which won the Stephen Leacock Award for Humour.

Fiction, 5½ × 8½, 211 pages, trade paperback